THE SCORPION'S ADVANCE

Ken McClure is an award-winning research scientist with the Medical Research Council of Great Britain. His medical thrillers have been translated in to eighteen languages and are all international bestsellers. He is the author of nine novels, and lives and works in Edinburgh, a city he loves with weather he hates.

D1369223

Also by Ken McClure

PESTILENCE
REQUIEM
CRISIS
CHAMELEON
TRAUMA
FENTON'S WINTER
PANDORA'S HELIX

KEN MCCLURE

THE
SCORPION'S
ADVANCE

POCKET
BOOKS

LONDON · SYDNEY · NEW YORK · TOKYO · SINGAPORE · TORONTO

First published in Great Britain by Fontana Paperbacks, 1986
This edition first published in 1998 by Pocket Books
An imprint of Simon & Schuster Ltd
A Viacom Company

07438608

Simon & Schuster Ltd
West Garden Place
Kendal Street
London
W2 2AQ

Simon & Schuster Australia
Sydney

A CIP catalogue record for this book is available from the British Library.

ISBN 0-671-85414 3

1 3 5 7 9 10 8 6 4 2

Printed and bound in Great Britain by Caledonian International Book
Manufacturing, Glasgow

. . . Changeable fortune, O unstable Chance,
Thine is the scorpion's treacherous advance!
Thy head all flattery, about to sting,
Thy tail a death, and death by poisoning.
O brittle joy, O venom sweet and strange,
O monster that so subtly canst arrange
Thy gifts and colour them with all the dyes
Of durability to catch the wise . . .

Geoffrey Chaucer
The Merchant's Tale

PROLOGUE

Tel Aviv

Dexter parked the car and got out with an awkwardness that said he was used to driving something bigger than the green Fiat. He walked along Ben-Yehuda Street with the slow, deliberate gait so typical of American men who had grown up in the shadow of Gary Cooper and John Wayne. It wasn't affectation, just the result of constant subliminal suggestion from an early age. The haircut, the smart light-weight suit, the crisp shirt with the button-down collar were what people in Dexter's position wore. It was as simple as that. No sartorial decisions had been necessary.

Dexter pushed open the door of the airline office and stepped into the cool, air-conditioned interior. He adjusted his glasses on the bridge of his nose while he took in his surroundings. There was one other customer being attended to at the desk. Dexter avoided eye contact with the assistant who rose to deal with him and picked up a leaflet which he studiously read until the other customer had completed his business. The door closed and Dexter put down the leaflet.

'Yes, sir. Can I help you?' said the clerk.

'I'm enquiring about flight LH 703,' said Dexter.

'We have no flight LH 703, sir.'

'Check for me, will you?'

'One moment, please.' The clerk left his post and disappeared through the back to return a few moments later. 'The manager will see you now, sir.'

Dexter nodded. He didn't waste words on people of junior rank where it could be avoided. He walked through the door that the clerk held open for him and turned right into a long corridor. He didn't need directions. He knew exactly where to go. He came here two or three times a year to deliver his report or when specially summoned as he had been this morning. He stopped at a blue door and pressed the buzzer outside. There was a pause while an overhead TV camera scrutinized him, then a noise like an electrical short circuit preceded a series of mechanical clicks as three thousands dollars' worth of electronic lock released the blast-proof steel door and let him in.

'Good morning, Mr Dexter,' said a smiling girl behind a typewriter.

''Morning, Miss Ling.' Gary Cooper was always polite to ladies.

'The chief said to go right in, sir.' Dexter smiled and entered the inner office.

'Good to see you, J.D.,' said the short, grey-haired man behind the desk. 'Like Tel Aviv any better?'

'No,' replied Dexter flatly. 'Worst station I've had.'

'Well, wouldn't do if we liked them all,' laughed the grey-haired man.

'No, sir,' agreed Dexter, though totally failing to see why not.

'Cheer up. Could be Paris next time!'

'With my luck it'll be La Paz.'

'Luck doesn't come into it. You're as good as your last assignment, J.D.'

'Then it'll be La Paz,' said Dexter.

'No progress, huh?'

'None at all.'

'Maybe this'll help,' said the grey-haired man, pushing a piece of paper towards Dexter. 'It came in from the London station early this morning. It's a response to your all-station request for information on peripherals. This one is dead.'

Dexter read the report and recognized Miss Ling's style in the decoding. 'SUBJECT: Martin Klein. STATUS: Peripheral in Tel Aviv file. MESSAGE: Subject died in St Thomas'

Hospital, Surrey, England. Cause of death unknown.'
Dates and times were listed.

Dexter looked at his watch and saw that Klein had been dead for six hours. 'Never heard of him,' he said.

'We checked for you,' said the grey-haired man. 'Klein was listed as a peripheral because he worked in one of the genetics labs at Tel Aviv University for two months earlier this year.'

Dexter nodded thoughtfully before saying, 'Probably nothing in it but we better have a look at the autopsy report.'

'I've asked London to lay hands on it.'

'Thanks.' Dexter got to his feet and buttoned his jacket while the other man leaned back in his seat and put his hands behind his head.

'I hear you've got an agent on the inside.'

'I have,' said Dexter. 'Not that it's made any difference. The target's still pure as driven snow.' Dexter leaned forward with his fingertips resting on the desk. He said, 'You are sure this guy is bent? There couldn't be some kind of mistake?'

The older man considered his words carefully before replying.

' "Bent" is the wrong word, J.D. He's a head case. What's more, he's a head case with a PhD and access to everything he needs. That, my friend, is a combination that could make La Paz seem very attractive.'

CHAPTER ONE

Sweat was beginning to glisten on John Fearman's forehead as he drew back for the third time. 'For God's sake hold him still, will you,' he snapped in an uncharacteristic show of temperament.

Sister Jane Long was not used to being spoken to that way by a junior houseman but, this time, she let it pass. She knew the pressure that Fearman was under. She said in a deliberate monotone, 'The patient is convulsing, Doctor . . . I am doing my best.'

Fearman noted the tone of her voice. 'I'm sorry. Let's try again.'

'One moment.' Sister Long summoned another nurse and the two of them put their weight on the patient.

Fearman brought the needle closer to the patient's bare back. He wanted a clean insertion into the space between the third and fourth lumbar vertebrae, a nice clean sample of cerebro-spinal fluid and then out again. The last thing on earth that he needed was the man to jump when he had a needle inside his spinal canal.

The patient seemed calm for the moment. Fearman held his breath and pressed the long aspiration needle into the cavity of his spinal column. The seconds ticked by like minutes before the needle was in place and the spinal fluid flowed out into the waiting test tube – only slightly tinged with blood through Fearman's hesitant entry.

Fearman withdrew the needle and let out a sigh of relief. The sigh had barely passed his lips when the patient gave a huge involuntary convulsion. Fearman had to add his strength to that of the nurses in trying to control him, shuddering to think what might have happened had the needle still been in the man's back.

The fit subsided. Fearman looked at the clock on the wall; it was 1.14 a.m. At twenty-six minutes past, the result came back from the biochemistry lab where the duty technician had been called out to run the tests. Protein: Normal; Glucose: Normal; Chlorides: Normal.

Fearman could not believe his eyes. 'But it *has* to be meningitis,' he said out loud. 'He has all the signs.'

'Except for a normal CSF,' said Jane Long.

'You have seen a lot of meningitis cases, Sister. I value your opinion.'

Jane Long was pleased. Fearman had atoned for his earlier indiscretion. 'I agree with you, Doctor. The patient is presenting as a classic meningitis.'

'But this says not,' said Fearman, raising the lab report.

'Maybe viral?'

'Maybe, but the onset was all wrong. Who is the duty bacteriologist?'

'Dr Anderson.'

Fearman gave silent thanks. Neil Anderson was his flatmate. Calling out other doctors was always a problem for housemen. Do it too often and you would get a reputation for it; the kind of reputation that could damage your career. Calling out friends did not count.

'Neil? I need you.'

'What's the problem?'

'I've got a patient presenting as a severe bacterial meningitis but Biochem. says his CSF is normal.'

'Maybe it's viral.'

'I think not. I still think it's a classic bacterial. Would you have a look at his CSF for me? See if you can find anything?'

'Be right there.'

Fearman came out of the ward side-room when he saw

Anderson appear at the window. 'Thanks, Neil. Here it is.' He handed Anderson a test tube containing cerebro-spinal fluid.

'Who is the patient?' asked Anderson.

'Martin Klein, aged twenty-two, an Israeli national. He's one of our medical students. His flatmate called an ambulance just before one and he's been going downhill fast.'

'Have you called Lennox-Adams?'

'Not yet. I'll wait until you have had a look.'

Anderson nodded. 'I'd best get started.'

He left the warmth of the hospital and ran across the cobbled courtyard to the medical school with the cold night air nipping at his eyes. When he got in, the lift was on one of the upper floors. It was old and slow so he chose to sprint up the stairs instead and was breathing hard by the time he reached the Bacteriology Department on the third floor.

The fluorescent lights stuttered into life as he found the switch at the second attempt. He transferred the fluid from the test tube to a centrifuge vial and set the machine in motion. If there were any bacteria in the sample they would be concentrated at the base of the tube within minutes. While the centrifuge was running he prepared a series of microscope slides and culture plates, ready for inoculation as soon as the sample was static.

The automatic brake on the centrifuge cut in and the room was filled with the decelerating hum of the motor. Anderson removed the vial and held it up to the light. Not much debris there, he thought, but he went through the motions of decanting the top fluid and inoculating what was left on to the culture plates and glass slides. He put the cultures in the incubator and stained the slides at the sink by the window before examining them under the microscope.

Anderson's fingers moved the microscope stage slowly in

12

a search sequence as he scanned the slide from right to left. He repeated the sequence in the opposite direction, still without success. There were no bacteria to be seen. After six traverses Anderson called Fearman. 'Sorry, nothing in the direct slide.'

'Shit.'

'I've prepared a ZN slide just in case it's TB meningitis, but I doubt it.'

'Me too. I think he's going to die. I've called Lennox-Adams.'

'I'll come down when I've finished.'

Anderson completed the examination of the second slide with the same negative result. He switched off the lights and returned to the hospital. As he approached the side-room where Fearman's patient was, he heard a scream of anguish and a loud crash. He opened the door to find that one of the nurses had been flung across the room. The patient's eyes were wide open and filled with fear; his arms flailed in all directions. Anderson rushed over to help Fearman and Sister Long restrain him. The fact that Klein was a well-built twenty-two-year-old did not help matters.

Anderson could feel Klein's muscles harden like iron as his body went into spasm. He could see the veins on the side of his neck swell up till it seemed that they must burst under the pressure. Whimpering noises came from his throat as Klein recoiled from some unspeakable horror that only he could see.

Fearman and Anderson had just begun to gain control of the situation when Sister Long, with an anxiety in her voice that neither had heard before, said, 'His tongue, Doctor! His tongue!'

In the throes of his seizure Klein had sunk his teeth into his own tongue. Anderson and Fearman, unable to let go of his arms, looked up to see the skin round Klein's mouth retract and his teeth sink deeper and deeper into his tongue. Blood flowed over his chin and down the myriad channels created by the cramp-locked sinews and muscles of his neck.

Jane Long threw herself across Fearman's back and attempted to prise Klein's jaws apart but with little success.

'Use the blunt end of the forceps, Sister,' said Fearman.

'I'll break his teeth.'

'He can talk without his teeth,' said Anderson.

Jane Long did as she was bid and succeeded in inserting her forceps into a gap between Klein's teeth on the left side of his mouth.

'What on earth is going on?' said a well-modulated voice behind them. It belonged to Nigel Lennox-Adams, the consultant physician Fearman had called. 'Why hasn't this man been sedated?'

'He has,' replied Fearman, still in the throes of a wrestling match.

'Well, give him some more!' boomed Lennox-Adams as if he were talking to an idiot.

'He's had the maximum . . . ' said Fearman.

'Give him more. I will take the responsibility.'

'Please, Sister,' Fearman said to Sister Long. She prepared the syringe with professional calm and called, 'Ready.'

Fearman was in two minds about letting go of Klein's arm to take the syringe.

'Oh, give it here,' snapped Lennox-Adams. He gave Klein the injection and dropped the empty syringe into the bowl that Jane Long held out to him. 'Now we'll have some order round here,' he said, stepping back from the bed and waiting for Klein to respond to the sedation.

Nothing happened. Klein's body continued to convulse as if charged with electricity. The fear in his staring eyes could only hint at the nightmare his mind was inflicting on him. Lennox-Adams watched in growing disbelief as he saw that the sedation was not going to work.

Klein's body went into spasm again. His back arched and his muscles locked in rigid seizure. The staff looked on helplessly as the skin on Klein's face was drawn further and further back to expose all his teeth. There was a rattle from his throat and the agony was over. Klein was dead.

'Thank God,' said Lennox-Adams quietly. No one else spoke. He approached the bed and looked at the hideous death mask of Martin Klein. 'Brief me, will you, Fearman.'

Fearman referred to his notes as he gave the information to his superior. 'The patient, Martin Klein, was twenty-two years old, an Israeli subject attending medical school in this country.'

'One of ours?'

'Yes. Third year.'

'Go on.'

'He became ill earlier this evening, complaining of severe headaches, sickness and stiffness of the neck. By midnight he had a high fever and was becoming delirious. His flatmate put in a treble-nine call and he was admitted to hospital at one o'clock. All the symptoms at that time pointed to severe meningitis.'

'In whose opinion?'

'Mine.'

'Go on.'

'I performed a spinal tap and requested biochemical analysis on the CSF.'

'And?'

'The values were normal.'

Lennox-Adams looked puzzled but did not say anything.

'I called out Dr Anderson – he's the duty bacteriologist this evening – and asked him to examine Klein's CSF for bacteria.'

'And?'

'I didn't find any evidence of bacteria in a direct smear

test,' said Anderson. 'Of course, something might grow up in culture.'

'I am aware of that possibility, Doctor,' said Lennox-Adams coldly. He pulled back the sheet from Klein's body. 'An Israeli, you say?'

Fearman concurred and exchanged glances with Anderson as Lennox-Adams proceeded to examine Klein's arms and legs. At length he stood back from the bed and nodded to Jane Long who put the sheet back in place. 'I was looking for bite marks,' said Lennox-Adams. 'I saw a rabies death once; it was like that.'

The consultant left, and Jane Long called for the duty porter to take Klein's body to the mortuary.

'I think I'll get back too,' said Anderson.

'Don't you want some coffee?' asked Fearman.

'Truth is . . . I wasn't actually alone when you called . . . '

'You weren't . . . Oh, I see. Anyone I know?'

'Angela Donnington . . . ward seven?'

'Oh, I know, blonde, posh voice, nice legs.'

'We were having a late supper.'

'Of course you were,' leered Fearman. 'See you in the morning.'

Anderson got back to the flat to find Angela fast asleep, her fair hair spread out on the pillow and her clothes strewn at intervals over the floor where, earlier in the evening, they had progressed, with the aid of a Carol King album, from the couch to the bedroom. Anderson undressed and slipped in beside the sleeping figure. She stirred as he put his arms round her and said sleepily, 'Oh, you're back.'

'I sure am,' said Anderson, in what he hoped was a low, sexy voice.

Angela giggled and put her hand down to rub his thigh. The phone rang. Anderson cursed and fumbled for the receiver.

'Neil? It's me, John.'

16

'You are doing this deliberately, Fearman!' hissed Anderson.

'No, I'm really sorry to disturb you but it's important. I've been going through Martin Klein's things and I've discovered that he was one of the student volunteers on the Galomycin trial. You are involved in that, aren't you?'

'Yes,' said Anderson. His annoyance had disappeared. 'Thanks for letting me know.' He put down the phone and switched on the bedside lamp.

Angela screwed up her eyes and protested. 'What's the matter?' she asked.

'A medical student died tonight, meningitis they think, but he was a volunteer on the Galomycin trial.'

'The Gal . . . ? Oh, the new antibiotic they're trying out.'

Anderson nodded.

'You don't mean to say that the drug killed him?' said Angela, her eyes opening wide.

'No, of course not, but it will be really important to establish just what did before anyone else starts saying what you said.'

'But isn't that why you have volunteers? To find out if new drugs are safe or not?'

'God, no,' said Anderson. 'New drugs have to be proven safe long before they ever reach hospitals. We give them to volunteers for much less dramatic reasons, to look for minor side-effects – If you give a new drug to a patient and he starts to feel dizzy you can't be sure if it's the drug or his illness, but if you give it to twelve healthy students and they all feel dizzy, it's the drug. Again, with a new drug we have to work out the correct dose to give so we give it to volunteers and then collect samples of blood and urine to see how much gets into their system.'

'Neil?'

'Yes?'

'You are boring me.'

Anderson switched off the light and snuggled down beside Angela in the darkness. He put his hands down on to her buttocks and pulled her into him. 'And now . . . I'm going to bore you some more . . . '

Angela giggled. 'That was a very bad joke . . . but a very nice idea.'

Anderson got into the lab just after nine. Before doing anything else he examined the cultures he had put up the night before from the Klein case. There was no sign of bacterial growth on any of them. They were still perfectly sterile. At nine-thirty the internal-mail system delivered a directive that all personnel connected with the trial of the antibiotic Galomycin should present themselves at ten-thirty prompt in the medical superintendent's office.

Anderson spent the intervening hour on the project he was most concerned with at the moment: the problem of why so many infections in the hospital were failing to respond to standard treatment. This morning's lab cultures had yielded two more strains of bacteria that had apparently developed immunity to first-choice antibiotics. That made a total of eight in the last twelve days. He set up tests to establish alternative treatment for the patients.

Anderson left the lab at twenty-three minutes past ten and crossed the courtyard to the hospital. He made his way along the corridor in an easy slalom between trolleys bearing patients and trolleys carrying stores and stopped as he passed the main staircase when he heard his name being called. Mary Ryle, the hospital pharmacist, was hurrying after him. She was a thin, spinsterish woman in her late thirties whose life had been dedicated – and wasted in Anderson's opinion – to the care of her aged mother. She seemed relieved to see Anderson. 'Thank goodness,' she twittered nervously, 'I thought that I was going to be late.'

Anderson smiled at the idea. Mary Ryle was the last

person on earth to turn up late for anything. 'We still have a few minutes, Miss Ryle.'

'I must say, this is all very mysterious,' said the pharmacist.

Anderson did not bother to explain why the meeting was being called for they had reached the medical superintendent's office. They went inside to find the other four already there. James Morton, the medical superintendent; Nigel Lennox-Adams, consultant physician; John Kerr, consultant bacteriologist – and Anderson's chief; and Sister Linda Vane, in charge of the ward where Galomycin was under test.

Linda Vane made sure that everyone had coffee, then Lennox-Adams cleared his throat loudly to make sure he had their attention.

'I won't beat about the bush,' he said. 'One of the student/staff volunteers we have been using for the Galomycin trial is dead.' He paused while Mary Ryle injected a few variations of 'how awful'. 'There is, of course, no suggestion that taking the drug had anything whatever to do with it but, statistically, it is absolutely imperative that we establish the exact cause of death.'

'Does that mean that you don't know why he died?' asked James Morton.

Lennox-Adams told him of the circumstances surrounding Klein's death.

'I see,' said Kerr. He turned to Anderson. 'You say you found nothing in the slide?'

'Absolutely nothing.'

'And the cultures?'

'Negative this morning.'

'You've arranged a post-mortem?' Kerr asked Lennox-Adams.

'Two-thirty this afternoon. Quite frankly it's down to lab tests now. Fearman said that the patient presented as a

19

typical bacterial meningitis when he came in. When I saw him it looked like the final stages of rabies. I think that means that, as physicians, we simply don't know.'

Anderson walked back to the lab with Kerr, pausing to let Kerr light his pipe. After a few rapid puffs to verify that it was alight, Kerr said, 'I want you at the Klein PM this afternoon. Take the specimens yourself, everything you can think of.'

'Very well,' said Anderson without much enthusiasm. He decided to give lunch a miss.

The Pathology Department was in the basement of the medical school. It had originally been sited there so that horse-drawn hearses could use the back door to collect or deliver their cargo out of sight of curious eyes. The reason still held good, only the horses had gone.

Anderson asked the reception technician about the Klein post-mortem.

'Number five,' he said, inclining his head to the left.

Anderson followed his direction and went through the green swing doors marked with a white '5'. He found himself alone in the changing-room but could hear voices coming from the post-mortem suite beyond. They had already started. Anderson changed into gown and Wellingtons and joined them after a brief pause to steel himself for the sights and smells of Pathology.

The pathologist looked up from the table as Anderson entered and regarded him through half-framed spectacles.

'Anderson, Bacteriology, to take specimens.'

'Gelman,' said the pathologist.

The mortuary attendant adjusted the water supply to the table so that it settled down to a steady gurgle as it sluiced through the drainage channels.

Anderson looked at the face of the corpse and saw again the mask of terror that he had seen in the early hours of the morning. If anything, the yellow-white pallor of dead flesh made the spectacle even more horrible.

'An unpleasant death,' said Gelman, noting the look on Anderson's face. He opened up the cadaver with a strong sweep of the knife.

Gelman removed the internal organs, examining them visibly then weighing them before recording his findings on tape. At intervals Anderson would ask him to pause while he moved in with scalpel and pipette to take samples of tissue and body fluids and deposit them in small, sterile glass bottles for transport back to the lab. The head was done last; the air filled with the smell of burning bone as Gelman trephined round the skull and removed it as a complete cap.

At length Gelman stood back from the table and stripped off his gloves. 'Well,' he said with some resignation, 'I hope you lot can come up with something. I've just cut up a perfectly healthy twenty-two-year-old boy.'

Anderson took the last of the samples he wanted before joining Gelman in washing up at the sink. 'Dr Lennox-Adams thought it might be rabies,' he said.

'Doubt it,' said Gelman. 'No bite marks on him.'

'But rabies can have a very long incubation period, can't it?' said Anderson, knowing that it could but not wishing to offend the senior man.

'True,' said Gelman, drying his hands. 'But I still doubt it. Death followed too rapidly after onset . . . more like toxic shock.'

'So poisoning is a possibility?'

'I think it has to be, but God knows which one. That's something for the labs.'

Anderson returned to the Bacteriology Department and washed again, despite having just done so. He scrubbed his hands and arms till he was satisfied that no trace of the smell of the post-mortem room remained on them. He sluiced warm water over his face and gargled with cold water from the fountain before spitting it out into an adjoining basin with satisfying accuracy. 'Sweet Jesus,' he growled under his breath, finding that the disposable towels were inserted the wrong way up in their dispenser. 'A fifty-fifty chance, and she never gets it bloody right . . . '

Anderson asked one of the junior technicians to take some of the specimens back to the Virology Department before getting down to work on setting up his own tests. It was well after seven before he had the racks of culture tubes and plates safely in the incubator. He met John Kerr on the way out; they were the last to leave the building.

'Get everything you needed?'

'All set up.'

'I see you reported two more cases failing to respond to treatment in the wards,' said Kerr.

'It's a mystery,' said Anderson. 'The patients were responding well to antibiotic treatment then suddenly they stopped getting better and relapsed.'

'Did you come up with alternative therapy?'

'Yes. But I'd still like to know what the hell is going on.'

Kerr nodded. 'Any ideas at all?'

'Not yet. You?'

'No. We must talk.'

It was five days before the Galomycin group met again, five days during which Anderson had failed to find any evidence of bacterial infection in the specimens taken from Martin Klein at post-mortem. He knew that the Virology Department had come up with a similar blank, although they had managed to eliminate rabies from the running. Lennox-Adams announced similar reports from Pathology and Biochemistry with an air of barely suppressed irritation.

'Five days of investigation and we have discovered precisely nothing. Damned annoying. If anything is to be taken from the lab reports at all, it is that death was probably caused by some powerful toxin. As Biochemistry have failed to identify it, my own personal view is that it was probably bacterial in origin.'

Anderson heard the ball plop into his court, with some surprise. He scraped together a lob. 'I found no evidence of bacteria being involved, sir.'

'Are you saying that you found no bacteria at all in Klein's body?' Lennox-Adams asked with affected incredulity.

Anderson bit his tongue and held his temper in check. He said, 'No, sir, I am not. I found the normal organisms I would expect to find in the human gut. I meant that I did not find any evidence of disease-causing bacteria.'

'Perhaps Dr Kerr might care to take a look at the cultures,' said Lennox-Adams dismissively, adjusting his glasses and flicking through his papers.

Anderson bit his tongue again.

'I have confidence in Dr Anderson's ability,' said Kerr.

'Nevertheless . . .'

'Nevertheless, I have confidence in Dr Anderson's ability,' repeated Kerr coldly.

'Of course,' said Lennox-Adams with an unconvincing little smile. He changed the subject to bring them up to date with the overall progress of the Galomycin trial. 'To date, we have treated thirty-six patients with the drug and all of them have showed remarkable progess with, I think I'm right in saying, no side-effects?' He looked around the group with raised eyebrows.

Kerr said, 'One developed thrush but that's par for the course with any antibiotic.'

'Excellent. What about the blood levels in volunteers, Dr Anderson?'

'It's very good. I think we could cut the dose to, say, two hundred and fifty milligrams instead of five hundred.'

'Very well. See to it, Miss Ryle, will you?'

'Yes indeed, Dr Lennox-Adams, right away,' said Mary Ryle, barely avoiding genuflection in her anxiety to please.

Anderson left the meeting with John Kerr. 'Thanks for standing up for me in there,' he said, while Kerr fumbled in his pocket for matches.

'That's all right,' said Kerr, having once more achieved pipe ignition. 'Mind you . . . I want to see those cultures . . .'

Fearman was cooking spaghetti when Anderson got in. 'Want some?'

'No thanks.' Anderson flung himself down in a chair. 'Christ, what a day.'

'Problems?'

'Tell me. Is Lennox-Adams a natural son of a bitch or does he work at it?'

'What's he done?'

'Suggested that Kerr check my results like I was some kind of . . . fucking schoolkid!'

'Oh dear,' said Fearman, stirring his spaghetti and stifling a smile.

'One day I'll snap his bloody double-barrelled name in two and stuff half up each nostril.'

'That's what I like about the Scots . . . such a gentle race.'

'And your spaghetti up yours!'

'C'mon,' soothed Fearman. 'Don't take it personally. He's like that with everyone below the rank of senior registrar.'

Anderson closed his eyes and rested his head on the back of the chair. 'Suppose you're right,' he conceded. 'On top of that I've had half the medical staff on the phone today asking me what I'm playing at.'

'What d'you mean?'

'I recommend a course of treatment. Three days later the patient relapses; the infection has become resistant to the antibiotic. It's happened ten times in the past few weeks.'

'And you don't know why?'

Anderson shook his head.

'What does Kerr think?'

'We're both in the dark.'

'Well,' said Fearman, finishing his spaghetti and getting up with his plate. 'I've got lives to save.'

'Working tonight?'

'All week. You entertaining this evening?'

'I might ask Angela over if you are going to be out.'

Anderson changed his mind about calling Angela Donnington for the problem of the relapsing patients was too much on his mind. Instead he decided to catch up on his reading of current medical journals. He poured himself a whisky and settled down with notebook and pen at the ready. After half an hour or so his attention was taken by an article in one of them entitled 'Plasmids'. The author, a research geneticist, was attempting to bridge the gap between pure research and clinical medicine by suggesting the relevance of such entities in patient treatment. Anderson read that just as bacteria infect people, so plasmids infect bacteria. These tiny elements could spread through a bacterial population like wildfire conferring new properties on their hosts. Among these new properties was antibiotic resistance.

Anderson felt good for the first time in days. This could be the answer. If there was a plasmid at large in the hospital this would explain why the character of some infections would change after a few days and become resistant to treatment. He decided that he needed more information. He copied down a list of references from the end of the article. They would have the journals in the medical school library. He checked his watch; it was coming up to eleven o'clock. He could go first thing in the morning . . . No, he would go right now.

25

A bitterly cold wind was blowing as Anderson made the five-minute walk to the medical school. The streets were practically deserted; he only met one person along the way, a drunk going home and using the wall for support. Anderson entered by the side door and climbed the stone steps, worn down in their centres by generations of medical students taking the same shortcut to the library.

He found the journals that he was looking for and took them to a seat by a radiator. It was barely warm for the heating system was antiquated, but it was better than nothing. It took him forty minutes to find and copy out all the information he needed to set up tests for the presence of plasmids. He replaced the journals on their wooden racks, taking care to insert them in correct sequence, and switched out the light.

As he locked the library door Anderson heard the sound of breaking glass. He froze, listening at the head of the stairs, but all was quiet again. He felt sure that the sound had come from the Pathology Department on the floor below but could not remember having seen a light on when he crossed the quadrangle.

Anderson went quietly downstairs and stopped outside the heavy oak doors marked 'University Department of Pathology'. He tried the brass handle and found it open. Strange, he thought, someone must be working but there still did not seem to be a light on in any of the labs. He went inside, his feet squeaking on the polished linoleum as he walked down the corridor and entered the museum hall, a large square room with a statue in the middle to Sir Henry Struthers, first incumbent of the chair of pathology at the university. All around the walls were examples of human organs and tissue, fixed in formalin and displayed in glass cases for the benefit of medical students.

There did not appear to be anything amiss; all was quiet. There was enough light coming from the hospital across the courtyard so Anderson did not switch on the lights. He read the labels as he walked slowly past the cases and found himself wondering if the owners in life of the exhibited organs could ever have dreamed in their wildest nightmares of the 'immortality' that had been in store for them. Could 'male aged 49' ever have thought that his cancer-scarred lungs would one day swim in formolized eternity under public gaze? Did the parents of 'Foetus: Rubella Damage' know that their hideously deformed offspring would sit blindly in a glass-sealed vacuum for ever? Anderson hoped not.

As he passed the frock-coated figure of Sir Henry and moved into the shadow of the statue he saw what appeared to be an area of wetness on the floor at the far end of the room. Light was being reflected in a puddle. Anderson's first thought was that a window had broken and let in the rain, but that part of the room was the furthest from any window and consequently the darkest. The only reason that he had seen a reflection at all was due to light being reflected down from a white wall-mounted tray containing examples of gall stones. He approached slowly past a rack of excised and sectioned bladder tumours and saw that he had found the source of the breaking glass.

One of the display tanks had smashed on the floor, spilling out its contents. Anderson turned his head to read the floating label: 'Cirrhosis of the Liver: Male, aged 59'. He looked at the space where the display had stood. Why had it come down? Some fault in the glass? A weak mounting? He stepped gingerly round the spillage and ran his hand along the shelf, feeling for clues. The exhibit had been standing at the end of the row, just where the shelving curved into deep shadow . . .

Suddenly a dark shape erupted from the darkness and pushed him aside as it shot past on its way to the door. Anderson crashed back against a case containing the complete skeleton of a dwarf but was unaware of the rattle of protest as he fought fear and surprise. He made to give chase but forgot about the mess on the floor. His leading foot came down on the specimen and slid away from him, sending him tumbling to the floor where his momentum carried him across the wet linoleum till, finally, his head met the stone feet of an uncaring Sir Henry Struthers.

Anderson calculated that he had been unconscious for ten to fifteen minutes. He had a splitting headache and his right leg hurt where glass from the smashed exhibit had cut him. He got slowly to his feet and found the light switch. There was no telephone in the museum hall so he walked through the door by the niche where the intruder had sprung from and called the hospital operator from the Pathology Department office. He said that he would stay until the police arrived.

Anderson spent the short time he had to wait looking for any other signs of damage caused by the break-in; there did not appear to be any. The only odd thing to strike him was that, in the filing-room, three Anglepoise lamps stood together on a small table near the cabinets. He walked over and felt the shades; all three were still warm. Someone had wanted a lot of light concentrated on a small area . . . but for what? Anderson noticed that one of the filing cabinets was open a fraction. He pulled the drawer out a little further and saw that one of the folders was standing a little proud of the others, as if someone had hastily replaced it. He took it out and opened it. It was the post-mortem report on Martin Klein.

Anderson looked at the little table again. Someone had been reading the PM report on Klein, but why three lamps? Had they just been reading it? Or had they been photographing it?

CHAPTER TWO

'A bloody weirdo, if you ask me,' said the detective sergeant, viewing his surroundings with obvious distaste.

'You could be right,' agreed Anderson, who had decided to say nothing about his suspicions surrounding the reason for the break-in. He saw no point; it was only going to delay his getting to bed if he had to explain who Martin Klein was and about the circumstances of his death. At the end of it all he knew that the police would have no more idea than he as to why someone should want to see the Klein PM report that badly.

'And you say there's nothing missing, sir?'

'Not as far as I can tell but, as I said, this is not my department. You'll really have to ask Professor Flenley that.'

'Yes, sir, we've sent a car to pick him up,' said the sergeant.

'Some nutter after kicks, Sarge?' suggested the constable who had been taking notes.

'More than likely,' murmured the sergeant. Then, turning to Anderson, he said, 'We see a lot of funny people in our job, sir.'

Anderson smiled and waited for it to occur to the policeman that some of the people *he* met in *his* line of work might not appear on the invitation lists to royal garden parties – but it did not.

'Now if we can just go over these times again, sir?'

'Of course,' said Anderson, now working on grin-and-bear-it philosophy. He told the policeman once more what he had been through before, following every laborious curve of the constable's pen as he copied it down. A

29

uniformed man appeared to say that Professor Flenley had arrived, and Anderson was relieved to hear the sergeant say, 'I don't think we need detain you any longer, sir.'

Anderson went to the washroom to clean up. An examination of his head wound in the mirror told him that it did not need any treatment other than cleaning; the cuts on his legs were also superficial. He returned to the flat and took a sleeping pill.

Anderson got to the lab at seven-fifteen and found the morning cleaner sitting in the common-room having a cigarette. She got to her feet hurriedly when he looked in, brushing ash off her green overall. Anderson smiled. 'Aye, the early bird catches the cleaner having a fly fag, eh?'

The woman gave a bronchitic cackle. ''Ere, you're a Scottie,' she said.

The first of Anderson's many curious visitors that morning came in just after nine. By eleven he was fed up to the back teeth with people asking about the break-in at Pathology. There was only one person he wanted to see, John Kerr, and he did not arrive in the lab till half past eleven; he had been at a heads of department meeting to discuss the relapsing-patient problem.

Kerr came into Anderson's lab carrying four culture dishes. He put them down on the bench and said, 'These are the Klein post-mortem cultures you left out for me. I agree. Nothing but normal gut bacteria. I hear you had an exciting evening?'

Anderson told Kerr about the break-in but said nothing about the filing cabinet. In the cold light of day he had begun to think that it might have been his imagination. The Klein file *might* have been the last one put in the drawer by one of the secretaries. The Anglepoise lamps *might* have been stacked on one table while a cleaner polished the desks.

Kerr asked him what he had been doing in the library at midnight and Anderson told him of his plasmid theory.

'Now, that sounds interesting,' said Kerr.

'I hoped you'd think that. I'm setting up the tests today.'

'These plasmids don't confer resistance to all antibiotics, do they?' asked Kerr.

'No, usually only one or two.'

'Thank God for that.'

'If we can identify the plasmid involved in the hospital, and find out what antibiotic resistance it carries, we can simply avoid using those drugs on the wards.'

Kerr nodded. 'Can you do the tests here?'

'I can determine whether or not a plasmid is present, but I'll need expert help to identify it. Perhaps you could fix it with the Molecular Biology Department?'

'Will do.'

Anderson set up plasmid tests on lab cultures from four of the relapsed patients and included two cultures of normal bacteria as test controls. One was the Klein post-mortem culture that Kerr had just returned, for it was close to hand, and the other was a harmless stock strain to which he appended the name 'J. Smith'.

It took until seven in the evening for Anderson to finish getting the tests underway, by which time he was very tired, his headache having managed to defy frequent doses of aspirin throughout the day. The tests in themselves had not involved an enormous amount of work but the mere fact that he was not set up to do such analyses had meant constant sorties to other labs to seek chemicals and equipment not on his shelves. He was relieved when all the samples were loaded into the electrophoresis tank. He set the current to run overnight, washed up and locked the lab.

John Fearman was sitting drinking coffee when Anderson got back to the flat. He swivelled round in his chair and smiled. 'Well, I never thought I'd see it,' he said.

'See what?' asked Anderson, with the feeling that he was taking the bait.

'A bacteriologist working a twelve-hour day . . . '

'Just what I need, a comedian.' Anderson poured himself a drink and gestured with the bottle to Fearman who shook his head.

'I forgot. You are working tonight.'

'How about you? I suppose it will be on with the cape and mask and off to fight crime in the city.'

'You heard, huh?'

'I heard you'd tackled Sir Henry Struthers single-handedly . . . with your head.'

Anderson gave a smile of resignation. 'I suppose I'm never going to live this down.'

'Not if I can help it, old son.'

Anderson sat down and told Fearman about his plasmid theory to explain the relapsing patients.

'Sounds good. When will you know?'

'In the morning.'

When Fearman left for the hospital, Anderson ran a hot bath and relaxed in the suds till the water started to cool. His headache had gone but he was now plagued with recurring thoughts about the break-in at Pathology. In the quiet of the apartment he no longer found it possible to dismiss the open drawer in the filing cabinet and the concentrated illumination as coincidence. He reverted to believing that the intruder's target had, in fact, been the Klein PM report. But why? Who, apart from the Galomycin group, would have a desperate interest in the cause of Martin Klein's death? It was not as if there were anything secret about PM reports. Anyone with a legitimate reason for knowing could simply ask Pathology for a copy. That implied that someone without a legitimate reason for knowing was interested. But that conclusion only brought him round in a circle to the inevitable question: Why? It was still niggling at him when he finally turned over on to his side and went to sleep.

It was another early start for Anderson for he was anxious to know the result of the plasmid tests. He was delighted with the unequivocal nature of the way things had turned out. All four problem patients gave a clear indication of plasmid activity in their infections. The 'J. Smith' stock culture was blandly and pleasingly negative; in fact, the only problem at all was that the Klein culture, which he had put in as a second negative control, was showing a positive result. Could he have mixed up two strains? He decided that the question could best be answered in the identification procedure. He called the number left for him by John Kerr and spoke to the man who was to be his contact in Molecular Biology, Frank Teasdale.

Teasdale said that he would be happy to include Anderson's samples in a batch of tests he would be setting up that same day. He would get in touch with Anderson when he had some news, probably Thursday or Friday.

An internal-mail envelope landed on Anderson's desk on Thursday, just after lunchtime. It contained the results of Teasdale's analysis. Anderson's theory was confirmed in full. The patients who had relapsed were all carrying plasmid R76, a known antibiotic-resistance transfer factor and almost certainly the cause of the problems that had arisen in their treatment. The Klein culture had also carried a plasmid; it had been identified as 'cloning vector PZ9'.

Anderson's initial euphoria over having solved the problem died a little when he read the Klein result. There had been no mix up over the cultures; the Klein culture really did carry a plasmid of its own. But it was a cloning vector . . .

Anderson only knew what he had read recently about

plasmids but he did know that cloning vectors were rather special. They were manmade plasmids, designed for the transfer of genes in modern genetical research. As yet there had been no direct medical application for them so they were still very much the province of experimental biologists. He phoned Teasdale.

No, there had been no mistake, the sample marked 'Klein' did carry cloning vector PZ9. How could he be sure? There was a computerized register of all known cloning vectors; Klein's plasmid had been a perfect match. It had an insert of 2.7.

'You've lost me,' said Anderson.

'Sorry. The vector is carrying a gene sized at two point seven kilobases of DNA.'

'What gene?'

'No way of knowing.'

Anderson explained where the culture had come from.

'I see,' said Teasdale. 'Well, if he was a medical student I can only suggest that he must have swallowed something he shouldn't have in some practical class.'

'Could it have caused him any harm?'

'Shouldn't think so but it really shouldn't have happened.'

'Agreed. Do you think you could find out for me who works with PZ9 and what class it might have been used in?'

'I can try.'

'Thanks.' Anderson put down the phone and rubbed his temples lightly with the heels of his hands. The uneasy feeling that he had experienced first in Pathology had returned.

John Kerr put his head round the door. 'Well?'

Anderson smiled and said, 'It's been confirmed; a plasmid's been causing all the trouble.'

'Well done,' said Kerr, grinning and coming into the room. 'So we know what antibiotics to avoid in the wards?'

Anderson nodded and pushed over a piece of paper.

'Excellent. But you don't seem too happy about it.'

'Oh, I am,' said Anderson. 'It's just that something else has come up.' He told Kerr about the other plasmid in Klein's gut and what Teasdale had said.

'So he was a careless young man. But there's more?' said Kerr, sensing Anderson's mood.

Anderson confided in Kerr his suspicions about the break-in at Pathology.

'Did you tell the police about this?'

Anderson confessed that he had not, saying that it sounded fanciful unless he could think of a reason to back it up, and he couldn't. Kerr nodded his agreement and asked to be informed of the source of PZ9 when Teasdale called back.

Teasdale phoned at four-thirty; he sounded apologetic.

'I'm sorry. I misled you.'

'Then it wasn't a cloning vector after all?' asked Anderson.

'Oh yes. There's no doubt about that. It's just that PZ9 isn't used in this university at all. In fact, it isn't being used anywhere in the United Kingdom. It's an Israeli vector. It originates in Professor Jacob Strauss's laboratory at the University of Tel Aviv.'

'I see,' said Anderson slowly as he saw the pieces fit. 'That makes sense.'

'How so?' asked Teasdale.

'Klein was an Israeli.'

'Ah,' said Teasdale. 'Then I think you have your answer.'

Anderson thanked him and put down the phone. He was relieved that Klein had not contaminated himself here in the medical school for now there would be no need for embarrassing probes into the safety of practical classes, no tiptoeing through the minefield of colleagues' sensitivities.

On the other hand it also meant that there was no one he could ask about the gene in the Klein plasmid. Only the Israeli lab would know that.

'Well, what now?' said Kerr when Anderson told him.

Anderson screwed up his face. 'I've got a bad feeling about this whole Klein thing.'

'You mean you think that this cloning vector thing killed him?' said Kerr, lighting his pipe.

'I know it sounds overdramatic, and Teasdale didn't seem to think that it would do Klein any harm, but the fact remains: we don't know what the foreign gene is. I would like your permission to do a few animal tests. I'd feel a lot happier if I knew for sure that the Klein plasmid was harmless . . . '

'All right. Go ahead.'

It was after five; the animal technicians would have gone for the day. Anderson resolved to set up the tests first thing in the morning.

Anderson took the shortcut to the animal house. He went down to the basement of the medical school and along one of the maintenance tunnels, stooping as he did so to avoid hitting his head on the steam pipes that clung to the rounded ceiling. The smell of wet sawdust and the sound of the scratching inhabitants told him that he was getting near before he finally came to the frosted-glass door that always reminded him of a school classroom.

The chief animal technician came over as Anderson went in and asked what he could do for him. Anderson asked for a series of guinea-pig inoculations and asked how quickly they could be set up. Ray Allan checked his stock chart and said, 'Soon as you like.'

Anderson thanked him and said that he would send the samples down as soon as they were ready. Almost as an afterthought he turned as he got to the door and said, 'Be

careful with them. They may turn out to be nothing, but
. . . don't splash them around.'

'Understood.'

Anderson phoned Angela Donnington at seven. Her
flatmate said that she had gone out and volunteered the
extra information that she was with Phillip Green, a
surgical registrar on James Morton's staff. 'She expected
you to call on Monday.'

'I got tied up.'

'Any message?'

'No message.'

C'est la guerre, cookiewise, thought Anderson as he put
down the phone. He went out for a walk. The air was cold
but it was clean and crisp . . . all right if you keep on the
move. The phrase made him think of home. His mother
used it.

Anderson came from a family who farmed dairy cattle on
the rolling pastures of Galloway in the Scottish borders.
His older brother, Tom, was destined to take over the farm
one day; he had never considered anything else, but Neil
and his sister, Annie, had marched to a different drum. He
had studied medicine at Glasgow University and Annie,
two years his junior, had done veterinary science at the
Royal Dick Veterinary School in Edinburgh.

Like so many people, Anderson had not fully appreciated his family and upbringing until he had left home. It
was a good relationship: they were proud of him, he was
proud of them. Christmas anywhere other than at Leitholm
Farm would be unthinkable. No one in the family was keen
on letter writing. It was assumed that, if you heard nothing,
everything was as it always was, and that was comfort
enough.

Anderson's thoughts came back to Martin Klein. He
wondered what Klein had been like, where he had been
brought up. He presumed that the dean of the medical

school would have written to his parents and imagined their grief at receiving the letter. Had he been an only child? Or did he have a sister, too? Anderson wanted to know more about Klein. If he knew more he might be able to rid himself of this constant feeling of unease, the feeling that there was much more to the Klein affair than just the tragic death of a medical student.

Anderson ran his fingers along the wire of the guinea-pig cage; the animals dived under the straw.

'Fit as fleas,' said Ray Allan, who came over to join him. 'If anything, the injections did them the world of good.'

'So much for that idea,' said Anderson with a shrug. He returned to the lab. He contacted the student accommodation service and sought their help in finding the student who had shared a flat with Martin Klein. They responded with a name that Anderson traced to a third-year biochemistry class in the afternoon. He was waiting outside the lecture theatre when the students emerged. He asked one of them and was pointed in the direction of a tall blond boy. Anderson introduced himself and asked if they might talk.

'You were Martin Klein's friend?' Anderson asked in the empty lecture theatre as rain began to patter off the windows.

'As much as anyone was. We shared a flat.'

'Not popular, huh?'

'He wasn't actually disliked. It was more a case of him not fitting in, really – or not wanting to fit in would be more accurate.'

'How so?'

The boy made a face as if to illustrate his difficulty in explaining. 'Martin was middle-aged before his time. He never did anything on impulse, always looked at all the angles, weighed up the pros and cons of any situation before committing himself. Apart from that he never intended to practise medicine anyway.'

'So why a medical degree?'

'Martin was interested in molecular biology. You know, the science of the future, genetic engineering and all that. He figured that having a medical degree would stand him in good stead when it came to the scramble for research grants.'

'Astute.'

'Like I said, all the angles.'

Anderson asked if Klein had been home at all in the last year.

At first the boy said no, but then changed his mind. 'Yes, he went home at Christmas, said it was no time for a good Jewish boy to be sitting around. It was the only joke I ever heard him make. He fixed himself up with some kind of vacation job at the University of Tel Aviv, but I can't remember who with . . . '

'I can,' said Anderson. 'Professor Jacob Strauss.'

'Actually, I think you're right.'

Anderson told Kerr what he had discovered; the plasmid in Klein's gut was harmless, and Klein had, in fact, worked in the Tel Aviv lab where the vector had originated. 'Do we tell Strauss or let the matter drop?'

'Tell him,' said Kerr. 'Harmless or not, the fact remains that a student in his lab contaminated himself with a cloning vector. It should not have happened.'

'Will you write?' asked Anderson.

'No, you do it but go easy; Jacob Strauss is a very distinguished man. On the other hand, don't kiss ass.'

'Scotsmen don't kiss ass.'

'But they can get up noses sometimes.'

Anderson drafted his letter three times before he was satisfied that it was both polite and to the point. He initialled the envelope and tossed it into the mail tray. He stretched and leaned back in his chair, looking up at the ceiling. That still left one outstanding question. What did kill Martin Klein?

The same question was to come up again on Monday at another meeting of the Galomycin group. Ostensibly the meeting had been called to discuss progress with the new reduced dosage, but Lennox-Adams used it to point out angrily that, as yet, the hospital labs had completely failed to establish the cause of Klein's death.

Kerr said that Anderson had discovered something, obliging him to relate the tale of the cloning vector plasmid.

'Very interesting,' said Lennox-Adams in a voice that said the opposite. 'Perhaps something of a more practical nature might emerge before our next meeting.'

Anderson returned to the medical school alone; Kerr remained for a working lunch with the medical superintendent. As he entered the stairwell behind the side door, Anderson thought he heard something and stopped to listen on the first step. Nothing. He paused again on the landing, convincd once more that he had heard something. The wind moaned as it searched out the gaps round the fire-escape door, then he heard the sound again; it was coming from the dark shadow of the stairwell, a gentle, sobbing cry that vied with the wind for his attention.

Anderson descended and moved into the darkness, asking if anyone was there. As his eyes became accustomed to the gloom he saw what he thought was a white lab coat and moved towards it. He recognized the slight figure as one of the juniors from the animal house. She was in a state of shock, her eyes wide with disbelief, her fingers held to her mouth.

Anderson's questions failed to elicit anything at all from the girl for a few minutes, then she said, 'Mr Allan . . . it's Mr Allan . . .'

'The chief technician?'

'Mr Allan . . . Mr Allan . . . '

At that moment one of the department secretaries came into the building.

'Look after her, Sheila, will you?' said Anderson, ushering the girl towards the startled woman and running off towards the basement steps. He narrowly missed hitting his head on one of the tunnel's bulkhead lights in his haste to get to the animal house. When he got there the door was standing wide open. The guinea pigs stopped their ridiculous cries as he stepped inside, leaving the scratching of the mice the only sound apart from the intermittent buzz of a faulty fluorescent light.

'Mr Allan . . . ? Are you there . . . ?'

There was no answer.

Anderson walked slowly through the animal house calling the chief technician's name. He looked into one of the side-rooms and recoiled at the sight of a rat spread-eagled on the examination board, its insides exposed through a long mid-incision, a bloody scalpel lying by its side. Anderson closed the door and continued through the passage towards the back of the animal house. He turned left at the end and stopped dead in his tracks. Ray Allan, the chief technician, was staring at him through the glass-panelled door of his office, only . . . the eyes looked straight past him at the bleak prospect of eternity.

Allan's nose was pressed against the glass and his lips were drawn back over his teeth in a silent scream of agony. He looked like some fearsome medieval demon snatched from the crumbling stonework of an ancient cathedral. Blood dripped slowly from his mouth.

Anderson swallowed hard to contain the urge to vomit and started making frantic phone calls. He had managed to push Allan's body back from the door by the time Kerr arrived and, together, they managed to get inside the room.

Lennox-Adams appeared and examined the body. 'Poor chap's had a heart attack,' he said, getting to his feet rather stiffly after kneeling for a few minutes.

'What about the blood from his mouth?' asked Kerr.

'He's bitten through his tongue. Must have been the pain.'

'He looks like Klein did,' said Anderson.

'He looks like anyone who has just died in agony,' said Lennox-Adams. But Anderson's comment had germinated inside his head. He said, 'He wasn't one of the Galomycin volunteers, was he?'

'No,' said Anderson, 'he wasn't.'

The post-mortem on Ray Allan failed to establish the cause of death; his heart had been perfectly sound. The words 'possible toxic shock' leapt out at Anderson from the report and triggered off the thought: just like Klein. He went to see John Kerr with the report still in his hand. 'It's that bloody plasmid!' he said.

'Shut the door,' said Kerr. Anderson shut it. 'Now, what do you mean?'

'Don't you see? Klein dies in agony – I find PZ9 in his gut. I give PZ9 to Allan to test – Allan dies in agony. The plasmid is the link! It must be . . .'

'I presume Mr Allan did not inject it into himself?' said Kerr with consummate calm.

'No, but . . .'

'And the guinea pigs he did inject it into remained alive and well?'

'Yes, but . . .'

'You are a scientist, Anderson, not an astrologer. Science says that the plasmid is harmless.'

'Yes, sir.'

'Mind you,' Kerr continued, pausing once more to put flame to tobacco, 'I'm not saying that there isn't a place for intuition in science, gut feeling, hunch, call it what you like,

42

but pursue it quietly. Let it show you the target but keep your mouth shut till you've hit it.'

'Yes, sir.' Anderson closed the door behind him.

Anderson came in next morning to find an air-mail letter bearing the crest of Tel Aviv University. It was from Jacob Strauss.

> Dear Dr Anderson,
> I was saddened to hear of young Klein's death. It is always a tragedy when a young person dies, all the more so when it is someone of Klein's undoubted ability. He worked in my laboratory for a period of six weeks during December and January.
>
> The plasmid you mention does indeed originate from my laboratory: Ref. PZ9. The inserted gene is, in fact, taken from the harmless gut organism *E. coli* and therefore poses no danger. Indeed, Klein, being an undergraduate, would not have been permitted to work with anything that posed even a remote threat to his health. It is interesting to note, however, that plasmid PZ9 can survive in the human gut and I am grateful to you for the information.
>
> Yours sincerely,
> Jacob Strauss

Anderson tapped his pen on the desk and read the letter again; he found it reassuring. The niggling doubts that he had felt about the plasmid were beginning to fade. There was something very comforting about seeing things in black and white. He opened his desk drawer and took out the file on Martin Klein, flicking briefly through the lab test reports before removing the most recent one, a computerized printout of Teasdale's analysis from the Molecular Biology Department. He was about to staple Strauss's letter to it

43

when he thought again and decided to show it to John Kerr.

Kerr grunted and threw it back across the desk at him. 'Satisfied?'

'Yes.'

Anderson decided to close the file on Martin Klein and checked through the paperwork to make sure that it was complete. It was not; the post-mortem report on the test guinea pigs was missing. It was customary practice, even when test animals showed no ill effects, to kill one and examine it for hidden internal damage. Anderson phoned the animal house and said that he was coming down.

He was met by a tall dark girl whom he had not met before. She came towards him and smiled at the uncertainty in his eyes.

'I'm Ann Veitch,' she said, 'on secondment from Immunology until you get a replacement for Mr Allan. Can I help you?'

Anderson said who he was, taking a liking to the girl, who exuded an easy self-confidence. 'How are you finding things?' he asked.

'With difficulty,' Ann Veitch laughed. 'Very much the new girl, I'm afraid. Still, I'll learn.'

Anderson didn't doubt it. 'I'm looking for a path. report on one of my guinea pigs,' he said, handing over a copy of the request form with its reference number.

Ann looked at it briefly and said, 'Karen will know more about this than I do.' She called over one of the other technicians. It was the girl from the stairwell. Anderson noted the name, Karen Davies, on her plastic lapel badge and asked about his missing report.

'Sorry. We're a bit behind at the moment.' The girl led the way to where Allan had kept his animal post-mortem reports, a large green metal filing cabinet which defied the diminutive Karen's attempts to pull open the bottom drawer. Anderson squatted down and did it for her then stood up and waited while she thumbed through the files and extracted a blue folder.

'Here we are. Report three-one-two . . . guinea pig . . . requested N. Anderson, Bacteriology. Result, negative . . . No abnormalities.'

Anderson copied down details of dates and reference numbers for his own file and handed the card back. He was about to leave when Ann Veitch came into the room looking very angry. She was holding a small brown bottle.

'You did it again!' she said to Karen Davies. 'The prep-room this time!'

Anderson looked on as a spectator as the junior apologized and looked at her feet. 'What was all that about?' he asked as the older girl left.

Karen looked sheepish. 'I'm a volunteer on the Galomycin trial,' she said. 'I keep leaving my capsules all over the place. I left them in here last week and Mr Allan took one in mistake for his own. If you think Miss Veitch was angry you should have heard him!'

'He had a point,' said Anderson.

'I know.'

'Why was Mr Allan taking capsules?' asked Anderson, remembering that the pathologist's report had made no mention of any medical condition requiring treatment.

'As a precaution. He cut himself while he was examining one of the animals. He had to get an anti-tetanus shot and . . . an antibiotic umbrella, I think he called it.'

Anderson nodded. 'Do you know what the animal had been infected with?'

'No, but Mr Allan didn't seem too concerned. It'll be in the accident book.' Karen brought down a rather tattered hardback notebook from the shelf above the desk and flicked through the pages. 'Three-inch cut between thumb and forefinger of left hand sustained from scalpel during post-mortem examination of guinea pig, ref. three-one-two

45

. . . animal disease-free . . . no known hazard. What a coincidence, Dr Anderson . . . That was your one.'

The colour drained from Anderson's face as he sat down slowly in the swivel chair that had been Allan's and rested his elbows on the desk. He rubbed his forehead with the tips of his fingers as he came to terms with an awful truth that swirled before his eyes like wet fog.

'Are you all right, Dr Anderson?'

Anderson did not reply for his mind was reeling with the implications of what he had just heard. Allan had been examining the PZ9-infected guinea pig when he had cut himself. He could have introduced the plasmid into his body – not that that would have done him any harm, but he had subsequently taken Galomycin and that was what had killed him! The combination of PZ9 and Galomycin! In Martin Klein's case he already had the plasmid in his gut when he took Galomycin as a volunteer on the trial. The combination of PZ9 and Galomycin was lethal!

Anderson became aware that Karen Davies was looking at him strangely.

'Karen, I want you to come into hospital for a few days.'

Karen's eyes filled with questions. 'But why? There's nothing wrong with me.'

'It's just . . . a precaution,' said Anderson, trying desperately to delete urgency from his voice. 'A few days' observation, that's all.'

He failed to convince Karen whose face now showed fear. She backed away slightly. 'There's something wrong, isn't there? I'm in some kind of danger . . . Tell me. I want to know . . . I have a right . . . '

Anderson put his hands on her shoulders. 'It's probably nothing to worry about,' he said gently, 'but there may be some kind of problem with Galomycin. If there is, I want you in the best place to deal with it and that's here in the hospital. That makes sense, doesn't it?'

The girl nodded and attempted a small smile.

'Good,' said Anderson. 'Now, telephone your mum and then go up and see Sister Vane. I'll tell her to expect you.'

'Yes, Doctor.' Karen turned to go.

'Oh, Karen?'

'Yes?'

'Give me your capsules.' The girl handed over the bottle.

Anderson called the senior technician into the office. 'Miss Veitch, I'll explain all this later but right now do three things. One, close the animal house when I leave; no one, but no one, is to come in. Two, trace the cultures used to inject animals for test three-one-two. Three, find out exactly what happened to the three guinea pigs used in that test. Understood?'

'Understood,' said Ann Veitch coolly.

Anderson ran back along the basement corridor and heard the door being locked behind him. He burst into Kerr's room but found it empty. 'Shit!' Snatching the receiver from its cradle, he asked the operator for Lennox-Adams.

'Dr Lennox-Adams is out at the moment,' said his secretary. 'Can I take a message?'

Anderson put the phone down without speaking. He lifted it again and called Linda Vane. ' . . . For observation please, Sister. A side-room . . . on her own.'

A striking match announced the return of John Kerr. He was surprised to find Anderson in his office and let the match go out before it reached his pipe.

'The plasmid did kill Klein and Allan,' said Anderson. 'It's the combination of Galomycin and PZ9 that's lethal.'

Kerr listened while Anderson told him what he had discovered. 'What have you done so far?'

Anderson told him.

'Good. I'll get the trial stopped and telex the company.

Contact Pharmacy and get them to impound all stocks of Galomycin.'

Three hours later, with all sources of Galomycin collected and under lock and key, the Galomycin group met to hear from Anderson in person.

'My God!' said Lennox-Adams. 'Have you any idea what's happening?'

Anderson said that he had not.

'Perhaps the drug is altered in some way by the plasmid,' suggested Mary Ryle.

'Good point, Miss Ryle,' said Lennox-Adams. 'Has the company been informed?'

Kerr said that it had.

'And Professor Strauss?'

'Not yet,' said Anderson, 'but we are the only group with access to Galomycin. There is no immediate danger to the Israelis.'

Kerr knocked out the spent contents of his pipe into the ashtray that Lennox-Adams pushed towards him and said, 'It seems to me that we can't be sure if it's the plasmid that makes the drug lethal or vice versa. It is in everyone's interest to find out quickly. I suggest that we arrange for the drug company to send some Galomycin to Professor Strauss and ask him, as originator of the plasmid, to find out what is going on.' The meeting broke up with everyone agreeing to Kerr's suggestion.

Anderson called Ann Veitch at the animal house as soon as he got back.

'I thought that you had forgotten about me,' she said. She had the information that Anderson had requested. One of the three guinea pigs had been killed and examined – the one that had infected Allan. The other two were still alive. The cultures used to inject the animals had been sterilized by autoclaving.

'Good,' said Anderson. 'See you in ten minutes.'

Anderson called in on Kerr and told him that two of the test animals were still alive. He suggested that they could prove the combination theory by injecting them with Galomycin. Kerr agreed and said that he would come with him to the animal house. Anderson explained to Ann Veitch what was going on and asked her to prepare isolation cages for the new experiment.

'This means that Karen is in danger,' said Ann Veitch. 'She has been working with plasmid-infected animals and taking Galomycin.'

'Yes,' said Kerr, 'she's in danger.'

'How long . . . I mean, when will you know?'

'After thirty-six hours the Galomycin will have cleared from her system and she will be safe,' said Kerr. 'It really all depends on how careful she has been around here and whether she has picked up the plasmid.'

Anderson remembered Karen's carelessness in looking after her capsules and saw that the same thought had been going through Ann Veitch's head. They exchanged an uncomfortable glance. He noticed that Kerr seemed very morose when they returned to the department. 'Something bothering you?' he asked.

'That junior technician, Karen Davies,' said Kerr.

Anderson could think of nothing reassuring to say.

The flat was cold and quiet when Anderson got in and he found a note from Fearman saying that he was going home for a couple of days. He lit the gas fire and shivered involuntarily as he poured himself a drink, causing a little whisky to slop over the side of the glass. It was six-thirty; Karen Davies had taken her last Galomycin capsule at three in the afternoon. Anderson started to read the evening paper but found that he could not concentrate and flung it across the floor. He tried television and had the same problem; his eyes kept straying to the mute telephone as if it were about to ring. He had asked the hospital to phone him immediately if Karen Davies should become ill, but in the end he could not accept the silence as assurance that all was well and called to ask. Karen was watching television and eating peanuts; did he want to speak to her?

Anderson called again as soon as he woke in the morning. Karen was fine. She remained very much on his mind throughout the morning but by five in the afternoon he had become confident enough to broach the subject with John Kerr. 'Looks like she got away with it,' he said.

Kerr nodded. 'She's a lucky girl.'

Anderson had been asleep for a little over an hour when the phone rang. It was Staff Nurse Donovan, the night nurse in charge of Linda Vane's ward. Karen Davies was complaining of a stiff neck and her temperature was rising; Doctors Kerr and Lennox-Adams had been informed.

At three in the morning, tears of winter rain ran down the windows of Karen Davies's room as her life came to an end. Her body arched in uncontrolled spasm as unimagined terrors filled her mind in response to the brain damage wrought by the toxin. Although warned of what might happen, the nurses were still badly shaken by the sight of their patient's agony. For the first time in their career the young ones found themselves praying for death to stop the suffering. Anderson left the room and gripped the handles of a trolley outside till the whites of his knuckles showed through.

'What luck . . . what rotten, fucking luck.'

Kerr put a hand on his shoulder as he passed but did not say anything.

At two on the same afternoon, Anderson received a telexed reply from Tel Aviv. In it, Strauss expressed astonishment that plasmid PZ9 could be lethal under any circumstances. It was his considered opinion that the antibiotic, Galomycin, must have been responsible for the

50

deaths after some chemical change had occurred. Naturally, he would carry out experiments as soon as he received a supply of Galomycin and let them know his findings.

'I hope to God he's right,' said Kerr when he read the telex.

'Why so? asked Anderson.

'If Galomycin is at fault we can all take a course of treatment with another drug, just in case we may have infected ourselves with the Klein plasmid. But if it's the plasmid that's lethal we can't be sure that another antibiotic won't trigger it off.'

'What a thought. Do you want me to screen the staff to find out if anyone's carrying it?'

Kerr stayed silent for a long moment. He finished scraping out the bowl of his pipe with slow deliberation before looking up at Anderson and saying, 'I think not. If it *is* the plasmid that kills, and some of us are contaminated, there's not a damn thing we can do about it . . . '

Anderson was suddenly aware of the tick of the large, Roman-numeralled clock on Kerr's wall. 'It's like having an unexploded bomb inside you,' he said.

'Crudely put, but accurate.'

'So you think it's better we don't know?'

'Don't you?'

Anderson sighed and nodded. 'But we'll have to warn everyone about taking medication.'

Kerr nodded. 'No antibiotics for any of us unless it's life or death.'

'And if it is?'

'Then you can screen the person involved.'

Anderson left Kerr and went down to the animal house. He chose not to take the shortcut through the basement, opting instead for the longer walk along the top corridor and down the main stairs with its busts of past medical deans on every landing. As he reached the front door he

51

looked up at the great, wooden war memorial board to those who had fallen in two world wars. The first name on it was 'Anderson'. 'Christ,' he muttered as he walked out on to the wet cobblestones of the quadrangle.

Ann Veitch looked pale and drawn but was running the lab with the cool efficiency that Anderson had come to expect of her. They spoke briefly about Karen's death but both knew that there was little to be said that helped.

'Your animals are dead,' said Ann Veitch, leading the way to the isolation cages.

Anderson looked at the cold, stiff corpses of the two guinea pigs. They were lying on the floor of their cages, teeth bared in what was now becoming a familiar death mask.

'Incinerate them,' said Anderson.

He had his proof.

Two weeks passed, during which Ann Veitch was appointed to the vacant chief technician's post in the reopened animal house. Things were returning to some semblance of normality, but, when three weeks had gone by with still no word from Israel, Anderson's impatience bubbled over into irritability. 'What the hell are they doing?' he exploded to John Fearman.

'Maybe the drug company were slow in sending the Galomycin,' suggested Fearman, saying the wrong thing.

'Are you kidding?' exclaimed an incredulous Anderson. 'That company must have ten million quid tied up in Galomycin! They would have rented a bloody Concorde to get it there if necessary!'

'All right, all right,' snapped Fearman, 'but for God's sake stop taking it out on me! You've become a pain in the arse!'

Anderson was struck dumb. It was the first time he had ever heard his even-tempered flatmate raise his voice. He

52

stared out of the window, calming down in the icy silence and realizing that Fearman was right. 'I apologize,' he said. 'Would six pints and a Chinese takeaway make amends?'

'You're on,' smiled Fearman.

On the Thursday of the fourth week, Anderson received his long-awaited report from Tel Aviv. He was absolutely shattered when he read it. Strauss had carried out extensive animal tests using a variety of plasmid and Galomycin combinations. All the animals had survived without showing the slightest ill-effects; doubling the Galomycin dosage had made no difference. He concluded that both the drug and the plasmid were quite, quite harmless.

Anderson cringed inwardly with humiliation. He concentrated his gaze on the notepad in front of him and drew a series of concentric circles in the top right-hand corner while trying to maintain a suitably inscrutable expression.

'It appears that Dr Anderson's conclusions were perhaps a little precipitate,' said Lennox-Adams to the assembled meeting.

'There may indeed be more to it than was first thought . . . ' continued James Morton.

Anderson sensed that Lennox-Adams was enjoying it all, playing with him, circling him like a hyena round a wounded animal, darting in to strike home with key words . . . headstrong . . . inexperienced . . . mistaken. 'Now that Professor Strauss has demonstrated that this plasmid thing . . . ' Lennox-Adams made a dismissive gesture with his hand, 'is completely harmless . . . '

'No, he hasn't,' said Kerr, attracting all eyes. 'What he has done is to come up with a different answer to Anderson.'

'Yes, but a man of Strauss's stature . . . '

'Can be mistaken like anyone else.'

'But surely in this case . . . '

'In this case, Nigel, there are three people in the

cemetery who don't think that Anderson was mistaken.'

There was absolute silence in the room. Mary Ryle shifted uncomfortably in her chair.

'Then what do you suggest, Dr Kerr?' asked Lennox-Adams in a cold, flat voice.

'I suggest that we send Dr Anderson to Tel Aviv so that he and Jacob Strauss can sort out this mess,' said Kerr.

'I hardly think that the Regional Health Board will look too kindly on that suggestion.'

'The drug company will pay.'

'Will you ask them?'

'I already have.'

Kerr grunted in response to Anderson's thanks for having defended him. 'You had better telex Strauss to see if it's all right with him.'

'Right away,' said Anderson, getting up.

'One thing,' said Kerr as Anderson reached the door. 'If it does turn out to be your mistake . . . Start looking for a locum in the Hebrides.'

Anderson had a reply to his telex on the following morning; Jacob Strauss agreed to the proposed collaboration. One week later, Anderson left for Tel Aviv.

CHAPTER THREE

Anderson looked down in response to the announcement from the First Officer and saw the lights of Tel Aviv appear in the blackness below; flight BA 576, London Heathrow to Ben-Gurion International, was coming in to land. The journey had done nothing to modify his dislike of travelling, regarding it as he did as an endless monotony of queuing and waiting, and the Israel flight had been worse than most. Much more time had been taken up with security and baggage checks. Determined to avoid yet another queue, Anderson sat still till the other passengers had filed out. The company smile on the face of the stewardess changed to a real one when she heard the croak from Anderson's throat when he tried to speak; it had been a long time since he had said anything.

Anderson stood at the top of the steps and let the Israeli night surround him. God, it was hot. No longer protected by the cabin conditioning of the Lockheed Tri-Star, he felt the humid warmth creep into the space between his collar and his neck. Perspiration was trickling freely down his forehead by the time he had collected his baggage and cleared Customs. He walked out on to the concrete reception area which was now crowded with embracing groups of people as sons and lovers were welcomed home.

Anderson stopped and looked around, a gesture that immediately marked him out as a target for a competing horde of taxi drivers, who surrounded him, tugging at his arm and rhyming off a discordant chorus of destinations.

Throughout the pantomime, which strained his patience to the limit, Anderson had been aware of a tall, bespectacled man hanging back beyond the edge of the group. A slight smile on his face said that he was enjoying the display. Anderson looked directly at him and the smile disappeared. The man approached and rasped something in Hebrew. The taxi drivers melted away.

'Dr Anderson?' enquired the man, without smiling. 'I am Arieh Cohen, one of Professor Strauss's colleagues. He asked me to meet you.'

The fact that Cohen did not smile convinced Anderson that he had been right in thinking that Cohen had hung back deliberately. It had been on the cards that there might be some resentment in the Israeli lab to an outsider questioning their results. He wondered if Cohen's hostility might be general. If it was? Well, he was no schoolgirl; he could take any shit they cared to throw, do his job and then get out.

The Volvo pulled out on to the highway and Anderson tugged at his collar as the heat of the night began to stifle him. Incredibly, the car heater seemed to be on. Anderson put his hand in front of the grille in disbelief.

'I'm afraid the ventilation system is faulty,' said Cohen.

Anderson did not know whether to believe him or not. He wound down the passenger window without the nicety of asking first and took deep breaths of the warm breeze. Fearing a complete breakdown in relations between them, Anderson tried to feign some semblance of normality. 'Forgive me, I'll just have to take off my jacket.' He smiled.

'That would be the intelligent thing to do,' said Cohen coldly.

Anderson ignored the jibe. 'Is it always this hot?' he asked.

'In Tel Aviv, yes. It's the humidity that's bothering you, not the heat. You'll get used to it.'

'If you say so.'

The drive into Tel Aviv took fifteen minutes. Cohen did not say much so Anderson just took in the road signs as they flashed by and was suddenly aware of being in the

Holy Land. The names on the boards made him think of days gone by, cold mornings in the school hall in Dumfries with infant voices raised in programmed praise. That 'Green Hill' was no longer so far away; it was thirty-seven kilometres east at the last intersection.

As they entered the outskirts of Tel Aviv, Cohen explained that Professor Strauss had arranged for him to stay in university accommodation, conveniently near the university itself. The students, he said, were still on vacation so it would be relatively quiet and he would have an apartment to himself.

'Sounds fine,' said Anderson.

'It's rather basic.'

They were now deep in Tel Aviv traffic and moving slowly.

'The university is on the north side of the city,' said Cohen, 'perhaps you would care for a cold drink before we go up there?'

Anderson, who was becoming more and more conscious of the stifling heat now that they were caught up in traffic, readily agreed. Cohen turned off the main street and twisted in and out of a maze of side-streets before they reached the waterfront and the slightest suggestion of a cool breeze flirted with Anderson's cheek.

'Atarim Square,' announced Cohen, as they walked towards a brightly lit area full of bars and cafés. 'Tourist Tel Aviv, tourist tastes, tourist prices.'

Anderson was sure an insult had been intended but for the moment thoughts of cold beer took precedence over everything else. They found a table by the sea wall overlooking the yacht marina and ordered drinks; Anderson asked for beer, Cohen had orange juice.

'You don't drink beer, Dr Cohen?' asked Anderson.

'I don't touch alcohol.'

Anderson could see that the prospect of fun-filled nights with Cohen in downtown Tel Aviv should be filed under 'remote'. He asked a few polite questions and received polite but curt answers in reply, so, deciding that he was running in mud, he did not launch any more initiatives and drank his beer in silence.

'Shall we go?' asked Cohen, eyeing his watch. Anderson nodded.

The car picked up speed as they left the town traffic and headed towards the northern suburb of Ramat Aviv. Anderson paid scant attention until they slowed and turned off into a broad, tree-lined avenue marked 'Einstein'.

'The university is at the top of Einstein,' said Cohen, 'and this . . . ' he continued as they turned right into a wide compound surrounded by high concrete buildings, 'is where you will be staying.'

Anderson was told that he was to have the roof apartment in the French Building, each block having been named after countries whose governments had been sympathetic to the establishment of the Israeli state, and who had backed up their sympathy with hard cash. The term 'apartment', as it turned out, referred to a single room furnished with the bare necessities of civilized life, a small bed, a table, a chair, a cooking stove and a sink. It did, however, have a toilet and shower cabin and it was the prospect of a shower that held Anderson's complete attention.

As he put down his bags, two large cockroaches scuttled across the floor forcing him to make an involuntary sound of disgust. He looked at Cohen and saw the amusement in his eyes.

'Stand on them,' said Cohen, turning to go. 'Someone will come for you in the morning.'

The door clicked shut and Anderson tore at his clothes in his haste to get into the shower. He turned his face up to the sprinkler head like an Inca sun-worshipper, letting the water cascade over him, bringing freedom, albeit temporarily, from the cloying heat of the Tel Aviv night. He turned the regulator to 'cold' and surveyed his feet for a few minutes till his body temperature had cooled. Feeling better, he wrapped a towel round his waist and padded over to the bed where he lay down and looked up at the white, featureless ceiling until the day stopped swirling inside his head and sleep invaded his tired mind.

Anderson woke just after five, with the rays of the morning sun streaming in through the slit window some eight feet up the wall and playing on his eyelids. Realizing that getting back to sleep would be impossible he got up, washed and pulled on a pair of shorts. The words 'roof apartment' sprang to mind. Did he really have access to the roof? He opened the door and looked left and right; the stairs down were to the right, but on the left was a small corridor which he followed and found led to the wide, flat roof of the French Building. The concrete surface, baked by a sun that was already very hot, threatened to burn the soles of his bare feet as he walked across to the parapet and looked over, following the broad sweep of Einstein down to the Mediterranean in one direction and up to the campus buildings of the university in the other.

Anderson returned to his room and looked through the cupboards – crockery, hardware . . . and food. Someone had stocked the cupboard above the sink with coffee, eggs and Syrian pitta bread. Another small cupboard turned out to be a fridge. It contained orange juice and milk. Anderson revised his hastily formed opinion of Israelis based on his experience with Cohen. He mellowed considerably over boiled eggs, toast and coffee.

When he had finished eating, Anderson took his chair out on to the roof and sat there with a second cup of coffee. He felt better with the food inside him and ready to face anything the day had to offer. As the sun climbed higher in the sky he moved his chair back into the shade of a water tower and used the time in hand to reorientate himself to the reasons for his visit.

Just before nine he heard laboured breathing coming from the stairs and turned to face the door. After what seemed to be an age the figure of an elderly man appeared in the entrance, obviously struggling for breath after the climb. He patted his chest as if in explanation for the delay before he spoke.

'Good morning. I am Jacob Strauss.'

Anderson ushered Strauss over to the chair he had been occupying and the old man sat down gratefully; he began to use his Panama hat as a fan and continued until· he had sufficiently recovered to speak. He nodded to the stairs and said, 'To you some steps, to me . . . the Eiger.'

Anderson smiled. So that was Jacob Strauss, a name which had appeared regularly throughout his student years in lectures and textbooks.·Not at all what he had expected. Strauss seemed to be a rather benevolent old gentleman, the sort you would find on park benches on summer afternoons, patting dogs and lifting their hats to passing mothers with prams.

Strauss outlined plans for the day. 'First, the damned paperwork . . . ' He made a gesture of annoyance with his hat. 'Then I show you my lab and we talk, yes?'

'Fine,' said Anderson.

Strauss's car, a very dusty Mercedes, was waved to a halt at the entrance to the university by an armed guard. Anderson thought that the guard seemed old and fat, but the gun he was carrying looked real enough. Strauss got out and approached the man who, in turn, saluted him. They had a short conversation in Hebrew, which Anderson guessed was about him, then he was asked to get out and his flight bag was searched.

'I hope you will forgive the impoliteness,' said Strauss as they drove on through the gates.

'Of course.'

Strauss listed the various buildings on the campus as they passed by on their way up a tree-lined avenue. They stopped at the administration building and spent half an hour on the 'damned paperwork' before proceeding to the medical school which turned out to be a multi-storey tower block.

The elevator rose silently and swiftly to the sixth floor where Strauss had his laboratory and where they were met by a number of people wearing white lab coats. He was introduced to everyone, although there seemed little hope of him remembering all, or indeed any, of the phonetically strange names.

'You already know Dr Cohen,' said Strauss.

'Yes, indeed.'

Cohen nodded curtly but did not smile.

Lastly, Anderson was introduced to a woman in her late twenties.

'And this is my right hand,' said Strauss, smiling broadly and putting his arm round the woman's shoulders. 'May I present my research assistant, Myra Freedman.'

Anderson shook hands with her and thought the wide smile genuine enough.

'It's a pleasure to meet you, Doctor,' said the woman.

Anderson was surprised at her American accent for, of all the people he had met so far, Myra Freedman would have been the one he would have picked out as looking typically Israeli. She was small and sallow-skinned with dark, curly hair that licked along her forehead and tumbled down on to her shoulders. She wore gold on both wrists and round her neck.

'You are an American?' said Anderson, betraying his surprise.

The wide mouth laughed, revealing well-cared-for teeth. 'Chicago,' said Myra. The telephone rang in Strauss's office and he excused himself, leaving Anderson and Myra alone.

'So what's an American doing here?' Anderson asked.

'I'm not an American any more,' insisted Myra with mock firmness. 'As of two years ago I'm an Israeli. Sam and I thought it was time.'

The name rang a bell for Anderson. 'Sam Freedman? Not the research biochemist?'

The woman smiled. 'The same.'

Anderson had started to say, 'But why should . . . ' when he stopped himself. He was too late. Myra Freedman completed his question.

'Why should a top-flight researcher like Sam give up everything and come to a backwater like Israel?'

'I'm sorry. I didn't mean to be rude.'

'Don't apologize, and don't think there haven't been times when I've asked myself the very same question, on days when it's a hundred and twenty degrees and one hundred per cent humidity and the air conditioning breaks down because there's a powercut and so on. But basically it's because we're Jewish and we both felt that supporting Israel with words just wasn't enough any more. Israel needs people, not just stateless, displaced people, people starting from scratch or running from some oppressive regime, but established, professional people, people who *want* to work here. These are the people who will give credence to Israeli science, medicine and the arts. These are the people who will provide the infrastructure for our future. Does that make sense?'

Anderson said that it did. He asked if her husband also worked in the university.

'No. Sam is director of the Kalman Institute in Hadera. It's a commercial concern doing contract research and the like but Sam still continues his work.'

'Does he like it here? Do you like it here?'

'We both do,' smiled Myra. 'People do things in Israel; they don't just sit around all day talking about it.'

Strauss rejoined them, rubbing his hands. 'Good,' he said, 'I see you two are getting to know each other.' He turned to Anderson and said, 'I have asked Myra to assist you with your experiments while you are here. Do you think you can work together?'

'I'm sure we can,' Anderson said with a smile, looking at Myra and getting a smile in return.

'Good, then I'll leave you to discuss details. Perhaps when you are ready we can talk?'

'Of course,' said Anderson.

Myra fetched her notebook and took down details of the kind of experiments Anderson would be likely to carry out during his visit. They discussed likely requirements in the way of glassware and specialized lab apparatus before getting round to talking about probable animal experiments. Anderson asked if the package containing plasmid cultures and Galomycin that he had sent on ahead had arrived.

Myra nodded. 'In the fridge.'

Anderson said that he had better go and talk to Strauss and asked her if she would check out the experimental animal situation.

'Guinea pigs or mice?'

'Pigs.'

'Will do.'

Anderson joined Strauss in his office where they spoke briefly of the magnificent view of Tel Aviv from the window before settling down to talk. For Anderson, it was a revelation. Here in his own environment, the research lab, Strauss was no longer the pleasant old gentleman from the park bench. He was a giant. They spoke, or rather Strauss spoke and Anderson listened while Strauss talked of science and medicine in general, highlighting the problems, the possibilities, the likelihoods, the uncertainties, with an ease and intellectual insight that left Anderson in awe of the man. There just did not seem to be any area of investigation that Strauss was not familiar with, and not just in general terms, for he appeared to be conversant with state-of-the-art research in any branch of medicine that Anderson cared to mention.

The pleasure Anderson took in listening to Strauss seemed to accentuate the dull, boring nature of so many of the seminars that he had attended back home where he would applaud politely at the end of yet more dotting of 'i's and crossing of 't's. He would grin and bear it as questions were asked dutifully by students who had been taught that asking questions proclaimed intelligence.

Since qualifying, Anderson had discovered that research was not the fast-flowing current that many imagined it to be. In many ways it was a log jam of mediocrity, with too many researchers wallowing happily in little eddies by the bank. Strauss was different; he had vision. He could see a long way downstream, pick out the rocks on which projects would founder, identify the difficult bends where more knowledge would be required than existed at present.

Anderson was sorry when Strauss came to the point and said, 'And now, my friend . . . the plasmid problem.' He rose from his chair, opened the door of his office and asked Arieh Cohen to come in. 'Dr Cohen conducted our experiments with plasmid PZ9, Dr Anderson. Perhaps you two should begin by exchanging details of technique.'

Strauss fixed his gaze on the tooled leather surface of his desk while Anderson gave the unsmiling Cohen information about volumes, concentrations, and animal weights used in his experiments. When he had finished, Cohen shrugged his shoulders and turned to Strauss. 'No significant difference.'

Strauss nodded thoughtfully and said to Anderson, 'I understand you have brought your own cultures with you?'

'They were sent on ahead. Myra tells me they've arrived.'

'Good,' said Strauss. 'Then you had better repeat your experiment using our animals.'

When Anderson returned to the lab, Myra Freedman told him that there would be no problem over animals. They would be available whenever he needed them.

'I'll set up some plasmid cultures for injection,' said Anderson.

'I took the liberty of doing that for you,' said Myra Freedman, 'they should be ready by late afternoon.'

At lunchtime Anderson gratefully accepted Myra's offer to show him the way to the university refectory. In the end he enjoyed the company more than the food but felt under a diplomatic obligation to force down as much as possible before giving in and pretending that he was not very hungry.

As they walked out into the blazing heat of the midday sun, Myra said, 'Congratulations.'

'What for?' asked Anderson.

'You ate seventy per cent of it; that's some kind of record.'

Anderson laughed for the first time in Israel. 'My tourist book says that the Israelis have taken the cuisine of eight cultures.'

'What it didn't say,' added Myra, 'is that we fucked up all of them!'

They had walked less than fifty yards from the refectory building when Anderson found himself forced to pause in the shade of a tree.

'Takes a bit of getting used to,' said Myra.

Anderson mopped his brow and squatted down on the grass to watch the sprinklers at work, through eyes narrowed against the sun. 'How come you don't work beside your husband?' he asked.

'We'd go mad,' smiled Myra. 'We've got a good marriage but it wouldn't stretch to twenty-four hours a day contact, so Sam works up in Hadera and I work with Jacob Strauss here in Tel Aviv. What did you think of Professor Strauss?'

'He strikes me as brilliant,' said Anderson.

'You're right. He is.'

Anderson left the lab at six when it had already been dark for an hour, but the setting of the sun appeared to have made little or no difference to the temperature. He found his skin becoming moist within minutes of leaving the building, but apart from this discomfort, which made him look forward to a shower, he felt good. The plasmid cultures had grown up on time and three test animals had been injected and put into isolation cages.

The green 'Walk' sign at the traffic lights flashed on and Anderson crossed over to stroll slowly down Einstein through the early-evening crowds. The avenue seemed surprisingly quiet for the number of people in it, so quiet that it puzzled him till he realized that nearly everyone was wearing sandals and moving much more slowly than would an evening crowd back home. He made for the supermarket at the corner of Einstein and Brodetsky; he had noticed it when Cohen had brought him from the airport.

With his fridge and cupboards well stocked, Anderson showered and took a cold beer out on to the roof where he leaned on the parapet wall and watched the lights of the traffic on Einstein. The fate of the guinea pigs was uppermost in his mind. This result was probably the most important one he had ever waited on, but then, he reasoned with the philosophy of a beer drinker, they probably all were at the time. Still, three live animals in the morning would probably have him wiping egg off his face for some time to come . . . and in the Hebrides.

'Hello,' said an American voice.

Anderson turned in surprise to find a tall Negro in his late twenties standing before him.

'Miles Langman.' The man held out his hand.

'Neil Anderson. I thought everyone here was on vacation.'

'The Tel Aviv people are but there are quite a few Americans around, mainly students pretending they are Israelis for a year – makes their folks feel good.'

'And you?' asked Anderson, thinking that Langman seemed a bit old to be a student.

'I'm a researcher in Talmudic law, on sabbatical from the University of California.'

'Talmudic law? Then you are . . . '

'Yes, I'm Jewish, black and Jewish. When God throws a curve ball . . . '

Anderson grinned, taking a liking to Langman. 'Beer?'

'Please.'

Anderson fetched two more beers from the fridge in his room and asked, 'How many American students are there?'

'Thirty or so, with maybe another thirty exchange students from Europe.'

The two men killed another couple of beers before the American left, telling Anderson that he lived on the second floor of the building and inviting him to 'shout out' if he needed anything.

Anderson wrote up his lab notes before turning in early to find that he could not sleep for the heat. He got up and, once more, sought the sanctuary of the roof where he sat with his back against the parapet wall looking up at the stars in a black velvet sky; somewhere below him the Americans were singing folk songs. After an hour or so he took a cold shower and got into bed again, hoping that he would fall asleep before his body temperature rose. He did.

His original plan to get into the lab early foundered when he did not wake till after nine. But his annoyance faded when he realized just how well he felt after such a good sleep, and how an early start was not going to influence the guinea-pig outcome one way or the other. He felt hungry after having eaten so little the previous day on account of the heat so he delayed even further and cooked himself a large breakfast.

The medical school was sited at the back of the campus so Anderson had a good distance to walk through the grounds to reach it. He enjoyed it, passing as he did along paths lined with exotic trees and shrubs and constantly aware of the cool, wet mist from the sprinklers before finally exchanging the heat of the morning for the air conditioning of the medical school. As the elevator climbed to the sixth floor, Anderson wondered if he would feel good in a few moments' time.

Myra Freedman looked up as he walked in. She said, 'You've created quite a stir. Cohen's with the Professor.'

'The pigs?'

'All dead.'

Anderson had to see for himself. Navigating from memory of his trip with Myra the day before, he made his way to the animal laboratory alone and looked at the carcasses of the dead guinea pigs. They were lying stiff in their cages, teeth bared in typical plasmid death. 'Thank Christ,' he muttered as he closed the door and returned to the lab to join Strauss and Cohen.

Strauss pushed his glasses up on to his forehead and leaned back in his chair. 'So, we have a real problem, gentlemen. There is now no difference in experimental conditions so there must be a difference in the components of the experiment. What do you suggest?'

Anderson said, 'I suggest two more animal experiments. One injected with your plasmid, my Galomycin; the other with your Galomycin, my plasmid.'

Strauss looked at Cohen. 'Do you agree, Arieh?'

'It's the obvious thing to try,' said Cohen.

It is when I have just told you, thought Anderson

uncharitably and without any real cause, for Cohen, as yet, had not said enough for Anderson to reach any kind of conclusion about his ability or competence. The thought had been born out of a growing dislike for the cold, sullen Israeli with whom he would now be spending the rest of the day in preparation for the new experiments.

By the middle of the afternoon Anderson had to admit that Cohen was competent enough – in fact, if pushed, he would have had to concede that watching him work had been a pleasure. His large, seemingly ungainly hands had assumed the dexterity of a Swiss watchmaker when handling bacterial cultures. But apart from the professional respect which Anderson now had to accord him, he still thought him a cold son of a bitch who had not said two words more than were necessary.

Anderson returned to the main lab with Cohen just after five, having injected a new series of animals. He found Myra Freedman preparing to leave for the day and stopped to have a few words with her. Cohen walked on.

'He's a lot of laughs,' said Anderson.

'He's a good scientist, but with a chip on his shoulder.'

'What about?'

'Search me. He never talks.'

Anderson was walking on when Myra called after him, 'Hey, you're invited to dinner Friday. Come and meet Sam.'

'Thank you.'

The thought of going back to his sweat-box apartment made Anderson loth to leave the cool air conditioning of the medical school. He took the elevator to the top floor where the library was situated and sat for a while, thumbing through the current copies of the medical journals when he was not being distracted by the views of the lights of Tel Aviv. He stayed there till seven when hunger dictated that food was now more important than temperature and it was merely a question of whether he should eat out or make his own. In the event, Miles Langman was to settle the matter for him. He heard Anderson wearily climbing the stairs of the French Building and put his head round the door. 'Had a hard day, dear?' he mimicked.

During the ensuing conversation Anderson confessed that the only thing stopping him from eating out was his fear that the food might turn out to be like that of the university refectory.

Langman rolled his eyes. 'No way,' he said, 'that place is special. Even the cockroaches don't eat there.' He suggested that they take the bus down to the port of Jaffa and dine on Arab food. Anderson agreed.

The service bus hurtled through the town traffic, the driver's foot either hard on the accelerator or hard on the brake. Anderson took what little comfort he could from the fact that neither Langman nor his fellow passengers seemed to notice anything amiss. He tried to concentrate on the sights that were flashing by, silhouetted date palms, neon signs in Hebrew, the splash of light from a pavement café, until Langman eventually nudged him as the bus lurched to a halt. As they climbed down, Anderson was aware of the driver tapping the inside of his signet ring against the steering wheel in his impatience to be away from his enforced pit stop. The pavement felt wonderfully still.

'So you were right and they were wrong,' said Langman when Anderson had finished telling him what he was doing in Tel Aviv.

'It's not that simple,' replied Anderson. 'I've shown that there is some kind of serious problem connected with the plasmid or the drug but we've still to find out what it is.'

'How long will that take?'

'We should know tomorrow whether it's the drug or the plasmid.'

70

'What's the betting?'

'Evens.'

Anderson insisted on paying for the meal and they left the café to walk through the narrow lanes of the restored artists' quarter of old Jaffa, flanked by minarets and towers of an age gone by.

Langman said, 'I guess if it turns out to be the drug, the pharmaceutical company are in big trouble.'

'Agreed.'

'Mind you, it would be an interesting case,' said Langman.

'How so?'

'From what you have said, this plasmid thing is required to induce lethal changes in the drug.'

'Yes.'

'But you also said that the plasmid was manmade?'

'Yes, it was.'

'Then the drug company could argue that there is nothing wrong with their drug at all. It's perfectly safe with anything in the natural world.'

Langman had stressed the word 'natural' and Anderson took his point. 'Maybe the company will brief you for the defence,' he said.

Langman's job prospects disappeared at eight on the following morning when Cohen and Anderson inspected the test animals; three were dead and three were alive. The test using Anderson's plasmid culture and the Israeli Galomycin had proved lethal. The Israeli version of PZ9 had had no effect on the animals.

Cohen said that he would inform Strauss while Anderson went to the telex office to send a message home. He addressed it to John Kerr and it said simply, 'PLASMID LETHAL NOT DRUG'.

For once Anderson was not conscious of the blistering

heat as he walked slowly back across the campus carrying the full implication of what had been discovered on his shoulders. Martin Klein had been carrying a cloning vector in his gut and it had killed him. Could the thing have mutated inside him? Could a harmless bacterial gene really have become so deadly through spontaneous change? It was a straw that Anderson felt unable to grasp with any degree of conviction, but on the other hand, alternative explanations had all the attraction of a field full of stinging nettles. There had to be something wrong with the Israeli explanation of what gene the plasmid was carrying . . . Could Strauss and Cohen be lying?

'Dr Anderson,' said Strauss, 'tell us again how you came to conclude that the plasmid found in Martin Klein was our PZ9.'

Anderson went through the story, step by step, of how he had isolated a plasmid from specimens taken from Klein at post-mortem. The Molecular Biology Department had performed restriction analysis on it and identified it positively as PZ9, an Israeli cloning vector. Klein was an Israeli; Klein had worked in the lab in Tel Aviv where the plasmid originated. It all fitted.

'It seems watertight,' said Strauss with a sigh of resignation. Cohen shrugged in agreement.

'Do you have a copy of the analysis with you?' Strauss asked Anderson, who said that he had and excused himself while he went to fetch Teasdale's report. He handed it to Strauss who read it quickly, his head moving slightly from side to side as he scanned the data. His head suddenly stopped moving and he frowned as if deep in thought.

'Is something wrong?' asked Anderson.

'The size of the insert,' said Strauss slowly. 'Your colleague found it to be two point seven kilobases of DNA. We know it to be two point nine.'

'So the British measured it wrongly,' said Cohen.

'A difference of nought point two,' said Strauss, still deep in thought.

'Perhaps it underwent some kind of change in Klein's gut,' suggested Anderson.

'A spontaneous deletion of part of the gene? It's possible, I suppose,' said Strauss.

'But unlikely,' added Cohen, satisfied with his own explanation of a British error.

The room lapsed into silence again as Strauss considered and Cohen and Anderson waited. The air conditioning fan seemed to get louder as the minutes ticked by, and Anderson took to watching the progress of a small, stone-coloured lizard as it climbed up the sun-baked exterior surface of the building.

At length, Strauss threw his pen down on the desk and pushed up his glasses to rub his eyes. 'There is no easy way,' he said through stretched lips. 'We must analyse the DNA from both versions of the plasmid and find out the difference for ourselves.'

Strauss's decision sentenced Anderson and Cohen to three days' hard work with little or no rest, days that were made more difficult by Cohen's stubborn refusal to thaw in the camaraderie of joint effort. Anderson was glad when Friday evening came round and he went to have dinner with Myra and Sam Freedman.

The arrangement was that Sam Freedman would pick up Anderson at seven on his way home from the Institute at Hadera. He was ready by a quarter to and waited out on the roof until he saw a white Mercedes glide silently to a halt outside the apartments. He ran down the stairs to save Freedman the trouble of climbing up and was met by a short swarthy man with hawklike features and darting eyes that analysed everything they saw.

'Sam Freedman?' enquired Anderson.

'Neil Anderson, I presume,' said Freedman, stretching

out his hand. 'Good to meet you.' As they shook hands Freedman slapped Anderson on the shoulder, a gesture that made Anderson mark him down as an extrovert. The slightly proud walk and exaggerated swing of the arms as they walked to the car added weight to the diagnosis.

There was an eerie silence about the streets as they sped across the city. It prompted Anderson to say that it seemed more like two in the morning than early evening.

'*Shabbat*,' said Freedman, 'the Jewish Sabbath. Sundown on Friday till sundown on Saturday. If you think this is quiet, you should see Jerusalem. Nothing moves.' Freedman took a hand off the wheel to make a chopping gesture. 'We would risk being stoned driving through certain parts of the capital on *Shabbat*.'

'By whom?' asked Anderson.

'Religious nuts,' said Freedman.

Freedman's answer told Anderson what he wanted to know about the man's own religious commitment. 'I thought that Tel Aviv was the capital,' he said.

Freedman threw his head back and gave a guffaw. 'For Israelis, Jerusalem is the capital. The Americans and the British like to pretend it's still Tel Aviv. They don't like offending the Arabs.'

The car turned off the main thoroughfare and purred quietly through back streets before swinging round into the drive of a white-painted villa with a flat roof. It was surrounded by dense shrubbery giving off a heady mixture of scents.

'Here we are,' Freedman announced. He got out and slammed the door behind him. Anderson closed his with a gentle click and followed his host into the house. He waited while Sam and Myra embraced, before being welcomed by Myra and shown into a beautifully appointed room. The walls were pastel blue and hung with what Anderson considered to be better examples of modern art, while the seating, a variety of chairs and couches in matching soft leather, lined the walls in tasteful proximity to floor-standing lamps and spotlights. Here and there, religious items appeared and reminded Anderson that he was in a Jewish household. Their presence puzzled him slightly after what Freedman had said in the car. Freedman noticed him glance at the menorah, the Jewish candlestick, and appeared to read his mind. 'For a Jew it's hard to separate religion from tradition, they are so intermingled.'

'It must give you a sense of history,' said Anderson.

'Some of it offends the intellect,' said Freedman. 'On the other hand, it's comforting to be part of something that has spanned the centuries. We all need a sense of belonging though we might not care to admit it.'

Sam Freedman, it turned out, was as different from Cohen as Anderson could have possibly hoped. Whereas Cohen found it difficult to speak, Freedman found it difficult to stop. His quicksilver mind darted from one subject to the next without pause and, unlike Jacob Strauss who considered everything before speaking, Freedman would say the first thing that came into his head and modify it rapidly in succession as objections arose in his own mind. Anderson experienced at first hand the restless intellect that had made Sam Freedman one of the world's foremost researchers in medical biochemistry. He asked him about the Kalman Institute.

'We supply technical expertise and research facilities to companies who can't afford, or don't want, to set up their own,' said Freedman.

'Sounds interesting,' said Anderson with as much enthusiasm as he could muster.

Sam Freedman laughed out loud and said, 'Thank you for your politeness but we both know that it's anything but interesting. In fact, testing other people's cosmetics for potential allergy problems is possibly the most boring job on earth. But it makes a lot of money for the Institute and provides a lot of employment.'

'What about your research work?' asked Anderson.

'I get a small grant from the Institute which enables me to carry on my own work, and the facilities at the Kalman are second to none.'

'Doesn't the Institute have a say in what you work on?'

'No, I have complete academic freedom. The only restriction is financial; if I come up with anything that makes money, the Kalman gets sixty per cent, I get forty.'

'I'd like to see round the Institute before I go back,' said Anderson.

'You would be very welcome.'

As they relaxed after dinner, Freedman turned the conversation to the reason for Anderson being in Israel.

'I understand your visit here has something to do with the death of Martin Klein,' said Freedman.

'And the deaths of two other people,' agreed Anderson.

'Myra said that you found something strange in Klein's body.'

'A plasmid.'

'Lots of us have plasmids inside us.'

'This one was a cloning vector.'

Freedman gave a low whistle. 'I see, and you think it came from Tel Aviv?'

'Yes, it's one of Professor Strauss's – PZ9. Klein worked in that lab during his vacation.'

'Yes, I remember.'

'You knew Martin Klein?'

'Myra brought him home for dinner once. A very clever young man.'

'So I hear.'

It was well after midnight when Sam Freedman drove Anderson back to his apartment through streets that were deserted and silent. Freedman's Mercedes sped north like a white ghost through Ramat Aviv, along the broad sweep of Ha Universita and turned into Einstein to stop outside the university apartments.

'Don't forget. Whenever you want to see round the Kalman, just tell Myra and we'll fix something up.'

Anderson said that he would.

CHAPTER FOUR

Anderson's alarm went off at six and the headache, a legacy of the Freedmans' hospitality, made sure that he stayed awake. It faded after a long shower and a good breakfast and had completely gone by the time he set off for the lab. It was Saturday, *Shabbat*, and Anderson was alone on the streets as he walked up Einstein and crossed the normally busy intersection without having to wait for assistance from the traffic lights. He knew that he and Cohen would be the only two working today but that grim prospect was to some extent offset by the knowledge that today would see an end to their work and provide an answer.

An unexpected relief from the silent strain of Cohen's company came just after eleven when Myra Freedman came into the lab to deal with some work that Professor Strauss had asked her to take care of. Anderson joked about his hangover and thanked her for dinner.

'Glad you enjoyed yourself. How is the work going?'

'Another couple of hours and we should know.'

Myra had long gone when Cohen and Anderson watched the computer printer chatter into life and give them their answers.

SAMPLE ONE: PLASMID PZ9: INSERT 2.9
SAMPLE TWO: PLASMID PZ9: INSERT 2.7

Anderson looked at Cohen but the Israeli avoided his eyes. There really was a difference in the size of the inserted genes and, what was more, the computer agreed with the figure provided by Teasdale in the Molecular Biology Department back home.

'Well, well,' said Anderson, enjoying the moment.

Cohen ignored him and feigned deep concentration while he typed his next question into the computer. He sat with his arms folded and his glasses perched perilously near to the end of his nose while he waited for the answer.

The printer stuttered out its reply. GENE HOMOLOGY: NIL.

All thoughts of self-satisfaction left Anderson as he pushed himself forward in his chair. 'But that should read one hundred per cent,' he said quietly, but there was no mistaking the alarm in his voice.

Cohen did not say anything. He retyped the question.

Chatter . . . Chatter . . . GENE HOMOLOGY: NIL.

'But this is crazy!' Anderson protested. 'The computer is saying that there is no similarity at all between the two inserts. It's not just a case of a small piece of DNA being lost from one of them. They never were the same! They are entirely different genes!'

Cohen stared at the screen and shook his head. 'I do not understand,' he said, 'I simply do not understand. A small deletion of the original gene was possible . . . but this?'

Anderson looked for signs of acting on Cohen's part but could not be sure. It was difficult to spot any emotion in Cohen. He turned the screw. 'Correct me if I'm wrong, Doctor,' he said, 'but doesn't this mean that in the case of the Klein plasmid someone cloned a different gene into PZ9?'

Cohen moved in discomfort. 'Possibly Klein himself.'

'Who did he work with in the lab when he was here?' asked Anderson.

'Me.'

'Well?'

Cohen took a deep breath but fumed inwardly. 'Just what are you suggesting?' he said in a hoarse whisper.

'I think you know,' said Anderson.

Cohen's face quivered slightly as the anger within him

threatened to erupt. 'You think that I participated in an illegal experiment with the student Klein! You think that I am in some way responsible for the deaths of innocent people!'

Anderson's pulse was racing. To see such a usually unemotional man suffused with rage was unnerving, frightening even. He said, 'Someone in this place knows more than they care to admit and you were Klein's supervisor . . . ' For a moment Anderson thought that Cohen was about to strike him but, at the last moment, he turned on his heel and stormed out of the room leaving Anderson to expel his breath slowly in relief.

Anderson sat still for a moment feeling drained after the angry, unpleasant scene. He had remained outwardly calm but his heart was thumping and his stomach felt hollow. He hoped Cohen had left the building for anger and suspicion hung in the air like lightning looking for a passage to earth, and he and Cohen were the only people there. He collected the computer printouts and returned to the lab.

As he reached the bench, Anderson's preoccupation turned to terror for, as he moved his stool to open the drawer holding his lab book, a glass container came crashing down from the gantry above the work surface and shattered. The unmistakably acrid fumes of hydrochloric acid filled his lungs as the liquor turned to fire on his skin and nightmare thoughts of disfigurement and blindness filled him with panic. He groped his way to the sink with his eyes screwed tightly shut in a desperate attempt to save his eyesight, and clawed over the cold, smooth metal to find the taps. His hands were now smoking as the acid burned into the flesh and he let out a curse as a drop found its way into the corner of his left eye. The stream of water from the taps seemed painfully inadequate to his needs as he sluiced what he could gather in his hands up to his face.

All at once a great deluge of water hit Anderson, soaking

him from head to toe, then another as Cohen emptied a second twenty-litre carboy of distilled water over him.

'This way!' insisted Cohen as he dragged Anderson, who still had his eyes tightly shut, along the corridor to what, Anderson felt, must be certain death. He could see it now, an accident in the lab. Blinded with acid, frantic with pain, it would be assumed that he had stumbled and crashed through a sixth-floor window to his death.

Cohen pushed him and Anderson fell backwards, waiting for the crash of glass and the fall through space. He slid down the cold tiling of the shower that Cohen had pushed him into; Cohen turned on the water and said, 'I will be right back.'

Anderson tore at his smouldering clothes.

'Here, use this!' Cohen pressed a large sponge into Anderson's hands. 'It's mild alkali.' Cohen recharged the sponge at intervals as Anderson neutralized the remaining acid on his skin. 'Your eyes, Doctor, can you see?'

Anderson opened his eyes cautiously, one at a time, keeping the alkali sponge ready. 'Yes . . . I can see.'

'Mainly superficial, Doctor,' said Cohen, applying the final dressing to Anderson's hands. 'You were very lucky.'

'I'll say,' said Anderson quietly, still trembling with the after-effects of shock. 'I'm in your debt, Dr Cohen. If it had not been for you . . .'

'Please, say no more.'

Anderson's gratitude was qualified by a lingering doubt: despite Cohen's quick actions in saving him from disfigurement and blindness, he could still not believe that the Israeli was completely innocent in the affair.

'Perhaps you should be admitted to hospital,' said Cohen.

Anderson insisted that that would not be necessary; he

would much rather go back to his apartment.

'I have some spare clothing in my locker,' said Cohen and went to get it.

Anderson put on the shirt and trousers that Cohen returned with and looked at the charred remains of his own clothing. He shuddered.

'At least let me drive you to your apartment,' said Cohen.

Anderson declined, saying that a short walk in the sunshine was just what he needed to wipe out the trauma of the last half-hour.

Cohen shrugged. 'Very well. Until tomorrow then.'

'Indeed, and thank you again.'

Anderson walked slowly across the campus and paused to sit in the shade of a tree for a while before he left the grounds. He could now think objectively about what had happened. How had the acid fallen from the gantry? He had used it the previous day and was sure that the bottle had not been balanced near the edge. The container had crashed down when he had moved the stool, but he had not hit it against the bench; in fact, he had pulled it *away* from the bench. Curiosity persuaded Anderson to change his mind about returning to his apartment; he walked back to the medical school.

As he stepped out of the elevator on the sixth floor, Anderson heard a noise and stopped in his tracks; there was someone in his lab! He tiptoed to the door and looked in. It was Cohen; he was bending down near the bench where the accident had happened.

'Something wrong, Doctor Cohen?'

Cohen spun round in surprise and looked flustered. 'The acid . . . the cleaners in the morning . . . I thought I'd better check that none remained . . . '

Anderson walked towards him and squatted down on his heels to see what Cohen had been looking at. An electric cable was wound round one of the legs of his stool. He traced the cable up and over the gantry where it terminated in a plug socket on the other side. It was the supply cable for a small, under-bench fridge.

'Your stool was caught in the cable,' said Cohen. 'When you pulled it out, the cable brought the acid bottle down – most unfortunate.'

'Most,' said Anderson flatly.

Miles Langman was on the roof of the apartment building when Anderson returned; he was hanging out some newly washed clothes on an improvised line. He stopped when he saw Anderson and stared. 'I figured we Jews had some screwy customs,' he said, 'but we don't have one that says you bandage your hands and wear your trousers eight sizes too large . . . '

'Beer?'

'Please.'

Anderson got two beers from his fridge and told Langman about the accident.

'Shit! That isn't funny.'

'No,' agreed Anderson, 'it wasn't.' He took a long swig of the ice-cold beer, and Langman looked at his bandaged hand holding the can. 'Are your hands going to be OK?' he asked.

Anderson assured him that the damage had been restricted to superficial burns; it was what might have been that still kept getting to him.

'I can understand that,' said Langman solemnly.

Anderson sat down with his back against the parapet wall. 'It's been quite a day, all in all.' He told Langman about the computer report on the plasmids.

'You mean the kid was doing experiments on his own?'

'That's the story, but I don't believe it.'

'You think he couldn't have done it?'

'Oh, he could have done it all right, just as physics students are capable of building hydrogen bombs. I'm just saying that he could not have done it without someone knowing.'

'This "other gene" that he cloned, what was it?'

'Anybody's guess.'

'Can't you find out?'

'No. In theory it could have come from any living thing on earth, from a virus to a palm tree.'

'So what do you do now?'

Anderson shook his head slowly. He was trying to think of an answer to another question. Why did Langman want to know so much?

Anderson got in to find a letter lying on his desk, but the bandages on his hands made it difficult for him to deal with. He fumbled around till he found something to serve as a paperknife and slit it open. It was from John Kerr; he was relaying a request from the dean of the medical school that Anderson should visit Martin Klein's home in Caesarea and convey the sympathy of all the students and staff. He stuffed the letter into his desk drawer and sighed, ' . . . all the good jobs.'

Strauss arrived in the lab looking old and troubled. Anderson could see that he already knew. 'Come in, Dr Anderson,' he said, standing in his office doorway. 'Dr Cohen telephoned me last night.' They were joined a few minutes later by Cohen who enquired about Anderson's hands. Strauss, who had been deep in thought, looked up and asked the same question.

'I'm fine,' said Anderson.

'Dr Anderson thinks that we have been doing secret cloning experiments,' said Cohen, putting an end to the pleasantries.

'Really?' said Strauss, looking over his glasses at Anderson.

84

Anderson kept his cool and said, 'I do find it difficult to believe that a third-year medical student could carry out a sophisticated cloning experiment in this laboratory without anyone realizing it.'

Strauss continued to stare at him for a long moment before finally saying, 'Yes, Doctor, I think I agree with you.' It was Cohen's turn to receive the stare.

'I don't know how he did it, but he must have,' said Cohen.

A sudden silence fell on the room as the air conditioning fan ceased to function. 'A power failure,' said Strauss as, almost immediately, the temperature began to climb.

'Was Klein ever in the lab for long periods on his own?' asked Anderson.

'No, never,' said Cohen.

'Did he keep a lab book?'

'Of course.'

'May I see it?'

Cohen left the room and returned within moments to hand Anderson a dark-blue notebook. He opened it and began to read as a first trickle of sweat ran down the hollow of his back. The notes were a minor work of art, the product of a mind obviously obsessed with neatness. The cloning experiments were those outlined by Strauss in his initial correspondence; there was no mention of any private venture. Anderson leaned forward and placed the book on Strauss's desk saying, 'I wish all student notes were like that.'

Strauss nodded with a weak smile, and Anderson could see the sweat on his forehead as the temperature in the room continued to rise.

Strauss sat back in his chair and fanned his face with a sheaf of papers from the desk. 'Gentlemen, we must be realistic. We may never know what Martin Klein did, or why, or even how, but I have two suggestions to make.' The air conditioning moaned into life again as power was restored, bringing smiles from Strauss and Anderson but only a casual glance from Cohen. 'Firstly, I think that you should try producing toxin from the plasmid in test tubes. We might be able to identify the poison by its potency if it's a well-documented one.'

'Brilliant,' said Anderson.

'And secondly,' continued Strauss, 'we must investigate the action of other drugs on the plasmid.'

'I'll get started,' said Cohen, getting up.

'I'll join you,' said Anderson, but Strauss interrupted him.

'No, you have worked continuously since your arrival. You will take two days off.'

'But Dr Cohen has been doing the same,' protested Anderson.

Cohen turned back from the door. 'Go, Doctor,' he said. 'It only needs one of us to set up these tests and your hands are still bandaged – besides, if I need help I can get Myra Freedman to assist.'

Anderson looked down at his hands and reluctantly agreed. 'But I take over on Wednesday and you take two days off.'

'Agreed,' said Cohen, closing the door.

When he had left Strauss's office, Anderson took Kerr's letter from his desk and said, 'Myra, how do I get to Caesarea?'

'You can't go directly from Tel Aviv. First go to Hadera, then get a bus from there. Why?'

Anderson showed her the letter. 'I've got two days off. I thought I'd go and see Klein's parents tomorrow.'

Myra had an idea. 'The Kalman Institute is in Hadera,' she said. 'Why not travel up with Sam tomorrow? You could look round the place in the morning and then go on to Caesarea afterwards. It's not far.'

Anderson agreed that it was a good idea. He arranged a time for Sam Freedman to pick him up in the morning and left the lab as Cohen came in to request Myra's assistance.

Anderson felt lost with so much free time on his hands. His first inclination was to use the university swimming pool but his bandages said that that was not such a good notion so he settled instead for a bus ride down to tourist Tel Aviv and a walk round the market stalls. In the event, the lure of the nearby Mediterranean proved too much and he ended up taking off his sandals and walking along the sand at the water's edge to the old port of Jaffa where he and Langman had eaten a few nights before. The skyline of strange towers and turrets pleased him as the warm water rushed up the sand to swirl round his ankles.

'So you've just been bumming around all day,' said Miles Langman as he and Anderson met on the roof in what was becoming a regular evening meeting.

'More or less,' agreed Anderson. 'Enjoyed it too.'

'Same again tomorrow?' asked Langman.

Anderson told him about the planned visit to Klein's parents.

'Not so good,' said Langman, 'but the trip to the Kalman sounds interesting.'

Anderson could see why Freedman had said that 'it wouldn't take long', as the white Mercedes ate up the miles on the coast road north from Tel Aviv, its fat, black tyres frequently forcing the speedo into three figures.

'The Institute is just outside Hadera,' said Freedman as the car slowed to enter what Anderson assumed to be the concrete fringe of the town.

'On the other side,' added Freedman as they moved deeper into the streets of what appeared to be a dull, dusty, rather ordinary town.

The Kalman Institute turned out to be a long, low, white

building of two storeys. Freedman stopped the car at the gate while two men in green uniforms opened it and saluted as they drove past. Another green uniform held the door open for them as they entered a large, impressively modern reception hall with an ornamental pool in the middle and an abstract sculpture towering up from the centre of the pool to a green glass cupola some thirty feet above their heads.

Freedman led the way as they climbed one of the two semi-circular staircases that coiled round the back of the sculpture and led to a second-floor balcony which had been designed to bridge the gap that allowed the sculpture to rise from floor to ceiling.

'Here we are,' said Freedman, opening a door off the centre of the balcony.

The office came as a surprise to Anderson and it showed on his face.

Freedman laughed and said, 'I brought it with me from the States. You can keep that modern stuff outside.' He gestured to the door.

Anderson admired the Ivy League study with its green leather armchair and period furniture. 'I think I agree,' he said. 'That sculpture out there is a bit . . . a bit . . . '

'Looks like a giant prick,' said Freedman. 'Still, it impresses the clients.'

'You know, I still don't understand the economics of this place,' Anderson confessed. 'If your clients can't afford to do their own research, how come they can afford you?'

'I may have given the wrong impression when I used the term "can't afford",' said Freedman, sitting down in his swivel chair. 'All of our clients are very successful companies, many in the international big league, but from time to time one of them may come up with a discovery which is not directly related to their own sphere of business. For example, an oil company may come up with something which looks as if it may have applications in, say, pharmacy.

It just wouldn't make economic sense for them to build and staff pharmacy labs for a one-off product so they might contract us to do the research for them. Make sense?'

Anderson agreed that it did.

'Come, let me show you around.'

Freedman ushered Anderson out on to the landing. 'We have four main labs and one high-risk facility in the basement, a large animal house and all the usual services. This is one of the main labs.' Freedman opened a door marked 'L1'. The lab was obviously equipped to the highest standards and designed to accommodate ten workers. All were present and dressed in identical light-blue surgical slacks and tunics with a gold 'K' motif on the epaulettes. Anderson opened his mouth to ask what they were doing, when Freedman stopped him. 'Don't ask,' he said. 'A lot of our work is boring, but it's confidential boring. Our clients demand it and our reputation depends on it.'

Anderson nodded. 'I understand.'

Superbly equipped instrument-rooms appeared at regular intervals along the corridors. Centrifuges hummed as their motors multiplied the forces of gravity; scintillation counters chattered as their trains changed samples automatically; red, green and blue lights winked at Anderson from all directions. They came to another main lab where all the workers were dressed in green. 'Biochemistry,' said Freedman.

The two men came downstairs and Anderson could tell by the smell in the narrow corridor that they were approaching the animal house. It turned out to be the biggest he had ever seen, a huge, bright hall with a Disney-like quality given it by the different-coloured plastic panels on the fronts of the cages. Green for guinea pigs, red for mice, blue for rabbits, pink for rats, and yellow for something the empty cages said was large. 'Beagle hounds,' said Freedman. 'We're expecting a delivery.'

They left the animal complex and returned via corridor and stairs to the reception hall. 'Well, that's about it,' said Freedman, 'except for the high-risk suite in the basement. It's not being used at the moment and is all locked up, but you know the sort of thing – inoculation hoods, air filters, negative vents etcetera.'

Anderson nodded. Freedman led the way back to his office where he brought out a bottle of single malt whisky. 'A snort before lunch?'

'Can you imagine a Scotsman saying no?'

Freedman eased his large frame into his chair and poured two generous measures before the phone rang. He swung away to answer it, hoisting one foot up on to the corner of his desk.

As always in this situation, Anderson felt that he was intruding, although in this particular instance there was no need, for Freedman was speaking in Hebrew. Not a pleasant language, he thought, a bit like Afrikaans, definitely not the language of love. As the conversation continued, Anderson's eyes strayed to Freedman's bookshelves. He saw some familiar titles sitting there and got up to investigate further. As he walked towards them there came a sudden crash behind him which made him spin round in alarm. Freedman's foot had knocked the tray off the corner of his desk and Glenfiddich whisky was soaking into the carpet through a sieve of shattered crystal. Freedman fired a final guttural burst into the receiver and put it down. He was staring at Anderson.

Anderson said, 'I think you'd better turn your back for a moment.'

Freedman looked at him strangely. 'I don't think I understand,' he said.

Anderson smiled. 'You don't want to see a Scotsman cry . . . do you?'

After lunch, Freedman arranged for transport to take

Anderson back to Hadera where he was in time to catch an ancient service bus with 'Caesarea' listed on its destination board. The journey in the blistering heat was mercifully short, but the driver, assuming Anderson to be a tourist, deposited him at the ancient ruins outside the town, and in the middle of what seemed to him to be the desert.

As the bus rattled off in a choking cloud of dust, Anderson crossed over to a slight rise and climbed it. He could see the sea and, unlike the muddied waters that skirted Tel Aviv, here the water was bluey green with brilliant white surf that kissed the outer reaches of an old crusader fort.

Anderson approached the gatehouse and showed the attendant his piece of paper with the Kleins' address on it. The old man nodded and pointed with his finger along the shore. 'How far?' Anderson asked, getting a blank stare in reply. He tried holding up fingers. 'One kilometre? Two kilometres?'

The old man laughed chestily. '*Ken, ken*, two kilometre.'

Deciding to rest before attempting a two-kilometre walk in the burning sun, Anderson sat down in the cool shadow of a crumbling stone arch. The old man came over from his hut and offered him a flagon of water. '*Toda*,' said Anderson, using up his one word of Hebrew and gratefully accepting the offer. He took a long draught of the lukewarm water, returned the container and brought out his wallet, a move which brought an angry reaction from the old man. 'Sorry,' said Anderson, '*toda, toda.*'

Anderson walked through the leaning stonework of the fort till he got to the shore where he took off his sandals and padded over the burning sand to cool his feet in the dying eddies of the waves. He adjusted his bush hat to get maximum protection from the sun and set off in the direction that the old man had indicated, reluctant to stray more than a few metres from the promise of coolness that the water offered. After one kilometre he came to the remains of a Roman-built aqueduct and sat down in the shade of its arches to rest. He could now see the road that led inland.

When he came to them, Anderson found the houses to be as beautiful as their setting. Low white bungalows nestled in lush green foliage and the brilliant colours of exotic blooms as the sprinklers hissed in the soporific heat of the afternoon. Anderson found the house he was looking for and opened the gate, which squealed quietly on its hinges as if not to disturb the peace of the place. It allowed him to enter an immaculate flower garden where the neatness of the rows reminded him of the meticulous attention to detail he had found in Martin Klein's lab book. The analogy made him pause. Klein *must* have written down what he had done. It was in his nature. If it wasn't in his official lab book perhaps there was another one, and what was more, if the book wasn't in Tel Aviv it could be here, in his home. Anderson checked the dates in his diary. Klein had left the lab in Tel Aviv on the eighth of January, saying that he was going home to see his parents before returning to medical school in Britain. He had arrived back in the UK on the nineteenth. That meant he had been home for ten days. The book must be here!

'Yes, can I help you?' asked an elderly woman with grey hair tied back in a bun.

'I'm Neil Anderson, from St Thomas's Medical School.'

The woman's hands flew to her mouth. 'Martin's school?' she said in disbelief. Anderson nodded, steeling himself for the ordeal. 'Oh, my dear, come in, come in.'

Anderson stepped into the cool interior and followed the woman over tiled floors to an exquisitely furnished living area. 'Maurice!' cried the woman, repeating herself once more before they were joined by a man in his sixties who came in scratching his head as if he had been sleeping. He

92

was surprised to find they had a visitor and looked at his wife who came over and took his arm. 'Maurice, this young gentleman is from Martin's medical school,' she said with pride.

Anderson introduced himself and said how sad everyone at St Thomas's was over Martin's death.

'Did you know our son, Doctor?' asked Klein.

Anderson confessed that he hadn't and saw disappointment appear on the Kleins' faces. He added hastily that he had spoken to lots of people who had. Their son, he said, had obviously been very popular and was greatly missed by everyone. The couple smiled at each other and Anderson thought, Well, there are times in life when it's right to lie your head off.

Mrs Klein shuffled off to the kitchen to prepare cold drinks while Anderson and her husband chatted. Klein enquired about the dressings on his hands.

'A slight accident in the lab.'

'Then you are working here in Israel?'

'In Tel Aviv, Professor Strauss's lab.'

They were rejoined by Mrs Klein bearing a tray of drinks with ice cubes bobbing in them. 'Momma, Dr Anderson is working at the university in Tel Aviv . . . with Professor Strauss.'

Mrs Klein made clucking noises in admiration. Anderson should have sensed something amiss when neither of the Kleins picked up on Strauss's name, but he didn't. He said, 'I have something to ask you.' The Kleins looked attentive.

'Please, Doctor, ask.'

'When Martin came home in January did he leave a notebook here?'

The Kleins looked puzzled. 'January?' said Mr Klein.

'Yes, when he'd finished working in Tel Aviv.'

'Tel Aviv?'

Oh, Christ! thought Anderson as he suddenly saw the truth loom up like a rainy Sunday. Martin Klein hadn't come home at all, and he had just told the dead boy's parents that their son had been back in Israel and hadn't bothered to come and see them.

Anderson felt the perspiration of embarrassment on the back of his neck. The look on Mr Klein's face said that there was no way back. It was too late to pretend a misunderstanding. Klein had realized what had happened. His wife didn't; she looked at Anderson and said, 'But Martin hasn't been home in two years, not since he went to medical school . . .'

Anderson looked away as Klein explained to his wife what the reality was. The look of hurt that appeared in her eyes made Anderson feel even worse. Klein patted her reassuringly on the shoulder as he put his arm round her. 'Momma, we are being rude to our guest.'

Anderson was glad to be away from the house. He had stayed for another cold drink but had declined an invitation to join the Kleins for dinner. He had also turned down Klein's offer to run him back to Hadera, saying that he wanted to take a proper look round the crusader fort before returning.

As he reached the sea, Anderson kicked off his sandals and walked into the surf, bending down to fill his bush hat with water and putting it back on to empty over his face. He shut his eyes as the deliciously cool water rinsed the sweat from his face. The bastard! he thought, the rotten little bastard! Just how could a nice couple like the Kleins end up with *that* for a son? Anderson calmed down a bit as he meandered along the shore, kicking up water when he felt like it. There was now a new question to be asked. Just what did Klein do for ten days after he left Tel Aviv? One question led to another. Was Cohen missing at the same time? Could that be it? he wondered as pieces began to fit.

Maybe the secret cloning wasn't done in Strauss's lab at all. Could Cohen and Klein have done it elsewhere? It made a lot of sense.

A puff of sand distracted Anderson and made him stop to look for the little animal he supposed had made it. As he squatted down, a second spurt of sand flew up to the left of the original but this time Anderson correlated it with a distant sound. Someone was shooting at him!

He tried running and swearing at the same time and ended up doing neither successfully as his feet lost purchase in the soft sand and made him a rolling, tumbling, foul-mouthed shambles as he reached the cover of the Roman aqueduct. A bullet whined off the stone as he pressed himself to the ground and lay still. What now? he thought as he looked around. He was trapped with a kilometre of open beach between him and the fort in one direction and nothing between the aqueduct and the port of Haifa in the other! Moving inland was also out; the ground was as flat and as open as the beach.

Anderson didn't move; the sniper didn't fire; only the sound of the waves lapping the shore and Anderson's own heartbeat broke the peace of the afternoon. Any doubt that he might have harboured about the incident in the lab with the acid being accidental evaporated in the shimmering heat that rose from the sand. Someone was trying to kill him and the odds were all on their side.

His watch said that ten minutes had passed. Maybe his attacker had gone. He cautiously pushed his flight bag out into the open. Crack! The bag jerked as if someone had kicked it. Anderson pulled it in by its strap to find a black hole in the side. The sight of it made him feel sick in his stomach. This was it. He was going to die on the burning sands of Judaea, a long way from Dumfries, and he was no way near ready.

If only he knew exactly where the sniper was he might be

able to work something out . . . in fact, there was a chance he might be able to use the natural curve of the aqueduct to keep it between himself and the gunman while he made a run inland. But with over a hundred metres of open, flat ground between the beach and the nearest cover he would have to be very sure. A bullet from a high-velocity rifle was not going to leave him limping onwards with the 'flesh wound' so beloved of Western movies. It was going to bring him down, and if it did not kill him it would leave such a hole on exiting and make such a mess of his insides, that death might be preferable. But it was his only chance.

He would use his flight bag to induce the sniper to fire again. This time he would push it out suddenly while he himself looked out from the other side of the arch for a muzzle flash. Timing was going to be everything. If he looked out too soon the gunman would fire at his head instead of the bag.

He positioned the flight bag at the edge of the arch and located a long piece of driftwood behind it so that he could move it with his foot from the other side of the arch. When he was sure that everything was positioned as well as it could be, he mentally rehearsed exactly what he was going to do. Then he did it.

In one flowing move he hit the wood with his left heel to send the bag out into the open and then spun on his right to look out. He was in time to see the flash of fire in the scrubland as the gunman fired at the bag. He jerked his head back in not a moment too soon as a second bullet whined off the rock where his head had been.

Anderson let out the breath that he had been holding in and relaxed for a few seconds in the shelter of the stone. He felt a sense of achievement; he knew exactly where the sniper was. He calculated that, if he were two arches further along the aqueduct, he would be able to run across the open ground without the gunman being able to hit him.

But, and it was a big but, to get two arches further along would mean exposing himself completely for three or four seconds. Could he risk it?

Realistically, Anderson put his chances at zero. Each time his flight bag had been exposed it had been hit within a second. He would have to think again. Perhaps he could rig up some protection. There were plenty of rocks and boulders lying around in the shade of the arch. If he moved some of them to the mouth, perhaps he could form a small wall to crawl behind for a few yards? He started to shift stones and pile them up at the edge of the arch, taking care to keep his hands inside. If a bullet hit his hand he would lose it.

The sniper saw what was going on and loosed off a shot; it sent stone splinters flying in all directions and made Anderson hug the earth. When his courage had returned he continued his task, telling himself all the time that as long as he did not expose himself he would be all right. He pushed another rock out to extend his wall and the sniper fired again. This time a chip from the stone above Anderson hit him on the forehead. He fell backwards, still conscious but feeling dizzy. He put up his hand to wipe away the blood that was trickling into his eyes and heard the sound of an engine labouring along the sands. Was this the sniper coming to finish him off?

For Anderson, dizziness and fear seemed to merge with confusion as the air was filled with the sound of shouting and automatic weapons being fired in short bursts. He tried to move to the mouth of the arch but stopped as the pain in his head affected his vision. He contented himself with leaning his head against the stone and gazing at the cloudless blue sky.

The light was suddenly blotted out by a figure appearing in the entrance to the arch. A female voice said, 'Are you all right?'

Anderson strained his eyes and saw the epaulettes of a military shirt silhouetted against the sky. He thought that his ears had deceived him and said, 'I'll be OK. Just a cut on the head.'

'It looks nasty,' said the female voice.

'You *are* a woman,' said Anderson, now sure of what he had heard.

'Incredible, isn't it,' said the woman as she crawled inside the arch and examined Anderson's forehead. Anderson could not see her that well in the gloom but what he could see he liked.

'What happened to the bugles?' he asked as gentle fingers wiped away the blood.

'Bugles?'

'The cavalry always blow bugles when they come to the rescue.'

'Ah, I see. American movies. You don't sound American.'

'I'm not. I'm Scottish.'

'Sit still for a moment,' said the woman. 'We have some dressings in the jeep.' She crawled out backwards from the confines of the arch and ran down the sands to where a jeep was parked with its doors hanging open. She returned within moments carrying a small wooden box which she propped up against a rock and opened. She wiped some more blood away from Anderson's wound before deciding what size of dressing was needed.

Anderson tried to decipher the badges on her uniform but gave up when he realized that his failure to do so had little to do with the poor light in the shadows and much to do with the fact that they were in Hebrew. 'You're a nurse?' he asked.

'No, I'm not a nurse,' said the woman with a certain slow deliberation.

'But you're in the army?'

98

'Yes, I'm in the army.'

Anderson saw the pips on her shoulders as she reached round him to secure the dressing. 'I'm grateful to you, Captain,' he said. 'You saved my life.'

'We hate to lose tourists,' smiled the woman. 'We need the foreign currency.'

Anderson smiled back. 'Seriously . . . I'm grateful.'

'Can you stand?'

'No problem.' Anderson crawled to the edge of the arch and got to his feet in the sunlight. He could now see his rescuer properly as she stood, hands on hips, looking towards the scrubland where the sound of sporadic gunfire still came from. She was dressed in olive-green fatigues which in no way disguised the slimness of her figure, and she held her hand to her dark hair to stop the wind from the sea blowing it round into her face. Anderson thought that she could not be more than twenty-five or so but her proud profile and the slight haughtiness of her stance suggested a confidence and stature beyond her years.

'What's happening?' asked Anderson.

'My men are pursuing your attacker.'

Anderson noted the 'my men' but managed to contain his surprise.

'Which hotel are you staying at, Mr . . . ?'

'Anderson, Dr Anderson, and I'm not staying at a hotel. In fact, I'm not a tourist.'

'Then what?'

Anderson put his hand to his head as it began to throb in the blistering heat of the sun. 'Actually, I . . . ' The sand ran into the sea, the sea ran into the sky, and night fell with a sudden, total blackness.

Anderson woke up in hospital. He did not catch which one when the nurse told him but he managed to gather

99

that it was in Hadera. 'What time is it?' he asked.

'Eight in the evening.'

The door closed, leaving him alone to examine his surroundings. The walls were white, the ceiling was white, the floor was brown. That took care of that. He reached out and lifted his flight bag off the top of the bedside locker. The holes in it were real enough; it hadn't been a bad dream, it had really happened.

'Dr Anderson, you have a visitor,' said the nurse as she held open the sprung door. Anderson's rescuer came in, still dressed in dusty, olive drab.

'How are you feeling?'

'Much better, thank you. I'm afraid I don't know your name.'

'Mirit Zimmerman. You passed out before I could ask you some things I need for my report.'

'Did your men catch the gunman?' asked Anderson.

'I am afraid not, but all the shore patrols have been alerted in that area in case there are more.'

'More?'

'More terrorists. They come ashore in small boats along the coast, cause havoc then depart. It's supposed to undermine our morale.' Mirit Zimmerman said it as if that were the last thing on earth that it was going to do.

'I see. Then you think it was a terrorist?'

The cool, dark eyes looked straight into Anderson's. 'Don't you?' she asked.

Anderson held her gaze for a moment, wondering if she really knew more than she was letting on, but the features did not flinch. In fact, he felt sure that Mirit Zimmerman was appraising *his* reaction. 'You are the expert in these matters, Captain.'

Anderson gave Mirit Zimmerman the information she needed about his reasons for being in Israel and his address in Tel Aviv should there be any need to contact him again about the incident. As she got up to leave, Mirit turned and smiled as if something secret were amusing her. 'Can you think of anything else I should know, Doctor?' she asked.

'I don't think so,' replied Anderson. 'Except to tell you again how grateful I am.'

The slight smile was still on Mirit's face as she nodded and left the room.

Anderson felt distinctly uneasy. There was nothing he would have liked more than to believe it had been a terrorist that had shot at him in Caesarea, but he could not believe that and he suspected Mirit Zimmerman had some unspoken reason for not believing it either. He wondered what it was.

Anderson was discharged from hospital in the morning and returned to Tel Aviv, pausing only briefly at his apartment before going up to the university where he found Myra Freedman alone in the main lab. He had to explain the head bandage before finding out what stage the toxin tests were at.

'Cohen inoculated the animals last night and set up two drug tests, tetracycline and ceporin,' Myra told him. 'He said that he would be in to see you this morning but hasn't appeared yet.'

'I'll check the animals,' said Anderson.

The door to the isolation suite was locked when Anderson tried it but the rattle attracted a technician who came over with the keys. It was strangely quiet, thought Anderson. He read the labels on the cages and found the toxin tests. Cohen had inoculated six mice, each with a different dilution of the filtered fluid from the plasmid/Galomycin mix. In addition he had inoculated two control animals, one with the neat fluid and one with only sterile culture medium.

Anderson examined the control mice first. The one

which had received the undiluted fluid was stiff and dead, the other alive and well. Controls OK, now for the dilutions. One in a thousand . . . Dead. One in ten thousand . . . Dead. One in a hundred thousand . . . Dead. The hair rose on the back of Anderson's neck as he went along the line. Last one. One in ten million . . . Dead. Good God Almighty! said Anderson under his breath. 'Can't be . . . Please God, it can't be.' He rechecked the dilution figures on the labels. There was no mistake.

Before returning to the lab, Anderson looked at the two guinea pigs used for the new drug tests. Both were dead. Galomycin was not the only drug to trigger off the plasmid. Tetracycline and ceporin would be just as lethal. It was shaping up to be one of those days – with a vengeance.

'There must be some mistake,' exclaimed Strauss, when Anderson told him of the toxin tests. 'This would mean . . . ' He paused to reach behind him for a book, flicking through the pages till he found the information he was looking for. 'Yes, this would mean that the toxin from the plasmid is ten times more lethal than that from the bacterium *Clostridium botulinum*. And that, Doctor, as we both know, is the most powerful poison known to man.'

'I rechecked Dr Cohen's labels. There is no mistake.'

'Is Dr Cohen in the lab?'

'No,' said Anderson. 'Myra said that he hasn't been in this morning.'

'Repeat the experiment, Doctor.'

'Very well.'

'And, Doctor?'

'Yes?'

'What happened to your head?'

'I hurt it on the beach.'

Anderson told Myra of Strauss's decision. 'I'll inoculate the cultures,' she said. On finding the fridge empty Anderson asked her where the Galomycin was. 'In Cohen's lab. He used it through there yesterday.'

Anderson walked into Cohen's empty lab and looked in the fridge. He found the Galomycin but as he stood up again he thought he detected a peculiar smell, an unpleasant smell, a smell that filled him with foreboding. It was the indefinable smell that all medical people come to associate with death.

Anderson's increasing heart rate made his head wound pulse painfully as he walked slowly across the lab to Cohen's bench and looked down behind it to have his worst fears realized. Cohen was lying spreadeagled on the floor; he had been dead for some time and the bared teeth and agonized expression told Anderson exactly how he had come to die.

Before doing anything else, Anderson told Strauss what he had found. Together they returned to Cohen's lab and locked the door behind them.

'Plasmid death,' said Strauss, looking at the face.

'Unmistakable,' agreed Anderson.

Strauss knelt down stiffly beside the body and murmured, 'Poor Arieh. He was always so careful.'

'Yesterday we didn't know how powerful the toxin really was,' said Anderson. 'He must have been working with the pure stuff.'

Anderson was examining the bits and pieces lying on Cohen's work area, trying to deduce what had happened, when Strauss called him back to the body. He pointed to Cohen's right hand and to a cut in the surgical glove he was still wearing. Dark blood stained the inside where it had spread by capillary attraction between the skin and the tight-fitting glove.

Anderson nodded. 'That looks like it,' he said, looking around the floor by the body for something that could have made the cut. He found what he was looking for, a thin scalpel fitted with a number-eleven blade. He showed it to

Strauss who shrugged then shook his head in sorrow. 'Damn, damn, damn,' he said as he got unsteadily to his feet.

Anderson looked down at Cohen's body while Strauss picked up the phone. Poetic justice? he wondered. He heard Strauss say, 'There has been an accident in my laboratory. Dr Cohen is dead.'

CHAPTER FIVE

The death of Arieh Cohen put an immediate stop to working with the plasmid and its toxin in the open lab. Strauss insisted that the maximum-containment facility in the basement of the building be opened and used for all future work. It was agreed that only Anderson and Myra Freedman would work there, with a supply of lab animals being put in for them.

Anderson was depressed at the thought of having to work under the restrictions imposed by the containment suite but agreed that it was now imperative. Such facilities were designed for work with the most highly dangerous materials where the prime consideration was to prevent their escape to the outside world.

The first line of defence in the system was the use of differential air pressure. The suite was constantly maintained at a lower atmospheric pressure than the area surrounding it so that no air could escape. People working in the suite had to get in and out, of course, but such movement was restricted by the elaborate entry and exit procedures which demanded that workers remove all their outside clothes and pass through a series of airlocks and showers before donning the masks, coveralls and boots they would wear for the duration of their work period. Leaving meant stripping and showering again. No article was ever removed from the containment suite without first being rendered safe; in the case of biological contamination, by passage through a sterilizing autoclave equipped with double doors and embedded in the wall of the suite.

For the protection of workers inside the facility, innoculation hoods were standard for dealing with bacteria and viruses. These were glass-fronted cabinets fitted with armholes and a range of internal lighting options including ultraviolet for disinfection when not being used. The base was a watertight tray which could be flooded with an appropriate sterilizing agent should accidental spillage occur. The degree of protection afforded by these cabinets was, to a certain extent, offset by the loss of sensitivity imposed by using the gloved armholes. No one liked them. Everything seemed to take twice as long.

When the differential air pressure had stabilized in the containment suite, Anderson showered, donned protective clothing and passed through the airlock. He adjusted his respirator mask till it seemed comfortable but knew from past experience that there was no position that would seem right after a couple of hours. Myra Freedman joined him in similar garb, gown, Wellingtons and respirator. He saw her eyes smile above the mask and nodded. It was going to be a long day.

'Thank God!' said Myra as they met outside the airlock. 'I feel like a nun.'

The elevator took them up to the sixth floor where Strauss was waiting. 'Everything all right?' he asked them. Anderson told him that they had repeated Cohen's experiment with even more dilutions and set up two more antibiotic tests. 'Excellent. A word, if you please, Doctor.' Anderson made a face at Myra Freedman and followed Strauss into his office. 'I had a call from the military authorities in Hadera,' said Strauss.

'Oh,' said Anderson.

'Your "accident" on the beach was a little more dramatic than you had me believe.'

Anderson apologized, saying that he didn't want any fuss to distract them from the real problems.

Strauss smiled. 'The stiff upper lip of the English, eh?'

'I'm Scots,' said Anderson.

'Forgive me,' said Strauss with another smile. 'Mrs Strauss and I would be delighted if you would join us for dinner this evening.'

Anderson enjoyed the evening with Jacob and Miriam Strauss. He had hoped that Strauss might speak again of science and medicine as he had on the first occasion in his office, but it was not to be. Out of deference to Miriam, who was not a doctor or scientist, the conversation was kept more general. Anderson told them about his family home in Dumfries and what he and his sister had got up to when they were young and running free on the hills of Galloway. Miriam laughed loudly and shook her head in mock despair. 'I can sympathize with your poor mother!' she said.

'Do you have any family?' Anderson asked.

Miriam's face clouded a little before the smile returned and she said, 'Two boys. Dov, he's a biologist like his father. He works in America . . . '

Anderson looked at Strauss, expecting him to say something but he appeared to avert his eyes. He looked again at Miriam.

'And Jacob, our youngest son. He was killed in the war, doing his military service.'

Anderson felt bad. He wished that he had never asked. Now both his hosts were looking at the floor.

'Your glass is empty,' said Strauss, breaking the spell.

Anderson returned to his apartment building just after eleven-thirty and found that some of the American students were sitting on the lawn outside with guitars and the inevitable folk songs. Miles Langman was with them. He came over as he saw Anderson and greeted him like a long-lost brother, asking where the hell he had been for the last two days. Anderson looked at the smiling face and gave it the benefit of the doubt. Maybe Langman was just a friendly guy, interested in everything. Americans were like that . . .

'It's a long story.'

'Want to talk?'

'Sure.'

They stopped at the second floor while Langman collected beer from the fridge, then climbed up to the roof to sit with their backs against the parapet. Anderson let out a long sigh.

'Problems?' asked Langman.

'It's been one shit-awful day,' said Anderson. 'Make that two,' he added, touching the wound on his head. He told Langman of his trip to Caesarea and his discovery that Klein hadn't actually gone there when he had left Tel Aviv.

'A girlfriend?' suggested Langman.

Anderson shrugged. 'I think that's when the little bastard did the secret cloning along with Cohen from the lab, but now we'll never know.'

'Why not?'

Anderson told him of Cohen's death.

'Oooooeeeee,' sighed Langman. 'Acid. Terrorist bullets. People dropping dead. It's not much of a vacation.'

'It was never going to be that.'

'If Cohen and Klein are both dead, what are you going to do now?'

'Find a drug to wipe out that bloody plasmid and get my arse out of here.'

'Figures.'

'Mind you,' said Anderson, after a sudden thought about what Langman had suggested earlier. 'If Klein *did* have a girlfriend, she might know where his lab book was. She might even know where he went during the missing ten days . . . ' The idea brought Anderson out of his depression.

'How will you find out?' asked Langman.

'I'll ask Myra.'

Anderson had a restless night. His sleep was constantly disturbed by a dream of the beach at Caesarea in which he was running on sand so soft that it threatened to swallow him, and always, in the background, was the beautiful Mirit Zimmerman, smiling at him in a strangely distant way and moving slowly backwards into the sea. Anderson woke for the umpteenth time as the sand was about to cover his face. He got up, switched on the electric kettle and showered while it boiled. By the time he had freed himself of sweat and drunk his coffee he was sure of one thing. He had to see Mirit Zimmerman again and find out what she really knew about the attack in Caesarea.

Strauss provided Anderson with the telephone number of the military authorities in Hadera. He phoned before going down to the containment suite, using the pretext of a lost camera.

'One moment,' said the voice, 'I'll see if she's on duty.' The moment became a minute, then two. Anderson twisted and untwisted the phone wire round his index finger as he waited.

'You have lost a camera, Dr Anderson?' said Mirit Zimmerman's voice. She sounded puzzled.

'Actually . . . no,' Anderson confessed. 'I needed an excuse. I wanted to speak to you.'

'What about?'

'Did you catch the terrorist up in Caesarea?'

'No.'

'Did you find any evidence of terrorist activity in that region?'

'Really, Doctor, I don't think that I can discuss . . .'

'Forgive me,' interrupted Anderson, 'I know that this must sound most improper. It's just that . . . I don't think it was a terrorist who attacked me.'

'Oh?'

'And I don't think you do either.'

'I don't remember saying anything to give you that impression, Doctor.'

'You didn't have to. I saw it in your face.'

'I don't think that we can discuss this over the telephone.'

'Then will you meet me?' asked Anderson.

'Doctor, if you have any information that could be of use to the authorities you must . . . '

'I know what I should do, Captain, but I have no evidence, only bad feelings. Scared feelings. I would like to talk to you.'

There was a long pause before Mirit Zimmerman said, 'Very well. I'll be home in Jerusalem at the weekend; I'll meet you for lunch on Sunday.'

Anderson breathed a sigh of relief. 'Thanks. Where do I meet you?'

'The Jaffa Gate at noon.' The phone went dead.

Anderson found Myra Freedman, who had been waiting for him, and they took the lift down to the containment suite. He took the opportunity of being alone with Myra to ask if Martin Klein had had a girlfriend.

'Yes. Shula Ron, one of the undergraduates.'

'Where do I find her?'

'At home probably, it's vacation time. Why do you ask?'

Anderson told her about the missing ten days in Klein's life. 'I want to find out if she knows where he was, what he was doing.'

Myra pulled out the cage containing the mouse that had only received an injection of sterile culture fluid. It was alive and well and in a minority of one. By the end of the examination the bench was littered with the corpses of ten dead mice and two dead guinea pigs. Anderson lowered his respirator slowly and shook his head.

'Two more drugs today?' asked Myra quietly.

'Two more. But first I want to talk to Strauss.'

'So there's no mistake,' said Strauss when Anderson told him of the mouse tests.

''Fraid not. Botulism is no longer the world's most powerful toxin. We've got a new number one.'

Strauss said something in Hebrew but Anderson felt confident with the translation he guessed at. 'I have been doing some calculations,' said Strauss. He took a glass from the tray on his desk that held a water carafe. 'This much plasmid toxin,' he said, holding out the glass, 'would kill all of Tel Aviv.' Anderson stayed silent. 'The point is, Doctor, what do we do?' said Strauss.

'Have you informed the authorities?' asked Anderson.

'No, I have not,' said Strauss with great deliberation. 'I said Tel Aviv but I could have said Damascus or Beirut.'

Anderson was aware that Strauss was watching for his reaction but he still didn't say anything.

'How many people know about the plasmid?' asked Strauss.

'Quite a few,' said Anderson.

'How many people know of the toxin's true potency?'

'You, me, Myra Freedman.'

'So there's still a chance,' said Strauss thoughtfully.

'A chance?'

'Doctor, I will be frank. I do not want to hand this over to the authorities . . . any authorities. I do not trust the military mind.' He looked long and hard at Anderson before saying, 'I will undertake to destroy all sources of the plasmid in this laboratory if you will agree to do the same when you return . . . no reports, no paperwork, just a simple act . . . a simple human act for good.'

Anderson's mind played with the words. A simple act . . . a simple, unprofessional act . . . a simple, unscientific act . . . a simple, career-destroying act . . . but, an act for good.

'Very well,' he said, 'I agree.'

'Good,' said Strauss, with obvious relief.

'But,' said Anderson, 'there may be another source of the plasmid. We don't know for sure that Klein made it in this lab.'

'But where? When?'

Anderson told him about the missing ten days.

'I see.'

'To be brutally honest, Professor, I believe that Klein did the secret cloning during those ten days and I don't think he did it alone. I think Arieh Cohen was involved.' Anderson waited for an angry reaction but it didn't come. Instead, Strauss sighed deeply and said, 'I didn't know about the ten days, of course, but I am bound to say that I have nurtured similar suspicions.'

'But why would they do such a thing?'

Strauss shook his head. 'Why do men do such things? What a question to ask a Jew, my friend.'

'It's just plain evil,' said Anderson.

'It's also puzzling,' said Strauss. Anderson waited for an explanation. 'Has it occurred to you that such a weapon might be considered rather primitive for this day and age?' Anderson shrugged. Strauss continued, 'I just can't understand why anyone, even someone evil, should set out to design a toxin when binaries and nerve agents took over a long time ago in biological weapons.'

Anderson saw that the old man did have a point but said, 'The plasmid is cheap and easy. Anyone could make toxin with it, and it is very powerful.'

'And there you may have it, my friend,' said Strauss. 'Cheapness and ease of production. That, I think, tells us something about its potential users.'

'Terrorists,' said Anderson.

'Indeed,' said Strauss, 'and that is why we must destroy it. We must wipe it out before some idiotic bunch of political lunatics see fit to pour it into a reservoir, and hope that with Klein and Cohen dead there is no other source.'

Anderson agreed, shuddering inwardly at the consequences of failure.

'What happened in the antibiotic tests?'

'Two more failures. We'll try another two today.'

The day for Anderson and Myra Freedman was relatively undemanding with only the new antibiotic tests to set up, and they were able to leave the containment suite shortly after lunchtime. 'You look less like a road accident today,' said Myra as they returned to the lab, referring to the fact that Anderson had been able to discard his head bandage that morning in addition to the hand dressings which had gone the day before.

Anderson left the lab at three and went to the student administration building where he found out the home address of Shula Ron. She lived in Jerusalem. He copied the address into the back of his diary and started making preliminary plans for the weekend. He now had two reasons to visit Jerusalem, three if he counted the fact that he wanted to see it anyway.

Anderson went directly from the student building to the university swimming pool where he was content to wallow in the cool water for a few minutes before starting to swim up the length of the pool in a slow, lazy backstroke. The brightness of the sun demanded that he keep his eyes almost closed, but he enjoyed floating on his back and opening them just a little so that the reflections from the water made spectral patterns with his eyelashes. The world seemed marginally nicer today and the fact that he was going to see Mirit Zimmerman again had a whole lot to do with it.

The afternoon passed with appreciated slowness, Anderson alternately swimming in the cool green water and toasting himself on the poolside. He developed an ecosystem where he would bake on both sides then roll, like a lazy

113

seal leaving its rock, into the water to sink slowly to the bottom. One thrust with his feet and he would break the surface with enough velocity to pull himself out of the pool and start all over again.

Next morning, Anderson's spirits were to rise further when he found only one dead guinea pig. The other, which had received the plasmid plus a drug called Colomycin, had survived – indeed, it seemed perfectly healthy. Strauss was delighted. 'So, Colomycin does not trigger the plasmid. Excellent! But we must be sure.'

'I'll repeat it, of course,' said Anderson.

'Yes, and give the surviving animal another dose of Colomycin.' Anderson looked questioningly at Strauss. 'In a few days we can challenge the animal with Galomycin. If it survives it means that the Colomycin has cleared all trace of the plasmid from its body.'

Anderson told Strauss of his plans to visit Jerusalem and talk with Shula Ron.

'It would be nice to know,' agreed Strauss, adding that he was glad Anderson was going to see Jerusalem. 'Stay a few days. Your work here is nearly over.'

Another quiet day meant that Anderson could leave the lab at lunchtime. He decided not to spend another afternoon in the chlorinated waters of the pool but opted instead to walk the length of Einstein to the junction with the Haifa Highway where he caught a bus to the resort of Herzliya just to the north of Tel Aviv. There he bought sandwiches and cold Maccabee beer from a beach stall and ate under the shade of a canopy while he watched people at play beneath the apparently uninterested but ever-watchful eyes of two lifeguards who sat on raised platforms.

After an hour or so, Anderson renewed his life-long love affair with the sea, swimming out fifty metres to turn over on to his back and look at the land. There was always something pleasurable about the perspective that this view gave him, a pleasant feeling of detachment, a momentary escape from reality as if he'd just stepped off the world to take a breather and would catch it again next time around.

The bus to Jerusalem was packed. Anderson had been trapped in the middle of a great phalanx of people at Tel Aviv bus station and had been carried along in the crush as everyone made to board the bus at the same time. He found himself in a window seat halfway along on the left-hand side, though how he got there owed nothing to choice. An Arab woman displaying a mouth full of gold teeth was tumbled into the seat beside him as the harsh, guttural sounds of Hebrew and Arabic made it seem like the opening session of a convention for bronchitics.

The journey, a distance of about sixty kilometres, seemed long and laboured as the laden bus toiled uphill through the barren scrub of the foothills of the mountains of Judaea. Anderson, bored with the sight of sand, examined his fellow passengers without, he hoped, making it too obvious. The sunburnt skin, the hawk noses, the age lines – were these, he wondered, the faces that Jesus of Nazareth saw when he looked into the crowd?

Jerusalem appeared as a jewel in the morning sun, impressing Anderson with its cleanness and an aura of brightness created by the light-coloured stonework of its buildings. The bus station was the scene of yet another scrimmage as his fellow passengers all decided to alight at once, but this time Anderson remained aloof, or rather seated, until they had all gone and he could step out into the sunlit Jerusalem morning unaided.

It was hot but different from Tel Aviv in that the air was no longer heavy with moisture, making it seem fresher, drier, altogether more comfortable as he left the bus station and headed off in the direction of the Old City.

Anderson stood quietly and took in his first sight of

115

ancient Jerusalem with its huge ramparts stretching out to encircle what had been at the heart of so much history. He could see the sweating slaves of Emperor Suleiman as they toiled to build the great stone walls along lines originally decreed by Solomon and Herod, 'modern' sixteenth-century walls to protect a city chosen some three thousand years before by King David to be the capital of the first state of Israel.

Anderson checked his watch. Two hours to go. He entered the Old City at the Jaffa Gate and stepped back in time to a society that still drove donkeys with sticks through narrow, cobbled alleys. Only the anachronism of soldiers patrolling with machine pistols said that this was no biblical tableau resurrected from childhood memory. That, and the smell in the alleys which were crammed with Arab traders selling everything from leather to gold, from spices to china, from fish to linen.

The vendors vied with each other for the attention of passers-by, each so attuned to insincerity that the belief that showing their teeth constituted a smile seemed universal. Anderson moved from stall to stall, looking but ignoring the dentistry, feigning immunity to the crouching and the hand rubbing. He left the dappled shade of the alleys and climbed the steps leading to the precincts of the Dome of the Rock.

He stood stock still at his first sight of the great mosque, its huge golden dome throwing back the sunlight above the spot where Muhammad was said to have ascended to heaven. Well, why not? thought Anderson.

He climbed the steps leading up to the mosque itself and removed his shoes at the door before entering the cool, dark interior and walking round, finding the place surprisingly free of religious trinketry. It seemed to Anderson that all adornment and symbolism had gone into the building itself, leaving the interior with a not unpleasant air of emptiness. In this particular mosque the great expanse of carpeted floor was broken by the rock itself where it rose through the floor in the middle. Anderson saw that there were steps leading down to the base of the rock and descended to find himself in a smaller carpeted area. A man lay spreadeagled on the floor in prayer.

The sight made Anderson feel guilty. He was an interloper. This place obviously meant so much more to the man than himself. It didn't seem right that he was there just watching it all. He came up again quietly and walked out into the sunlight. It was time to keep his appointment.

It was coming up to the hottest part of the day as Anderson looked for a shaded place to wait by the Jaffa Gate. He was relieved to find a stone arch next to one of the great wooden doors where he could cower from the heat, albeit under the interested gaze of one of the patrolling guards who had noticed him lingering there. Anderson smiled; the guard remained impassive. Knowing that the guard was watching him made him feel uncomfortable; it forced him to look at his watch more often than he might otherwise have done in an effort to convince the suspicious man that he was waiting for someone. Mirit arrived and the guard was forgotten.

She had to pause for a suitable gap in the traffic outside the Old City before she could cross the road to where Anderson waited on the pavement. It gave him time to look at her. She wore a white dress that contrasted beautifully with her dark hair and showed off her smooth olive skin to advantage. She pushed her hair back from her face with the same gesture that Anderson remembered from the beach, and he saw again the same slight haughtiness in profile as she anticipated a hiatus in the rumbling traffic and skipped across lightly after a service bus had obscured her momentarily from view.

'It was good of you to come,' said Anderson, holding out his hand.

Mirit smiled in reply. 'Your first time in Jerusalem?' she asked.

'But not my last, I hope,' said Anderson.

Mirit smiled again. 'It does affect people that way,' she said.

'I'll have to rely on you to suggest where we eat,' said Anderson.

'Of course. Shall we eat in the Old City?'

They walked for a few minutes through narrow alleys till they came to a low wooden door, painted purple and furnished with a brass plate inscribed in Arabic. 'In here,' said Mirit.

Anderson had to duck his head to get through the doorway and then had to wait for a few moments till his eyes became accustomed to the gloom. A waiter wearing a long Arab gown showed them to a table; they appeared to be the only ones in the restaurant.

'Shall I order for us?' asked Mirit.

'Please,' said Anderson.

As the waiter went off with their order, Mirit turned her dark eyes to Anderson and said, 'Now, Doctor, who is trying to kill you?'

'I don't know who.'

'But you know why?'

'I think so. It has to do with the reason for my being here in Israel.' Anderson told her briefly about the death of Martin Klein and how it had led him to Tel Aviv and Professor Strauss's laboratory. He told her of the incident with the acid.

'But why didn't you tell the police?' asked Mirit.

'Because it could have been an accident. I couldn't prove anything. In fact, I almost believed it was an accident until the thing at Caesarea and even then there seemed a possibility that it was a terrorist until I saw in your face that you had some doubts.'

Mirit nodded. 'You're quite right. A terrorist would have been the usual explanation for the attack but there were certain things that didn't seem quite right in your case.'

'And these were?'

'To begin with, you don't even look like an Israeli. Why would a terrorist attack you? Secondly, you were on your own. Terrorists tend not to attack individuals unless they have some political significance. You have none. It didn't make sense for them to land on a lonely beach and kill a tourist; they had nothing to gain by it. You didn't see them land so why waste ten, fifteen minutes trying to shoot you? And then there was the weapon.'

'The weapon?'

'By the time I saw you in hospital in Hadera we had found the weapon used by your attacker. He got away but he dropped the gun in the chase. It was a high-velocity sniper's rifle, made in West Germany. Not the sort of weapon we've ever found on a terrorist before. They are almost invariably equipped with semi-automatic weapons of Eastern-bloc origin.'

Anderson looked down at the table and nodded in resignation. He said quietly, 'Thank you. You've told me what I wanted to hear, or rather what I didn't. But now I'm sure; someone wants me dead.'

'You have lots of company, Doctor,' said Mirit, getting a puzzled look in return. She explained, 'It's not much comfort to you but every Israeli in the country could truthfully say what you have just said. It might be less personal but it's the same feeling.'

'I'd never looked at it that way before,' smiled Anderson ruefully. 'Tell me about it. Tell me about your life.'

They paused while the Arab waiter came with the food

and set it before them. 'What do you want to know, Doctor?'

'My name's Neil and I want to know everything.'

'My parents are German Jews. They came to Israel in 1948 after surviving the camps and wandering all over Europe; they were present at the very birth of modern Israel. I was born in Jerusalem itself but the city was divided then; the Jordanians occupied the eastern half. It was like that until I was eight years old, then the six-day war broke out. The Arab assault on Jerusalem was repulsed and the city reunited. I remember my father crying that day, for the western wall of the temple had been in Arab hands until then. He went there to pray and came home with tears running down his face. I've never forgotten that. It was the day I really discovered what being an Israeli meant.'

Anderson noted the softening of her eyes when Mirit spoke of her father. He said, 'I wish I could say that I know how you must feel but the truth is that I don't. I couldn't possibly. You must have lived your entire life under threat of violence and war.'

Mirit smiled and leaned towards him. She said, 'I will confess a secret fear to you. Sometimes I don't think we could survive without the threat from outside. It's the thing that keeps us together. The will to simply survive is the most powerful force in Israel. Take away the threat . . . who knows.'

'I can't see the threat disappearing just yet,' said Anderson.

'You're right. The Palestinians are a problem.'

'They have a point,' said Anderson, taking a gamble on the intelligence he felt sure lay behind the dark eyes. For a moment he thought that he had got it wrong. There was an uncomfortably long silence during which Mirit stared at him stonily. Then she said slowly, 'Have you ever seen a bus full of children after it has been blown up by an Arab bomb?'

Anderson felt his pulse quicken but kept calm. He returned Mirit's stare and said, 'No, I haven't. But then I've never seen an Arab village when your air force has finished with it. The emotions of personal involvement never solve anything. Your answer was a cop-out . . . and you know it.'

The hardness left Mirit's eyes. She looked at Anderson as if seeing him for the first time. 'Yes, it was,' she said quietly. 'But what made you so sure?'

'I read it in your face.'

'You keep doing that,' smiled Mirit. 'So what is your answer to the Palestinian problem?' she asked.

'I don't know. Do you?'

'No, I don't know either,' confessed Mirit.

Anderson asked how long she had been in the army.

'Five years. I did national service then stayed on to make it my career.'

'Why?'

'You won't deny that we need an army?' smiled Mirit.

'No, I certainly won't do that,' agreed Anderson. 'But why you personally?'

Mirit smoothed the hair away from her forehead. She said, 'My parents owe everything to Israel. They went through hell on earth, like so many of our old people, before the foundation of our country. We, the younger generation, owe it to them to see that Israel survives, that what happened in the thirties and forties never happens again. I am an only child; I have no brothers, so it was up to me.'

'Do you like being a soldier?' asked Anderson.

'I am good at my job,' said Mirit.

Anderson believed her. 'But you don't have women in the front line?' he asked.

'No, we don't. But that doesn't mean to say that we wouldn't if the need arose.'

Mirît and Anderson left the restaurant and walked slowly back to the Jaffa Gate. They stopped on the pavement outside.

'I'm grateful to you for coming,' said Anderson.

'I'm sorry I couldn't be more helpful. I only wish we had caught your attacker. But you will go to the police now? They can obtain a copy of my report from Hadera.'

'Not just yet. I have something to do first. Perhaps you can help.' Anderson showed Mirit the address he had written down for Shula Ron.

'It's on my way. I'll take you there.'

It was a ten-minute drive from the Old City through the broad, busy streets of modern Jerusalem with its traffic and office blocks. Mirit pulled the white Fiat into the kerb and stopped.

'Along there,' she said, pointing with her finger. 'Third on the left.'

'Thank you again,' said Anderson, reluctant to get out and say goodbye. He wanted to see her again. 'Mirit . . . if I should need to get in touch with you . . . ' he began.

'What for, Neil?' asked Mirit, with just the hint of a smile in her eyes.

'To ask you out to dinner,' confessed Anderson, dropping the search for some kind of official excuse.

Mirit took a notepad from the dashboard and scribbled something down. 'This is my telephone number here in Jerusalem. Don't call me at the post.'

For a moment Anderson felt as if he were thirteen years old. He grinned broadly as he took the piece of paper. 'When would be a convenient time for you?'

'When did you have in mind?' asked Mirit.

'Tonight?' Anderson asked in mock trepidation and looked at her out of the corner of his eyes. She burst out laughing and Anderson followed suit.

'I think that would be very nice,' she said. 'Call me at that number when you have finished your business.'

Anderson stood on the pavement looking after the Fiat, still smiling till the peculiar looks he was attracting from passers-by made him stop. He walked along the street in the direction indicated by Mirit and found the address he was looking for. The flat, in an old building that smelled strongly of cats, was on the third floor. Anderson pressed the bell and the door was opened by a middle-aged woman wearing heavy, metal-framed glasses. He said who he was and asked to speak with Shula.

'Shula is working today.'

'Working?'

'She is a guide in the Old City during her vacation.'

Anderson smiled and said that he had just come from there. 'Whereabouts in the Old City?' he asked.

'She is one of the promenade guides.'

'The promenade?'

'Yes. It is the walk along the top of the old walls. Shula works from the Christian quarter. There's nothing wrong, is there?'

'No,' said Anderson, 'nothing at all.'

The bus journey back to the Old City took longer than the outward run, but Anderson wasn't complaining. He felt good. The mountain air of Jerusalem was like freedom after being trapped in the constant energy-sapping humidity of Tel Aviv. He got off the bus and asked for orange juice in a street café within sight of the walls. As he sipped his drink in the shade of an umbrella his attention was taken by a small convoy of military vehicles that seemed to materialize from nowhere and stop at a point some distance away. Soldiers jumped from the back of trucks and began cordoning off a fifty-metre stretch of road while some others unloaded what looked to Anderson like some kind of metal trolley.

As the trolley whined into life and began to obey the commands of its remote controller, it became obvious that this was the bomb-disposal squad. The trolley stuttered to a halt in the shade of the high walls and extended its spastic metal arms to embrace a package that was lying there. The moment of tension passed with a series of shouts that brought an instant relaxation in the atmosphere – nothing sinister, just a cardboard box, another routine job. The military packed up their gear with practised ease and disappeared as if they'd never been there. Anderson finished his orange and walked into the Old City.

Entering by the Damascus Gate he found his way to the Christian quarter and the Via Dolorosa. He followed the Stations of the Cross amidst tourists and pilgrims as he looked for a guide who might, by virtue of age and sex, be an undergraduate at Tel Aviv. The largest crowd was outside the Church of the Holy Sepulchre where Anderson found several guided tours converging. A group of African nuns in light-blue habits were being led by a young girl who looked as if she could be Shula Ron. Anderson waited until she had shepherded them safely into line to await admission before approaching.

'Miss Ron?'

'No.'

'I'm sorry. I'm looking for Shula Ron.'

'Shula is doing the wall promenade.'

'Yes. Where does it start from?'

The girl gave him directions and then checked her watch. She said, 'You will have to hurry; the next wall tour leaves in five minutes.'

Anderson thanked her and went off in the direction indicated by the girl. He got lost. He wasn't sure how, but he did and as one wrong turning led to another, and the alleys became quieter and quieter, his frustration pushed up the afternoon temperature still higher. Anderson was forced to rest in the shade of a stone arch until he felt better, but resting wasn't going slake the thirst that now burned in his parched throat. If only he could find some vantage point to get his bearings, but he seemed confined to an endless series of flat, blind alleys and hemmed in by walls.

At last! Steps! Anderson found himself at the foot of a flight of steps leading up what he took to be the inner face of the city wall. The steps were very old, judging by the dips in their centres and the fact that there was no guard rail, so Anderson had to climb cautiously, avoiding looking down and testing each crumbling stair before transferring his weight. He reached the top and looked around him. The great Dome of the Rock was now a very deep golden colour as the sun began to sink in the sky. He tried to work out which face he was looking at and reached a conclusion. He checked it by looking along the wall in both directions to ensure that, as he had predicted, he could not see the citadel. He could not. What he did see, however, was a group of people high up on the ramparts like himself, only a hundred metres or so further along and heading away from him. The coloured shirts and intensive camera activity told Anderson that he had found the wall tour. He looked at his watch and decided that it had to be the one after the tour he had set out to join and that they were on their way back. Probably the last tour of the day.

Anderson saw that he could not catch up with the tour along the top of the wall for he was standing on a very old part of the ramparts and the stone had crumbled away about thirty feet from where he stood, causing an interruption for at least thirty metres. He would have to descend and catch up with them on the ground.

Determined not to get lost again, Anderson kept as close

125

to the inner face of the great wall as was possible, only straying through alleys where there was no alternative. He found himself at the start and finish point for the tours as the last tour was descending from the ramparts. A young girl stood at the top, shepherding her people to the stairs and smiling at them as they said goodbye. Anderson felt a sense of relief; he had found Shula Ron.

The tourists seemed to take an age to descend from the ramparts, mainly because the stairs were narrow and the group had to move at the speed of the slowest member. There were several elderly people in their number and Anderson waited patiently as one particular lady tested each and every step before putting her weight on it. He walked across to the foot of the stairs to coincide with the last tourist leaving but stopped as he saw the last one in the group apparently change his mind and turn to climb back up again. The man sprinted up with an agility that said he was not one of the elderly Americans who had appeared to be in the majority. Anderson saw him ask Shula Ron something and saw her turn and point out over the city. The man took a photograph then asked something else. Anderson saw Shula smile and smooth her hair and dress before taking up a pose against the ramparts. The man raised his camera but seemed dissatisfied with what he saw in the viewfinder. He said something else to Shula who raised herself up on to the top of the wall and sat there with her hands folded on her knee. The man checked the viewfinder again then moved in to adjust the tilt of Shula's head with his fingertips. Anderson grew impatient. 'Get on with it,' he muttered as he waited in the shadow that had now overtaken the foot of the stairs.

The man raised the camera to his face again but Anderson could now see what Shula could not, since the man had profiled her head. He was not looking through the viewfinder. His head was turned slightly so that he could see down into the courtyard. What the hell is he playing at? thought Anderson, looking around him. What's he looking at? What is he waiting for? As the last tourist disappeared, the truth screamed through Anderson's head. He was waiting for the courtyard to empty! He did not want anyone to see what he was about to do!

Anderson ran out from the shadows and opened his mouth to shout a warning but he was too late. He saw the man move towards Shula, as if to alter her pose slightly, then pushed her hard in the face with the flat of his hand. A single scream rent the air as Shula Ron tumbled backwards from the wall and fell to certain death. The cry that had started out on Anderson's lips as a warning changed to despair as he realized that he had just seen a girl murdered. There was a momentary silence when the man on the ramparts looked down at Anderson and their eyes met.

Anderson took in the Mediterranean features and read fear and surprise in his nut-brown face. He obviously had not realized that anyone had been waiting at the bottom of the stairs. Anderson recovered first. 'You bastard!' he hissed and started to climb up. The man began to move off along the ramparts and, through his anger, Anderson could see that he was making for the next place he could descend, a crumbling stone stairway that had been fenced off from the unwary tourist with iron railings.

Anderson had got to within twenty feet of the killer when it became his turn to get over the railings. His hitherto sole purpose of getting to grips with the murderer was now tainted with acute feelings of vulnerability. He had never been fond of heights and now he had to get over a series of twisted iron spikes with a twelve-metre drop below him should he fail to reach the stone steps. The sight of his quarry accelerating down the steps gave him courage; he hoisted himself up on to the railings and prepared to jump.

Anderson thought about it too long. He froze on the

127

railings, unable to persuade his rigid muscles to relent and let him make the leap. The man had now reached the ground. He turned to see why Anderson had given up the chase and saw him silhouetted against the sky. It was too good a chance to miss. He picked up a series of rocks from the foot of the crumbling steps and thew them in quick succession at Anderson.

The second one hit Anderson on the head almost before he had had time to realize what was happening. It caught him on the exact spot of his head wound and reopened it. He saw the ground swim far below him; consciousness was slipping away. He knew instinctively that he could not go forward across the gap; he would have to try and get back from the railings. He tilted dangerously far forward as he tried to alter his position and again saw the ground below. There was a moment when he almost accepted that falling was now inevitable and relaxed his grip ever so slightly. At that moment another rock from below hit him in the chest and made him recoil automatically. It was enough to send him tumbling backwards off the railings and back on to the ramparts. He pulled himself up on to the wall but felt consciousness slip away fast. He had a sensation of grit in his mouth before he slid down the wall at approximately the same rate as the blood that had splashed on to it from his head wound. His last thought before passing out was of how red the dust looked in the sunset over Jerusalem.

Anderson awoke in jail. He groaned, alerting the guard, and put his hand to his head to find it bandaged. The guard looked in at him, grunted and left the room without saying anything. He returned a few minutes later with two other men.

'Why am I being held here?' asked Anderson.

The taller of the two men said. 'You are . . . Nile Anderrsson?' He made it sound foreign as he read from Anderson's passport.

'Yes,' agreed Anderson and repeated his question.

'You are being held in connection with the murder of Shula Ron.'

CHAPTER SIX

Anderson reacted with all the exasperation of the innocent. He repeated over and over again that he was not the girl's killer but that he had witnessed the murder and had given chase. He was met with blank stares and endless questions.

'Why were you in Jerusalem?'

'I had a lunch appointment.'

'Who with?'

'Captain Mirit Zimmerman of the Israeli army,' replied Anderson, hoping to impress. The expressions did not change but one man left the room briefly.

'After lunch, the Captain left you in the Old City?'

'No, she drove me downtown.'

'But you came back to the Old City?'

'Obviously.'

'Why?'

'To . . . find Shula Ron.'

'You knew the dead girl?'

'No,' said Anderson, walking deeper into the mire.

The policemen exchanged dull glances. 'Why would you look for someone you didn't know?'

Anderson took a deep breath. His head was hurting and his patience all but exhausted. 'Look, it's quite simple. I wanted to ask her some questions about her boyfriend. He was a medical student in England.'

'What did you want to know?'

Anderson let his head slump forward on to his chest. 'It's a long story and it wouldn't help your investigation.'

'We have all the time in the world,' said the policeman, lighting a cigarette.

'I want to call the British Embassy.'

'All in good time.'

'Now!' Anderson wished that he had not raised his voice; his headache had doubled in intensity.

One of the policemen got up and came towards him. He stuck his face in Anderson's and said quietly, 'We will decide when.' Anderson did not argue further.

'Get up!'

Anderson was held by both men and guided along a long corridor that led from the cells to a series of small rooms bearing Hebrew inscriptions. He was pushed into one of them.

'Stand there!'

Anderson stood in front of a white wall as directed. A woman was shown into the room; she wore metal-framed glasses. It was the woman he had taken to be Shula Ron's mother when he had met her at the apartment. The tears and the handkerchief said that he had probably been right.

'Is this the man?'

The woman looked at Anderson and nodded. She broke into fresh tears and was led out. Next came the young guide he had spoken to outside the Church of the Holy Sepulchre.

'Is this the man?'

'Yes, that's him,' said the girl with a look that said she would like to kill him.

Four other people were brought into the room in succession. They were from the tour party that Shula Ron had been leading. None of them recognized Anderson. The parade seemed to be over. One of the policemen closed the door and sat down beside the other, flicking some imaginary substance from the knees of his trousers before saying to Anderson, 'Two of these people recognized you.'

'Of course they did. I recognized them.'

'How did you recognize them?'

'Damn it! You must know that!'

'Tell us.'

Anderson told them.

The policemen spoke briefly in Hebrew. One left the room and returned with a small boy dressed in ragged clothes. He looked at Anderson and burst into a monologue punctuated with frequent pieces of mimed action. Anderson could not decide whether the boy was speaking Hebrew or Arabic but concluded that, in his present position, there weren't many things in the world that mattered less. The boy was taken out and the policeman returned.

'You are fortunate, Doctor. That boy saw two men up on the wall. One was chasing the other. The boy says that the foreigner was doing the chasing.'

Anderson sighed in relief. 'Then I can go?'

'Tell us about this other man.'

'For Chri . . . ' Anderson bit his tongue and started again, keeping his temper in check. 'Look, I must have told you at least a dozen times. My head hurts and . . . '

'Tell us again,' said the calm voice, 'you might remember something else.'

Anderson gave the description that he had given before. Tall, over six feet, sallow skin, Mediterranean features, well built, black moustache.

'You can go now,' said one of the policemen without bothering to look up.

'I can go?' repeated Anderson softly.

'Yes,' said the man, finally looking up. 'Go see Israel.' He returned to his writing.

'At this moment,' said Anderson, getting to his feet a bit shakily, 'seeing the back of it would be very nice.' He walked out, leaving both policemen looking puzzled.

'Not one of your better days, Neil,' said Mirit Zimmerman. Anderson spun round at a rate his head did not appreciate to find the white Fiat parked by the kerb outside the police barracks. Mirit was sitting in it, one hand on the wheel, her elbow resting on the open window.

'How on earth?' said Anderson.

'The police contacted me about our lunch date.'

'And?'

'I told them what I could, which wasn't much. I had to say that I had no idea why you had returned to the Old City.'

'Thanks,' said Anderson, without smiling.

'After all, you didn't tell me anything about Shula Ron.'

'No, I didn't,' agreed Anderson wearily, putting his hand to his head again.

'You look like you're . . . all in?' said Mirit, questioning the idiom.

'End of my rope,' agreed Anderson unhelpfully.

'Get in,' said Mirit.

Anderson got into the car and sat down with a long sigh. He was tired and thirsty and hungry and his head hurt a lot. He leaned his head against the window as Mirit pulled out into the traffic, and looked at the lights moving towards them in the rapidly falling dusk. Aware that they had just passed the bus station, Anderson pointed it out.

'We're not going to the bus station,' she said. Anderson put his head back on the window without further comment. OK, so they weren't going to the bus station.

The car eventually came to a halt in the pleasant leafy suburb of Beit Hakerem where Anderson experienced a sensation that he'd almost forgotten. As he got out of the car he felt cold. He rubbed his bare arms as he followed Mirit up a tree-lined path. 'It's because we're high up in the mountains,' said Mirit.

'Is this your house?' asked Anderson as once more he found himself having his head wound dressed.

133

'My parents'. They are in Europe.' She stepped back to assess her work. 'There, that should do. But you must be hungry. A lot has happened since lunchtime.'

Mirit left the room and Anderson got up and went over to the french windows. They led to a first-floor balcony overlooking a walled garden that seemed so beautiful in the twilight that Anderson just had to explore further. He went out on to the balcony and found the cool night air heavy with the scent of orange blossom. A spiral wrought-iron staircase led down from the balcony to the garden. Anderson descended and revelled in the silence while overhead the stars were becoming brighter.

'There you are!' said Mirit softly from the balcony. She came down and joined him.

'It's so peaceful,' said Anderson.

'Whenever I have a problem I come here. I have done since I was a little girl.'

'I had a hill,' said Anderson.

When they had finished eating, Mirit poured coffee and said, 'Tell me about Shula Ron.'

'I never even met her,' said Anderson, smiling at the bitter irony. 'I wanted her to tell me what her late boyfriend was doing for ten days last January.'

'Late boyfriend?'

'Martin Klein, the student I told you about at lunch.'

Mirit refilled the cups twice more while Anderson told her everything about the Klein affair, except how potent the toxin really was.

'So that's what you were doing in Caesarea,' she said, when he told her of his visit to Klein's parents.

'Another of my not so good days!'

'You've had a bad time in Israel.'

Anderson didn't deny it. 'If the Colomycin tests check out my job will be over. I can go home.'

Mirit looked at the clock. 'It's too late to return to Tel

Aviv. You can stay here tonight. I'll make up a room.'

Anderson lay awake for a long time. Shula Ron's death had raised a question which he had been avoiding all evening, but now, as he lay in the silver moonlight that filled the room, he met it head on. Was there a connection between the Klein gene and the young girl's death? There seemed to be a dearth of alternative reasons for her murder, but if there was a connection didn't that mean that Cohen and Klein were not the only ones to be implicated in the affair? Just who else had an interest in the Klein gene?

The answer wasn't written on the moonlit ceiling, neither was it on the walls which now held Anderson's attention as the trees outside began to move in a gentle breeze, making the shadow of their leaves a dark, tumbling waterfall.

Anderson awoke to sunshine, orange juice and Mirit Zimmerman's smile. 'Feel better?' she asked.

'Much,' he replied, deciding not to tell her of the thoughts which had plagued his mind in the night. Besides, the sight of her full hips in tight jeans and the rounded firmness of her breasts inside a dazzling white blouse did make him feel a whole lot better.

'Must you go back this morning?' she asked.

'No,' said Anderson, looking at the profile of her face as she looked out the window.

'When do you have to be back?'

'Never.'

'Neil. Be serious.'

'Tonight.'

'Good. Then I will show you my Jerusalem.'

For Anderson it was a day to remember, an enchanted day.

'Where are we going?' he asked as they started off in the car.

'A special place,' said Mirit, without offering further explanation. Anderson did not press her. He was content to take in the sights and sounds of the Jerusalem morning until they reached a car-park at the foot of an avenue of trees and stopped.

The 'special place' turned out to be Yad Va'shem, the museum of the Holocaust. Anderson's stomach reacted when he read the plaque outside the entrance. He looked at Mirit questioningly.

'I want you to see it,' she said softly, 'I want you to understand about Israel.'

Anderson followed her into the building, steeling himself for what was to come.

It was as awful as Anderson had imagined, but it was not so much the films and photographs of the death camps, with their cold captions, that shocked him; it was the little things that screamed their own story. Shoes that had been worn by a child, a cloth doll, limp and ownerless, a suit of striped Auschwitz pyjamas, their absent owner more present than the threadbare material. Mirit said nothing throughout and Anderson was grateful, for anything that he could have said in reply would have been inadequate. He tried to analyse his feelings. Revulsion? Horror? Certainly, but there was more to it than the obvious reactions. Embarrassment? Guilt? Detachment? Yes, detachment was there, a conscious feeling of not being Jewish, of failing to understand fully what a Jew must feel about Yad Va'shem.

Anderson felt the burning heat of the pavement through the soles of his shoes as they left the museum.

'Don't dwell on it, Neil,' said Mirit softly. 'Just remember.'

Anderson didn't reply. He just concentrated on walking away from the place.

'Well, what now?' said Mirit as they returned to the car.

'I'm in your hands,' smiled Anderson. 'Show me Jerusalem . . . your Jerusalem.'

136

Mirit took Anderson through the haunts of her childhood, an odyssey through winding streets and alleyways seldom if ever seen by the tourist. At his encouragement she reminisced freely, her recollections often accompanied by gales of infectious laughter as Anderson recalled some parallel experience. They had a long lunch in a small, intimate restaurant where Anderson agreed to sample anything Mirit suggested he should experience. More laughter accompanied the occasional strange looks on his face. They stayed in the garden of the restaurant, resting in the shade till the sun was well past its zenith, then continued.

Anderson found himself taking every opportunity to look at Mirit's face as she pointed out things of interest to him or explained the historical significance of what they were looking at. He only had eyes for her, the way she flicked her hair back, the curl of her lip when she smiled, the feeling he got when he made contact with her deep, dark eyes.

'And now the finest sight of all,' said Mirit as the sun went down. 'One you will never forget.'

Mirit drove the car up the winding road on Mount Scopus and brought it to a halt at a point high up on the hillside. She got out. 'Come with me,' she said. Anderson obeyed, moving round to join her. She led him by the hand through a small gap and said simply, 'Look.'

Anderson gazed down on the lights of Jerusalem, the floodlit walls of the Old City, the Dome of the Rock. He stood speechless at the sight. Mirit let him enjoy it in silence for a while before she said, 'Did you ever see anything as beautiful?'

Anderson looked at her and said, 'Yes.' He leaned down and kissed her gently on the lips. Mirit put her hand up to his face and ran her fingertips down his cheek gently before placing her hand softly against his chest. 'Neil, there can be no future in it.'

'But you will see me again?'

'Yes, but . . . '

'No buts. Yes will do.'

Mirit laughed and they kissed again before Mirit said, 'It's time. We have to go.'

Anderson's last view of Jerusalem was of Mirit waving as the red Volvo bus pulled out of the station at the start of the journey down through the hills of Judaea. Once again the bus was unpleasantly crowded, and with nothing to be seen from the windows in the blackness Anderson shut his eyes and did his best to rekindle visions of the day. By the time his fellow passengers had fought their way through the exit door he decided that he had had enough of communal transport and took a cab back to Einstein. The dampness round his collar, if nothing else, told him that he was back in Tel Aviv.

A knock on Anderson's door came just after eleven. It was Miles Langman; he held two beers in his hand.

'Feel like a jaw?'

Anderson's earlier suspicions about Langman came back in a sudden flood. This 'talk on the roof' business was just too . . . what was the word? . . . contrived. More like an interview than a chat. But there again it could be his imagination, paranoia even. 'OK.'

'So what did Klein's lady have to say?' asked Langman.

'Not a lot. Someone threw her off the city wall. She's dead.'

'You're not serious!'

The surprise seemed genuine enough, thought Anderson. 'I'm serious. She was murdered. I saw it happen.'

'Poor kid. Do you think this had anything to do with the Klein affair?'

Anderson got the feeling again. It wasn't his imagination, dammit. Langman was debriefing him. 'Who knows.'

'So you are no further forward?'

138

Anderson embarked on a lie. 'I wouldn't say that. Shula Ron's mother gave me a notebook that Martin Klein left at the house. I think it's going to tell me what he was up to.'

'Haven't you read it?'

'It's in some kind of code. I'll have to work on it.'

'That's great. Need any help?'

'I'll let you know.'

Next morning, before he left for the lab, Anderson took two pieces of adhesive tape and stuck them unobtrusively between the top of the door and its frame. He had thrown Langman the bait, now all he needed was a bite indicator.

At the lab Myra greeted him with the news that all the test animals were alive. She told him as soon as he walked through the door. There was now no doubt that Colomycin was safe to use in the presence of the plasmid and could therefore be used to eliminate the risk from possible carriers. Anderson telexed the news to John Kerr at the medical school back home with his customary brevity: 'COLOMYCIN CURES PLASMID SAFELY'. Some six hours later he was to receive an even briefer reply. It said, 'AGREED'. Kerr had obviously been conducting his own experiments along similar lines and had reached the same conclusion.

Anderson had to stall on the subject of when he would be returning home when Strauss and Myra asked him. Two days before and he would have been on the next flight out of Ben-Gurion but things had changed. Now his only desire was to be with Mirit. He put off telling Strauss about Shula Ron for as long as possible, but finally had to reveal all when Myra asked openly about his trip to Jerusalem. They were shocked. Strauss sat down in his chair as if his knees had given way.

The telephone rang, and Myra and Anderson returned

to the lab while Strauss took his call. 'Neil?' Myra began, but Anderson interrupted.

'You're going to ask me if there's a connection between the Klein gene and Shula Ron's death, right?' Myra nodded. 'I don't know, Myra, I just don't know.'

Myra wasn't satisfied. She said, 'But if there is a connection, surely it means that Cohen and Klein weren't the only ones involved?'

'Yes,' said Anderson flatly.

'But who?'

'I don't know who. I don't know where. I don't know how. I don't even know *what* was done. With the exception of one possible nigger in the woodpile I haven't found out a single, damned thing!'

'Who or what was the "exception"?'

Anderson told her about the inquisitive American in the university apartments who seemed to ask an awful lot of questions about the Klein affair for a researcher in Talmudic law.

'Maybe he's just a friendly guy.'

'Probably,' said Anderson, 'in fact, considering my success rate as a detective you're almost certainly right.'

The tape was broken on the door when Anderson got back. Langman had been in the apartment looking for the notebook bait! The black bastard! thought Anderson, without a trace of adjectival guilt. Just what the hell was his angle? Anderson quelled his initial impulse to rush downstairs and have it out with him. All he needed to do was deny it and then what? asked the voice of reason. He'd have to play it much more coolly, but what to do first, that was the problem. He lay down on the bed and thought it through. Well, Mr Langman, he concluded, if you are a researcher in Talmudic law . . . my grandmother is an Apache.

What did he know about Langman? Only what Langman

had told him himself, and that didn't count. He was American, of that there could be little doubt. His clothes, his speech, his mannerisms, all testified to that. Maybe that was the factor that would give him an edge? thought Anderson. As an alien, Langman would have had to register with the Israeli authorities. He could hardly have registered as a researcher in Talmudic law without having papers to prove it in some way. It would be very interesting to know just what was written on Langman's registration papers. But who could tell him? The police? Hardly likely. After yesterday's experience they'd probably open up his head wound if he as much as asked them the time. Mirit! She might be able to find out. After all, a captain in the army must have access to such information, mustn't she? Anderson had to admit to himself that what he knew about such matters could be comfortably accommodated on the back of a Tel Aviv bus ticket and still leave enough room for the names and addresses of the passengers. But he could ask Mirit. In fact, if he got a move on he could ask her that same evening.

Anderson signed the forms, paid with his Visa card, and took the keys to a dark-green Fiat Mirafiore. It had taken less than half an hour since he had thought of going to Hadera and now here he was, heading north on the Haifa Highway in a rented car with the windows open to attract the warm Mediterranean breeze. Myra Freedman was right. In Israel people did things.

Like a small western town before a gunfight, Hadera seemed dead. Anderson slowed the Fiat to a snail's pace and crawled through the deserted streets lined with shuttered houses which allowed only the tiniest cracks of light to escape into the dust-filled air. He made for the bus station on the assumption that he'd surely find some sign of life there, someone to direct him to the military post. He was about to ask a group of bus drivers when he noticed two soldiers sitting on one of the station benches munching felafel sandwiches. He asked them instead. One of them stood up and picked up the automatic weapon which had been propped against the bench. Oh Christ, here we go again, thought Anderson.

'Who are you?' asked the soldier. Anderson told him. 'Passport!' He handed it over. 'Why do you want to go there?'

'I want to see Captain Zimmerman.'

The questioner said something in Hebrew to his still seated, still munching companion. It got a toothy grin and a wad of wet crumbs fell out on to his trousers. 'OK,' said the soldier, putting down his weapon and giving Anderson directions.

The military post was outside Hadera on the west side. Anderson found it without difficulty and parked the car some fifty metres from the entrance to avoid obstructing traffic while he made enquiries at the gatehouse. A warm wind was blowing. It made the blue-and-white Israeli flag above the entrance flutter in the night air. The same wind threw up sand into Anderson's face and made him pause by the fence to remove some from his eyes. As he stood there blinking he heard the sound of a car slowing down. The car, a dark-blue Mercedes saloon, was leaving the base and had stopped at the gatehouse while the barrier was raised. The light from the open door illuminated the occupants. One was Mirit Zimmerman, the other was Miles Langman.

Anderson watched in utter desolation as the Mercedes roared off in a cloud of dust. Was everyone in this shit heap of a country descended from Judas Iscariot? he wondered as anger and bitterness filled him. The Fiat's wheels snarled and scratched at the dirt as he put his foot down and headed for the Haifa Highway. He broke his journey at Herzliya and went down to the edge of the sea where he found himself alone on the moonlit beach. He threw stones into the water until his arm hurt, then went on throwing. What possible involvement could she have in the Klein affair? Surely to God she was who she'd said she was. But how did she know Langman? Anderson swore out loud as he concluded that there was nothing he could be certain of. He took off his clothes and swam naked in the sea till, nearing exhaustion, he returned to the shore and waited for the warm wind to dry him. He was back in Tel Aviv by midnight.

Next morning, as he walked through the university grounds, Anderson paused to listen to the sounds coming from the music school. It was quite beautiful. A solo pianist was playing Chopin as Chopin would have liked his music played. Not even the burning sun could make him move before the end of the piece. 'Bravo,' he said under his breath as the music stopped. He had made a decision in the last four bars. The Israelis could have their Klein gene. He had had enough. He would clear away his things, sterilize every culture of the damned thing he could find and fly home in two days' time. Back home he would destroy all his own cultures as he had agreed to do and that would be his part over. No more sun, no more sweat and no more lies; it would be back to rain and reliability, pints of bitter with Fearman in The Angel, Chinese takeaways, nurses' parties. There would be no Mirit, of course, but he'd get over that in time . . . wouldn't he?

Anderson told Strauss of his decision and got permission to collect together all known sources of the plasmid containing the Klein gene. Shortly after three in the afternoon two trays of cultures were loaded into an autoclave in the sterilizer room. Anderson watched as the needle climbed to one hundred and thirty-one centigrade and knew that it wouldn't be that much longer till he was sipping gin and tonic aboard a British Airways Tri-Star.

Myra Freedman asked him to dinner on the spur of the moment, saying that he'd have to take potluck but that it would be nice if he could come and say goodbye to Sam. Anderson was happy to accept, knowing that it would be difficult to spend the entire evening brooding over Mirit in Sam Freedman's company as he would undoubtedly do if he were alone in his apartment.

True to form, the Freedmans' hospitality made Anderson's impromptu farewell dinner flow along in a tide of good conversation and malt whisky. Anderson was sincere when he thanked Sam Freedman for a great evening and waved as the Mercedes drove off down Einstein at one in the morning. Anderson had drunk more than usual, thanks to recurrent thoughts of Mirit which he had blotted out immediately by draining his glass. Myra Freedman had made sure that it hadn't stayed empty for long, which had led to the slight unsteadiness he now felt as he climbed the stairs.

As he fumbled with the lock on his door, Anderson became aware that he wasn't alone. There was a figure out on the roof, a man's figure. He stopped wrestling with the keys and walked through the passage to the roof. It was Langman! Good God, thought Anderson, not the 'beer on the roof' bit. The notion died, and Anderson sobered up as if immersed in ice as he drew closer. Langman wasn't really standing up. He was being supported by the clothes line which had been wrapped tightly round his neck and reattached to the parapet. Langman's limp, dead body was suspended in the middle like a puppet at rest.

Anderson recoiled as he saw Langman's eye move, but then realized that it was an impression given by a two-inch-long cockroach which had walked across the white of his eyeball on an inspection tour of the corpse. He turned and sought the support of the wall as he retched helplessly till his stomach was empty. Disgust was not the only feeling he had to cope with. Fear was there, fear such as he had never known before. It seemed that everyone he came into contact with in the Klein affair was being murdered and he didn't know why. Barely suppressed terror, ignorance of what was really going on, and the revulsion he felt at the sight of Langman's bloated features made a heady cocktail for Anderson to face in the black humidity of yet another Tel Aviv night. He rinsed his mouth out to clear away the taste of vomit and went down to telephone the police. It was going to be a long night.

Anderson showered while he waited for the police to arrive. He was putting his clothes back on when the wail of sirens cut the night air on Einstein. He went down to meet them.

As Langman's body was wheeled off the roof under a sheet on an ambulance transporter, Anderson reflected on how Cohen's body had been taken away in the same fashion. He could not avoid considering who might be next to lie under a sheet. He put a hand up to the back of his neck and rubbed it hard in a subconscious attempt to avert his train of thought.

Although it took nearly two hours before the police had completed their routine and got round to questioning him, the interrogation when it came was much shorter than Anderson had feared. To the police he was the tenant of the roof apartment, the bystander who had discovered the body. Yes, he knew Langman but only vaguely as one knows one's fellow tenants. A researcher in Talmudic law, he believed. Yes, he had been out all evening and yes, he could prove it. He gave them the Freedman's address and was allowed to return to his apartment.

As he lay on his bed, Anderson wondered what his chances were of being out of Israel by the time the Tel Aviv police found out about his encounter with the

Jerusalem authorities and started thinking along the lines of no smoke without fire.

It was after four when Anderson finally fell asleep. As a consequence he did not wake till after ten-thirty. The building was quiet with most of the Americans already away to lectures and classes, so he lay still and enjoyed the peace. He heard the clatter of a diesel engine on Einstein and assigned it to a bus. The sound of it labouring as it pulled away told him that it was heading up the road.

Anderson ventured out on to the roof with a mug of black coffee in his hand. For some reason the words on a tourist poster for Israel sprang to mind. It had said, 'You'll Never Forget It'. So true, thought Anderson with a wan smile. Thinking of the poster gave him the ridiculous thought that he had not sent any postcards. What on earth would he write on them?

He had started some preliminary packing when there was a knock on the door. First policeman of the day, he thought, and opened it to find Mirit standing there. His mouth fell open as a knotted fist turned in his stomach.

'You didn't call,' she said.

'No, I'm flying home tomorrow,' said Anderson flatly.

'I see,' said Mirit, looking puzzled.

'So if you'll excuse me . . . '

'Why are you behaving this way? Aren't you even going to ask me in?'

Anderson was in emotional agony. How could someone so beautiful be so devious? How could she stand there looking so concerned? He couldn't resist the urge to hurt her. 'Your friend Langman is dead,' he said. 'He was murdered last night.'

Mirit seemed stunned. 'Miles Langman?'

'Yes, Miles Langman.' At least she didn't pretend that she hadn't known him, thought Anderson.

'How did you know that I knew Miles Langman?' Mirit asked.

'I drove to Hadera last night to ask your help in finding out about him.' Anderson shook his head at the irony. 'I didn't believe he was what he said he was. Then I saw you both together.'

'I see,' said Mirit quietly. 'What did he tell you he did?'

'He said that he was a researcher in Talmudic law. But he asked too many questions.'

Mirit nodded. 'You were right. Asking questions was more Langman's business. He was an officer in the Tel Aviv station of the CIA.'

Anderson sat down slowly. This was all he needed. The CIA. To a man whose contact with the forces of law and order before coming to Israel had been a ticket for parking on a double yellow line in Chipping Campden, the mention of the CIA pushed his appreciation of the absurd to the outer limits. 'The CIA,' he repeated like a speak-your-weight machine. He had been drinking beer on the roof with CIA? Come on.

'It's true,' said Mirit, seeing the look on Anderson's face.

'And your connection?'

'I met Miles Langman for the first time in my life last night. The CIA were interested in the attack on you in Caesarea; they requested a copy of my report from the base commander last week and followed up yesterday by asking to speak to the reporting officer . . . me.'

'But why?' asked a confused Anderson.

'Ironically, Langman wanted to know much the same as you did about the attack. He didn't seem to think it was terrorists either. He wanted to know if I had any other ideas.'

'I thought that you and he were in league.'

'I know what you thought,' said Mirit.

'But why should the CIA be interested in me?'

'The simple answer is, I think, that they are not. You are a means to an end. It's the Klein thing they're concerned with. As far as I could gather from Langman he was letting you do his job for him. He said something about you being able to go places he couldn't, so he was going to let you and keep watch in the background. When I confessed that I had seen you again on a personal level, and would probably be seeing you some more, he asked if I would do the same. I said that I could not deceive you in any way. But as you are going home tomorrow the question no longer arises.'

Anderson felt so bad he could not say anything. Still sitting on the bed, he held his head in his hands and stared at the floor, desperately trying to get his thoughts in order. Mirit got up to go. She said quietly, 'May I wish you a safe journey.'

This parting was more than Anderson could bear. He got to his feet. 'God, Mirit, I'm so sorry. Can you forgive me for what I thought?'

'Is it so important?'

'Yes.'

'But why?'

'Because I'm in love with you,' said Anderson, confessing the fact to himself as much as Mirit. There was a long silence before Mirit said softly, 'I see.' Anderson had never felt so emotionally naked in his life. It was as if time had stopped at what he'd said.

Mirit said, 'It's unwise, even ridiculous after such a short time, and there can be no future in it, but for what it's worth and how ever long it lasts . . . I feel the same.'

Anderson kissed Mirit and felt as if he had flown to heaven on a wet afternoon. He ran his fingers through her dark hair and held her close, never wanting the moment to end. 'God, how I love you!' he said, so forcibly that Mirit was forced to laugh. Then they both laughed. Anderson kissed her again.

'Neil?'

'Yes?'

'Your breath smells like a camel.'

Anderson apologized. 'I had rather a lot to drink last night . . . I was trying to forget you.'

Mirit ran her fingertips lightly along his forehead and said, 'Never do that, Neil.'

'Never. I promise.'

Anderson cancelled his flight. It was about the only positive move he felt sure of making. 'Now what?' he said as he put down the phone.

Mirit said, 'I came here today to tell you that I had taken some leave. I thought that we might go away somewhere for a few days. I had hoped that we might be able to work out why you were in danger. What do you think?'

'I think that that is the best idea I ever heard,' said Anderson, unable to believe how the mood of the morning had changed.

'Where shall we go?' said Mirit.

'Anywhere.'

'The Red Sea.'

Anderson left Mirit in the apartment while he went up to the university to tell Professor Strauss that he would not be leaving Israel just yet, but that he would be gone for a few days. He paused briefly to speak to Myra Freedman on his way out.

'Change your mind?' she asked.

Anderson said that he had decided to stay on for a bit.

'Find out something?'

'About myself,' smiled Anderson as he left. 'I'm off to the Red Sea.'

149

CHAPTER SEVEN

As they got into the Fiat, Anderson leaned over and kissed Mirit. 'Camel?' he asked.

'No, toothpaste!'

He felt better with every mile that took them away from Tel Aviv and south into the Negev Desert, a burning landscape that freed his mind from all distraction. After an hour of comfortable silence Mirit said, 'Neil? Is there anything that you can't tell me?'

'What made you say that?'

'I was about to suggest that we be absolutely frank with each other but then I thought that you might have given your word to say nothing about some things.'

'Perhaps I should ask you the same question.'

'You should,' agreed Mirit, 'but I only know what you and Miles Langman told me, although Langman did think that you had some secret notebook.'

Anderson told her about the trap that he had set for Langman using the lie about Klein's notebook.

She smiled. 'Where did you learn that?'

'I saw it in a film.'

They lapsed into silence again till Anderson said, 'I didn't answer your question.'

'I noticed,' said Mirit, without taking her eyes off the road.

'There is something I haven't told you, but as I haven't given my word about anything other than something I'm going to do, I will tell you.' He told her of the real power of the toxin produced by the Klein gene and of his agreement with Jacob Strauss to destroy it.

'Isn't that unscientific?'

'Yes.'

'Won't your career suffer when people find out?'

'Probably.'

'Neil.'

'Yes?'

'I'm glad.'

They drove into the Negev town of Be'er Sheva and stopped for some cold orange juice. 'You know? I like the desert,' said Anderson, looking at the burning waste through narrowed eyes under the shade of his hat.

'Any particular reason?'

'No, I just like it.'

Dusk was falling when Mirit slowed the car and pulled off the road. 'Come on,' she said, getting out and walking over to a ridge in the sand. Anderson joined her. 'There! Over there.' Mirit pointed and Anderson saw the sparkle of the setting sun on water some twenty miles away. There was a little cluster of lights on the horizon. 'Eilat,' said Mirit, 'that's where we're going.'

As they stood there on the ridge, Anderson realized that he couldn't hear a sound. The air was perfectly still. It was like standing in a painted landscape, the only people on earth; or maybe it wasn't earth, another planet perhaps.

'Do you like what you see?' asked Mirit softly.

'I like,' said Anderson.

'It gets better.' They got back in the car.

'Where are we?' asked Anderson as they pulled into the drive of a hotel that seemed to be the only building for miles.

'Coral Beach,' said Mirit. 'You'll see why in the morning.' They showered, changed and went downstairs to dinner. They ate outside on a verandah beneath the stars and within earshot of the waves as they lapped the shore.

'Finished?' asked Mirit at the end of the meal.

'Yes.'

'Come with me.' Mirit led the way out into the grounds

where she pulled two sunloungers together and said, 'Lie down.' Anderson stretched out on one and Mirit joined him on the other. 'Now look up.'

Anderson looked up into the star-filled heavens. 'Beautiful,' he said.

'Keep looking,' said Mirit. They gazed in silence at the night sky like two medieval philosophers until a bright trail of fire suddenly raced across the velvet. 'There!' said Mirit with satisfaction.

'A shooting star!' said Anderson.

Both of them knew that they were going to make love so there was no awkwardness when it came to it. Undressed, Mirit's body was all it had promised to be and Anderson held the gaze of her deep, dark eyes as his fingertips explored her smooth, firm contours. His tongue traced a line from her ear down to her breasts, teasing her nipples into full erectness as his hand sought her thigh.

Mirit met Anderson on his own terms with an almost animal passion that demanded as much from him as he from her. When she began to tease him by alternately barely allowing him to penetrate her and holding him immobile deep within her, Anderson's male urge to dominate became so unbearable that he trapped her wrists on the pillow and took her hard. He burst within her and the violence receded into loving tenderness as he licked the salty sweat from the nape of her neck. 'I think I've bruised you,' he said.

'An honourable wound,' said Mirit in the darkness.

The sun came up, painting the mountains of Arabia red and waking Mirit and Anderson who were comfortably asleep in each other's arms. Anderson let out a great yawn of contentment which made Mirit smile. 'How do you feel?' she whispered in his ear.

'Hungry,' he said.

'How ungallant!'

'And – very much in love with you, my lady.' Anderson kissed her gently and sat up, looking around him. 'God! I feel good.' He got up and went over to the window where he looked out on the sparkling water of the Gulf of Aqaba and beyond to the hills of Jordan. 'I knew it! I'm in the Garden of Eden!'

'Shall we swim first or eat breakfast?' asked Mirit.

'Neither,' said Anderson.

Mirit smiled.

It was too late for breakfast so they swam in the water above the coral reefs using snorkelling equipment from the hotel and adding even more to the illusion that they were in a time-locked world of their own. They dived and merged with the shapes and colours of the reef. The fish didn't seem to mind; they accepted them as if they had always lived there.

They ate lunch on the beach beneath a sunshade and stayed there snoozing till the fierce midday heat passed and allowed them to venture out again to swim once more over their coral paradise. 'Mirit, we must talk,' said Anderson as they emerged from the water.

Mirit put her finger to her lips. 'Tomorrow,' she said, 'tomorrow.'

There was no reason to change the pattern of the previous evening. It didn't even occur to them. They had dinner outside and then lay prone beneath the heavens in their continued quest for shooting stars. Their vigil ended after two and they retired to their room to love each other with the intensity of feeling only known to those who are in danger or fear that their happiness might be brief. Once more the first red glow of dawn was chasing the blackness from the sky as they fell into a deep sleep still locked in each other's arms.

At Mirit's suggestion they joined a party of divers going out by boat to some reefs further offshore. There were eleven in the group and their gear, most of it a great deal more professional than the snorkelling stuff taken by Mirit and Anderson, was stacked on top of a life raft, making a black-and-yellow jumble of cylinders and wetsuits in the well of the launch. Mirit and Anderson remained seated in the stern as the bow lifted out of the water and the launch creamed out into the gulf. Unlike their fellow passengers they had nothing to check or prepare so they watched the others as they tapped dials and adjusted webbing.

Anderson turned to look at the wake behind them, but Mirit's attention was taken by the pile of equipment, in particular by a harpoon gun that she could have sworn was pointing to their right the last time she had looked. It appeared to have turned through forty-five degrees but there was no one near it. As she stared, it moved. Another ten degrees of arc . . . towards them. Almost mesmerized, she leaned forward and saw the cord that trailed from the equipment pile across the floor of the boat to a man who was pretending to check a depth gauge. The gun was now pointing at Anderson's back! Mirit pushed him violently over to the right, sending him sprawling as a bolt from the harpoon hammered into the wooden transom that might have been his spine.

Everyone looked at Anderson, save Mirit. She didn't take her eyes off the man who was shuffling the cord away from his feet as unobtrusively as possible. She took her ID card and a pistol from the canvas bag on her knee and stood up, pointing the gun at the man. He panicked and looked left and right in quick succession before making a headlong dash for the stern and leaping overboard. Unaware of what was happening, the skipper in the wheelhouse held course and speed.

Anderson struggled to his feet, a task made more difficult by the nylon line that was paying out from the equipment pile at a furious rate. His would-be assassin had

154

caught his ankle in the harpoon line in his rush to get overboard and was now taking out line like a hooked marlin. The skipper, alerted by the cries from the stern, cut back the revs and the bow settled down into the water causing the speed to die suddenly and a loop of line to form under the stern. It was only seconds before the rope fouled the propellers. The man on the end of the line cried out in pain as he was jerked viciously towards the boat for a few metres before the screws seized on their diet of rope, leaving him still some thirty metres adrift.

Anderson watched the man as he tried to free his injured ankle and saw sudden fear cross his face. He began to scream at the top of his voice. 'What's he saying?' Anderson asked Mirit.

'He says he's bleeding,' said Mirit. For a moment Anderson didn't see the relevance of her words or understand the panic, but as two dark triangular fins crossed behind the man in the water it became all too clear.

A crewman took a desperately long time to bring the rope, which was now taut between the propellers and the injured man, within range of the hands reaching down from the stern. The skipper was standing on the roof of the wheelhouse with a rifle to his shoulder as he followed the circling fins in their ever-tightening arc, but with fifteen metres to go the screaming stopped and the sea was suddenly empty. There was a moment when all was quiet and calm. The rope was slack and the rifle silent.

Anderson swallowed in an attempt to moisten his dry throat but didn't stop looking at the spot where the man had gone down. His vigil ended as the water erupted and the sea gave up a bloody, legless torso to stare blankly at the azure-blue sky for a few seconds before another shark slammed into it and took it down for good.

There was nothing to say. The occupants of the boat sat in silence as the launch bobbed gently on the swell in the blistering heat and they waited for the attraction of blood in the water to dissipate before a crewman could go down to free the propellers. When he did go over the side, the sounds of hacking and sawing that came through the floor did nothing to lessen the awful images that filled their minds.

A cloud of blue diesel smoke lifted gently into the air as the engines choked and spluttered into life, having to fight all the way against airlocks in the fuel lines caused by the intense heat. They headed back to shore still largely in silence, Anderson constantly finding his eyes drifting back to the harpoon bolt embedded in the stern and feeling his stomach turn over each time he did so. He found himself massaging the point in his torso where the bolt would have entered, his fingertips tracing out its entry mark. He saw himself pinned to the board like a butterfly in a schoolboy's collection. They were still trying to kill him and he was scared.

When he could see beyond his own fear, Anderson realized that Shula Ron had been murdered because of the Klein plasmid. She must have known too much about what Klein had been doing, and someone had killed her to keep her quiet. What a can of worms. Anderson became aware that Mirit was looking at him. He managed a wan smile but didn't say anything.

The skipper of the launch had radioed ahead, so the police were waiting for them when they tied up and filed out on to the wooden landing stage. Interviews began almost immediately, not that that seemed to make the time pass any more quickly. It transpired that no one knew the dead man; everyone had assumed that he had been with everyone else. The skipper said that the man had been the last one to request a place on the boat and he had assumed that he had come from the same hotel as the rest of the party.

When it came to his turn, Anderson stonewalled the police, stating simply that he had no idea why anyone should want to kill him. He said nothing about the Klein gene and had requested Mirit to do likewise. They were allowed to go but the spell had been broken. Coral Beach was no longer a place of magic; they had returned to the real world and, as they walked back from the quayside to the hotel, Anderson wondered if he would ever know such happiness again.

They packed their things and checked out to begin the return journey to Tel Aviv. It was late afternoon so the heat had ceased to be a real problem as they left Eilat and headed north into the Negev. With twenty miles of barren waste behind them Mirit said, 'You know, there's a fault in your logic.'

'Good. Tell me,' said Anderson.

'You have assumed from the beginning that Cohen was the scientist involved in the secret cloning with Klein.'

'Yes.'

'But from what you have told me there was never any proof that Cohen was involved.'

'Klein worked with Cohen in Strauss's lab. They were both using the PZ9 plasmid that the gene was cloned into.'

'Circumstantial.'

'When the acid fell on me, Cohen was the only other person in the lab *and* I caught him back there afterwards removing the evidence.'

'You *assumed* that was what he was doing. The facts say that he saved your sight if not your life.'

'Yes, but . . .'

'No proof, Neil! No proof!'

Mirit gave Anderson time to digest what she had just said, before continuing. 'Have you considered that Cohen's death might not have been an accident?'

Anderson confessed that he had not.

'He may have been murdered,' said Mirit.

Anderson considered the possibility in silence. The reason for Cohen's death had seemed so obvious at the time that neither he nor Strauss had looked for any other. Cohen had clearly cut himself while working with the plasmid. Was Mirit suggesting that someone else had cut Cohen with a contaminated blade to make it look accidental? But there had been no sign of a struggle in the lab, and death would not have been instantaneous. There would have been time for Cohen to fight back . . .

In dismissing Mirit's suggestion, Anderson had exposed the flaw in his own and Strauss's assumption. If Cohen had cut himself why had he sat still, waiting for death? He had not even bothered to remove his glove and wash the wound. Why not? Why hadn't he raised the alarm? There would have been time . . . Death would not have come instantly. Blood would have washed most of the toxin out. But death *had* been instantaneous and it *had* been due to the toxin. Anderson struggled to fill in the bottom line. The Klein toxin had been introduced to Cohen's body, but not through the obvious cut. That had been put there afterwards to make it look accidental. By Cohen's murderer? So how was the toxin administered? For it to act immediately . . . an injection would have been necessary! If he were right, somewhere on Cohen's body would be the tiny mark left by a hypodermic needle.

'Tell me about Jewish funerals,' he said.

As night fell in the desert and the Fiat's headlights illuminated a monotonous ribbon of tarmac, Anderson made plans for the morrow. He would return to the university and ask Strauss if Cohen's body was still in the mortuary and, if it was, ask permission to examine it. No, he wouldn't. Shit! He couldn't do that. He couldn't ask Strauss anything, for if it were true that he had been guilty of assuming Cohen guilty he may have been equally guilty of considering Strauss innocent. He voiced his fears to Mirit.

'You are right. Trust no one.'

'But Strauss wants the plasmid destroyed,' argued Anderson.

'It could be said that he wants *you* to destroy it,' said Mirit. 'If he were guilty that would make sense. After all, he wouldn't want anyone else to have the weapon, would he? So he tricks you into destroying your source while pretending to have destroyed his own.'

Anderson bit back a comment about Israeli minds and corkscrews and saw that she was right . . . yet again. If he was going to examine Cohen's body he'd have to make his own arrangements. 'Can we stop for a while?' he said.

Mirit slowed the car and pulled off the road. 'Want to stretch your legs?'

'No, I want to talk.'

The Fiat's lights were off but the desert around them was still bright in the light of the moon.

'We've talked of nothing but the Klein affair since the thing on the boat. I want to talk about us. I want you to know that the two days I've had with you were the best and happiest I've ever known. Every word I said to you I meant. I love you now, I'll love you always. I'm not going to ask you to marry me right now because I think you'll say "no", but I am going to ask you to think about marrying me. That's all I ask, just think about it.'

'I will, Neil. I promise.'

'Good, because now I can forget about it for the moment and concentrate on keeping my arse in one piece!'

Mirit dropped Anderson off at his apartment block in Einstein while she herself drove on the further forty miles or so to her parents' house in Jerusalem. She had invited Anderson to go with her but he had declinded, saying that he had to be alone for a bit to get his thoughts together. The

Americans were singing folk songs on the lawn as he climbed the stairs. 'Bloody noise,' he said under his breath. He locked his door using both locks and then snibbed the window, deciding that discretion was the better part of ventilation. He'd make do with the small grid up on the wall. No one could climb through that.

Anderson slept badly but hadn't expected anything else. He was glad when the sun came up and chased away the darkness which always seemed to exaggerate doubts and fears . . . by a factor of 2.7. He smiled as the figure came to mind. When he was a medical student he had once said to a tutor that things always seemed three times as bad in the night. His tutor had said, 'Two point seven,' and when asked why had confided the advice, 'Never use round numbers. People will think you made them up. Use fractions and they'll think you an educated man.'

Deciding to brass it out, Anderson got up early and went into the lab, planning to arrive before anyone else. He was successful and donned a crisp, clean white coat with which to play out his con. The mortuary was on the ground floor and situated near the back of the building, giving him plenty of time to concoct a story on his elevator descent and subsequent walk through the corridors. It was time wasted; the attendant didn't speak English. Anderson got a blank look when he launched into his spiel. Oh well, intimidate him, he thought, beginning to act as if he were very important and very annoyed. He wasn't too sure how successful he'd been, but the words 'Cohen . . . Arieh Cohen' elicited some reaction. The blank-faced man rose off his stool and limped through the back. Anderson followed. Strange, he thought, mortuary attendants were like hotel desk clerks – they all looked the same. They didn't all have hunchbacks and answer to the name of Igor, but they weren't that far removed.

'Cohen,' said the attendant, pointing to a refrigerated drawer.

'Good,' said Anderson pompously and pointing to an examination table. 'Here!' he said. The attendant looked at him for a moment without doing anything and Anderson felt the game slipping away from him, but then, with a shrug of the shoulders, the man opened the fridge and locked on the transporter trolley. The body, covered in a white sheet embossed with a blue Star of David, was slid out on rollers and settled with a metallic thump on to the trolley. In common with all trolleys the transporter was fitted with three wheels that wanted to go one way and one that didn't, making it difficult for the attendant to manoeuvre it towards the table. Anderson gave the rogue wheel a helpful kick and Cohen moved serenely across the floor. The attendant gave him a look that said the same in any language.

Cohen had been a big man. The attendant grunted with the effort of heaving his corpse on to the table, top half, then bottom half. He disappeared for a moment before returning with a box of disposable gloves which he slapped down in front of Anderson with an open-hand gesture that said, 'All yours'. Anderson donned a pair of the gloves and started his examination. Having no idea how to mime 'magnifying glass', he didn't bother going to look for the attendant but searched instead through the drawers until he found one.

'Not a bloody thing,' he concluded after ten minutes on Cohen's front. He heaved the cadaver over on to its face with more than some difficulty. At the last moment the body slipped from his grasp, slamming face first down on to the table with a sickening crack as Cohen's head caught the edge. An alarmed apology flew to Anderson's lips before he realized that Cohen was in no position to care. There it was. High up on the left hip, the unmistakable mark of an injection. Anderson examined it closely under the glass and found it still possible to tell the direction of entry. He

161

concluded that someone had come up behind Cohen and stuck the needle in with a strong downward thrust. Mirit had been right. Cohen had been murdered.

Anderson felt guilty. He had disliked Cohen so intensely that it had been easy to assume anything bad of him. He felt worst about the incident with the hydrochloric acid because, having thought Cohen responsible, he had been very sparing in his thanks when Cohen, at great risk to himself, had saved him from serious injury. 'Sorry, old son,' he said as he pulled the sheet up over the body. Anderson nodded to the attendant on his way out. The man looked up from his paper and then resumed reading.

Anderson left the medical school and sought the shade of a tree in the grounds that had become his favourite. Its thick, foreign foliage gave complete protection from the sun and its relative isolation from pathways allowed him to think in peace. What he needed was perspective, vision . . . the very qualities he admired in Jacob Strauss, thought Anderson, seeing the irony. Just how did he go about investigating an internationally distinguished academic like Strauss on his own patch? The experience with Cohen should have taught him to be absolutely dispassionate but gut feeling fought hard. He liked Strauss. If Strauss turned out to be guilty he'd never trust another living soul.

After half an hour of contemplation, Anderson decided that his best chance of success lay in Martin Klein's secret notebook. He could almost hear Mirit say, 'You've no proof it exists!' But still, he felt confident that it did. Chances were that Strauss had it hidden somewhere, possibly in his office, probably locked away in his desk. He would have to search the room. Having decided on a definite course of action, Anderson felt better.

Strauss went to lunch each day at 1 p.m. Anderson had noticed the ritual donning of the Panama hat and the collection of the cane from the corner outside his office door and had remarked on it to Myra in the past. She had told him that Strauss had lunch every day with his old friend Max Jungman, professor of surgery. The rest of the lab staff usually went between one-fifteen and one-thirty. Anderson reckoned that the lab was nearly always empty between one-thirty and two. That should be enough time, he thought, to get into Strauss's office and find the notebook.

At one thirty-five Anderson took the elevator to the sixth floor of the medical school and, as he'd hoped, found the labs empty. The door to Strauss's office was locked, but he'd expected that and knew that his secretary kept a spare key in her desk drawer. He'd seen her use it before when Strauss was out. He found the key without difficulty and let himself into the room. His pulse was racing with the panic of the amateur criminal and all his fingers became thumbs in his haste to complete his mission as he rifled through the contents of the oak desk. One drawer was locked, encouraging Anderson to think that must be the one.

He began attacking the lock with a heavy ornamental paperknife. It had just slipped off the brass tongue of the lock for the third time when Anderson got a grip on himself. Calm down. Take it easy. Do things slowly, deliberately. Take your time. But there was no denying the sweat on his brow. All Tel Aviv was about to burst through the door. The continued stubbornness of the lock made Anderson put too much pressure on the paperknife. It flew out of his hand and clattered across the room, hitting, to Anderson's way of thinking, every conceivable echoing object in it. He stared at the knife as it came to rest and saw malice in an inanimate object.

One more try, Anderson decided, and that would be it. His nerves could not stand it. The lock yielded. Personal letters . . . bank statements . . . chequebook . . . old photographs . . . nothing else. There was no sign of Klein's

163

lab book. He was looking at one of the photographs, a young man in uniform, when a voice said, 'My son, Dr Anderson. He was killed in the war.' Anderson looked up to see Jacob Strauss standing in the doorway, waiting for an explanation.

Anderson felt the blood rush to his face. He'd been caught red-handed with his sticky fingers still in the till. Oh, Christ! Please let the ground open up! 'I had to know, Professor,' he said, feeling shame wash over him like oil.

'To know what?' said Strauss quietly.

'If you were the one who was involved in the cloning of the Klein gene.'

Strauss looked at him for a few moments before saying, 'So you thought you'd find secret stocks of cultures in my desk?'

'No, Professor. I was looking for Martin Klein's other lab book. When I saw his official book I recognized a compulsively neat character who would have had to write everything down.'

'I understand you to have thought Dr Cohen guilty,' said Strauss, still in a very soft voice.

'I did,' agreed Anderson, 'until this morning.' He told Strauss of the injection mark on Cohen's body.

'So that left me,' said Strauss.

'That left you,' repeated Anderson.

'I follow the logic, young man,' said Strauss with a sigh, 'but alas, as in so many things connected with this affair, there is no place for logic. I am innocent.'

'I rather think you are, sir,' said Anderson, still feeling awful.

Strauss sat down in his swivel chair and pushed his desk drawers shut, one at a time, pausing briefly to look at the photograph of his dead son before dropping it into the last one. 'I think in similar circumstances,' he said, 'I might have done the same thing. We'll say no more of this.'

Anderson could hardly believe his ears. Strauss had caught him rifling through his personal belongings and yet here he was seeing things from his point of view. The man was incredible. A saint.

'Or a very clever sinner,' said Mirit, when Anderson told her of his awful day. He had telephoned her as soon as he had left the medical school and had told her that he was coming up to Jerusalem for tea and sympathy.

'Please, Mirit. No more. As far as I'm concerned, Jacob Strauss is clean. If he is guilty then I don't want to live in this world any more.'

'All right,' she smiled, 'we'll leave your old professor out of this, but I was right about Cohen . . . '

'Let's talk about something else, for God's sake.' He took her in his arms.

'Religion?' suggested Mirit.

'No.'

'Politics?'

'No.' Anderson nuzzled her ear. She giggled.

'The weather?'

'No.' Anderson dug his fingers into her buttocks and pressed her body to him till she couldn't fail to notice his erection.

'Couldn't possibly be . . . that.' Mirit giggled.

'Oh yes, it could,' said Anderson, starting to lift her dress by walking his fingertips on her buttocks.

'Do you want to go to bed?'

'No,' said Anderson, having raised her dress to waist level and slipping his hands inside her panties. 'I want you right here . . . and now.'

They showered together and then sat on the balcony above the garden, holding hands and sipping cold orange juice. There was no need to speak. Each knew how the other felt, making words an unnecessary and primitive extra form of communication. They went inside when the

165

sun started to go down. 'What shall we do this evening?' said Anderson.

Mirit looked guilty. 'I'm afraid I know exactly what we'll be doing this evening. I have to return to the base. I'll drop you off in Tel Aviv.'

Anderson was bitterly disappointed. 'I thought you were on leave,' he protested.

'I've been recalled,' said Mirit.

Anderson kissed her long and hard when she let him out in Einstein. 'Take care, my lady,' he said.

'You too,' said Mirit.

Anderson climbed the stairs, sorting out his apartment key from the bunch by the dim stair lighting which barely seemed to exceed forty watts at the best of times. He had reached the second top flat when one of the stray cats that roamed the city screeched and flew past him down the stairs. He smiled, but then froze as he realized that something must have alarmed it – something . . . or someone. He paused at the foot of the last flight and looked up into the gloom. It seemed quiet enough. Maybe a squabble with another cat on the roof had caused the commotion, but then again, maybe it hadn't.

Anderson was afraid; he didn't know what to do, so he did nothing but stand absolutely motionless, staring up at the landing outside his front door, waiting. But for what? Then he saw what. There was someone up there, hiding round the corner in the darkness. He had grown impatient in the silence and was edging out to take a look at the stairs. Anderson saw the gun first. It was being held at head height and was pointing at the ceiling as its owner inched forward.

The sight of it was enough for Anderson. He took to his heels and hurtled back down the stairs as fast as his legs could carry him. The clatter of feet behind said that he was being pursued. He burst out of the front door to find

166

the lawn deserted. Shit! Any other time it would be full of bloody folk singers.

The sound of rushing feet behind him spurred him into running blindly out the gate into Einstein. There was a bus approaching the stop some thirty metres below him so he made that his target and managed to leap on to the bottom step as the driver was about to press the hydraulic door lever. Looking back through the rear window he could see a man in a light tan suit standing outside the apartment block on the pavement. He was looking after the bus and had his right hand inside his jacket as if holding his armpit, but Anderson knew differently. Just before they turned left at the foot of Einstein his heart sank. He saw a car pull up and pick up the man in the light suit. He would be able to follow the bus!

There were only four other passengers aboard. Anderson asked, 'Does anyone speak English?' Blank stares. He moved forward and squatted beside the driver, 'Speak English?'

'No English,' said the driver.

Christ! thought Anderson. Ninety per cent of the population speak English and I draw five blanks. He moved back up the aisle, attracting anxious stares from the passengers who clearly thought that he was mad. He could see the widely spaced headlights of the car that was tucked in behind them as they hurtled towards town at customary breakneck speed.

As they slowed to meet the busy intersection with Dizengoff Street, Anderson saw that he had to act so he yelled to the driver to let him off but got nothing more than a sideways glance. He lunged forward and kicked the door lever himself before leaping out and running into the crowd that thronged the street. With a chameleon-like urge to merge, Anderson weaved in and out like a crochet hook for about a hundred metres before he dared to look back.

There was no sign of the light suit. Anderson realized that he was breathing heavily and attracting looks from the strolling crowds who paraded up and down Dizengoff in the evening to no particular purpose. He consciously controlled himself and sought refuge in the shadows of a shop doorway. He pretended to light a cigarette but didn't take his eyes off the street.

He had to find a policeman. It was as simple as that. There was no time for anything more sophisticated, not that he could think of anything anyway. He would walk up to the first policeman he saw and tell him that a man was trying to kill him. It didn't matter if he thought that he was crazy just as long as he stuck with him, put some kind of authority between him and that bloody gun.

Anderson ventured cautiously out on to the street, trying to adopt the same ambling pace as the Israeli crowds but all the time looking for a uniform. A police vehicle passed by on the other side of the street with its occupants lazily surveying the crowd, but Anderson could see that he had no chance of attracting their attention without bowling half a dozen people over and running out in front of the traffic. He watched it pass by as a survivor in a life raft might view a ship that hadn't seen him.

By now, Anderson had been exposed for a quarter of a mile. Something made him look up. There, on a pedestrian bridge, was the man. He was looking directly at him! A bus swerved and braked as Anderson dashed across the road and dived into the gloom of a side-street. He was aware of passing an illuminated sandstone house with a plaque proclaiming it to have been the home of David Ben-Gurion, but Anderson passed it in an Olympic sprint. He ran until his legs began to lose co-ordination, making him feel like a newborn foal. He turned off into a dark lane and pressed himself to the wall behind a stone arch, taking in great gulps of air. It was quiet, very still and very quiet.

Anderson listened for footsteps but couldn't hear any. All he heard was the chirruping of insects in some nearby bushes and then the sound of a car engine. It was barely ticking over. He saw the car slide past the end of the lane, its two occupants looking out of the windows. One was the man in the light suit. He pressed himself even closer to the wall. He couldn't hear the engine any more but he couldn't be sure that it hadn't just stopped.

Anderson ran off along the lane, knowing it to be too narrow for a car to follow. He turned left at the end and headed in the direction he hoped would take him to the shore. Ten minutes later he found himself in Atarim Square, mingling with the tourists and still trying to find a policeman. He had a vague recollection that there was some kind of police station near the tourist information centre at the foot of some wide steps leading down to the marina promenade. He got to the top of them and stopped. Standing at the foot was the gunman, a grin on his face. Anderson spun round but didn't start running. Behind him was a man in sunglasses whom he realized had been the driver of the car.

Without pausing to think, Anderson vaulted over the side rail and dropped ten feet to the promenade below. He'd never have done it if he'd thought about it but, with both ankles amazingly intact, he ran off round the marina basin with the two men hot on his trail. Time was running out for Anderson and he knew it. There were only two exits from the basin, apart from the front which demanded a boat. The two men could cover them both. He was considering a desperate attempt to steal a boat when he caught sight of his *deus ex machina*. There was a police launch in the basin, and it was manned.

Anderson flew out of the gangway calling for help. Two policemen stood up to meet him. 'Do you speak English?' Anderson gasped.

'Of course,' said the policeman.

'These men—' he pointed behind him. 'They're trying to kill me!'

Both policemen drew their pistols. One of them levelled his at the light-suited man who had stopped some thirty metres back. He slowly raised his hands and the policeman walked towards him. 'Be careful! There are two,' cautioned Anderson. The second policeman started looking around for the driver. Anderson watched from the side of the launch as his pursuer was searched. He saw the policeman take his gun and open up his wallet. There was a brief conversation before all three came back to the launch.

Anderson watched in disbelief as one of the policemen handed the gun back to the man and stepped back on board the launch. 'What the bloody . . . !'

'This way,' said the man, pointing the weapon at Anderson, who turned in appeal to the police. They turned their backs.

CHAPTER EIGHT

Anderson got in the car as directed and was joined in the back by the man with the gun, as the driver pulled out into the traffic. He'd stopped protesting. There was no point.

'You're a hard man to talk to, Dr Anderson,' said his captor. Anderson didn't reply. He was thinking of Mirit and St Thomas's and the farm in Dumfries, all the things that he wouldn't see again. The car turned into Einstein and stopped at the gate to the university apartments. 'Let's go back to your place,' said the man. Anderson got out and looked up, his insides turning to water as he realized that they might throw him off the roof. He looked at the dusty pavement and saw himself lying there like a rag doll. 'Move it!'

The man in the tan suit stopped at the second top landing and motioned to the driver to go ahead. He drew his pistol and did as he was bid, sidling silently up to the top and checking out the roof passages. 'OK,' he said.

'Now where is it?' said light-suit as they entered Anderson's apartment.

'Where is what?'

'Klein's notebook, asshole!'

'I've no idea,' said Anderson.

'Don't give me that shit. We know you've got it.'

'I don't have it.'

'Then you gave it to somebody else.'

'No. I never had it in the first place.'

'You told Miles Langman different.'

'Who are you?' asked Anderson, puzzled at how he could have known that.

'J. D. Dexter. I'm an American,' the man said, fumbling in his inside pocket for something.

'Really,' said Anderson. 'With your manners you could have passed for an Israeli.'

'Cut the shit!' He thrust an ID card under Anderson's nose. Anderson took in the American eagle and the initials CIA, but didn't bother with the rest. He looked up at the ceiling and shook his head. 'Sweet Jesus, what a disappointment. I felt sure it would be the KGB this time.'

'KGB? Where?' said the other man in alarm. 'What do you know about the KGB?'

'Christ, Hiram, it was a joke,' said Dexter.

'Limey bastard.'

'Scots bastard,' said Anderson. 'Surely the CIA can get something right.'

'Cool it!' said Dexter as tempers flared. 'Now look, Anderson, don't get the idea that we are the good guys all the time.'

'That thought never entered my head,' said Anderson drily.

'We'll kill you if we have to.' There was a little too much cold sincerity in the comment for Anderson's liking.

'Why?' he said quietly.

'We want that notebook.'

'I don't have it. I never did. I made up the story to test Langman.'

'What test?'

Anderson told them of the trap he'd set for Miles Langman and how he had fallen for it and broken into his room.

'Smells like shit to me,' said the man in sunglasses.

'Your shoes,' said Anderson.

'What about them?'

'With those glasses on you probably stepped in some you couldn't see.'

'Bastard! I'll . . . '

172

'Cool it, Hiram!' said Dexter. He turned to Anderson and said, 'Miles Langman was murdered trying to get into your flat to get that book.'

'No, he wasn't,' said Anderson. 'He broke into my flat the day *before* he was murdered. He knew the book wasn't there. He wouldn't have been trying to break in again.'

Dexter thought for a moment. 'Shit! What a mess.'

'Amen,' said Anderson. 'Drink?'

'Please.' Anderson turned to the man called Hiram to ask him the same.

'Not on duty.'

Dexter gave an embarrassed little shrug when Anderson looked at him. He poured two large measures of Scotch and asked, 'I don't suppose you'll tell me, but why was Miles Langman detailed to keep watch on me?'

'He wasn't,' said Dexter, 'he was on second-tier surveillance.' Seeing Anderson's blank look he continued. 'He was detailed to watch friends and relations of our prime target.'

'Who is?'

'I can't tell you that.'

'Well, that's that.'

Dexter thought for a moment before saying, 'Look, Doctor, you're an intelligent man. It must be perfectly obvious that there is a certain degree of . . . overlap in our interests. Perhaps we could collaborate?'

'What did you have in mind?'

'We need your expertise.'

'Like Langman, only he didn't tell me,' said Anderson.

'If you like. You are here in Israel to investigate the origins of a plasmid that killed one of your medical students.'

'Yes.'

'We are investigating a man who may have constructed

that plasmid, but we have no proof. Despite the fact that we have a man on the inside, our target hasn't put a foot wrong.'

'Where do I come in?'

'Our man has managed to lay his hands on the accounts for our target's organization. Could you tell just by looking at them if the place is conducting experiments in genetic manipulation?'

'It's possible.'

'Good. Now we're getting somewhere,' said Dexter. He said he would be back in the morning and that Anderson should get a good night's sleep. There would be no need to worry about attempts on his life. 'Hiram' would be acting as minder.

'A comfort,' said Anderson.

Mirit arrived back at the Hadera base at eight o'clock and was told to report immediately to the commanding officer. Assuming some emergency she hurried across the dusty compound to his office but saw no signs of any undue activity on her way. She saw a jeep fitted with a light machine gun mounting go out of the gate but that was a routine patrol. The time on her watch said so.

'I expect you are wondering why you were recalled from leave,' said Colonel Aarons, stating the obvious.

'I had assumed some trouble.'

'No, no trouble, but this gentleman would like to have a word with you.' The unsmiling man standing beside Aarons nodded briefly and held out his ID card to Mirit. She read the name, Moshe Viren, and noted the Israeli Intelligence Agency insignia.

'And what can I do for Mossad?' said Mirit.

'If you'll excuse us, Colonel?'

'Of course,' said Aarons, getting up and leaving the room. So you carry that much weight, thought Mirit.

174

The intelligence man waited till the door had closed before speaking. 'Our colleagues in the CIA informed us, of course, that they wished to interview an Israeli officer and told us something of what it was about.' He laboured the word 'something'. 'Not to put too fine a point on it, Captain, if the CIA are interested in something in Israel, so are we.'

'I understand.'

'We know, of course, of your association with the English doctor . . . Neil Anderson.'

'He's Scottish,' Mirit interrupted, having adopted Anderson's reaction to the label 'English'. She felt silly and apologized.

The agent didn't mind; it told him a lot about the relationship. 'Captain, neither of us is a scientist but neither of us is stupid. Certain key words stand out in this affair, bacteria, genetic engineering, death. The CIA's interest only confirms the implication of these words – that some kind of biological weapon has been created. We want it. It is your duty as an Israeli officer . . . '

'Don't tell me my duty,' interrupted Mirit.

'Very well, Captain. Report to your commanding officer when you have completed your mission. You may return to your leave.'

Mirit walked back across the compound oblivious to the sand that was being whipped up into her face by the strengthening wind. So this was it. The conflict of interests that she had known must be on the cards somewhere ever since Anderson had declared his love for her and she for him. At worst she had thought that it might come to the point where she would have to say 'no' when Neil asked her to marry him, and try to explain why she felt that she couldn't settle down to be a doctor's wife in the leafy lanes of Surrey. But this she hadn't foreseen.

For Mirit, life hadn't been the same since she saw her

father return from the western wall in 1967. Although only eight years old, she had realized just what Israel meant to her father and all those friends and relations with the strange, numbered tattoos on their inner arms. The tear-stained reminiscences, the missing members in her family and in those of her friends, the pain-lined faces of those who were old before their time, had all conspired to fill a young girl with a determination that she would grow up to do all she could to defend and preserve the state of Israel. But now this.

On the drive back, Mirit tried to console herself with the thought that the conflict might never arise. Maybe the riddle of the Klein gene would never be solved. Maybe all the cultures had already been destroyed. But if they hadn't and she and Anderson found them? What then? An articulated lorry blasted on its horn as Mirit's concentration wandered and the Fiat strayed too far over the highway. She snatched the wheel back and thought of what might have been. Maybe death was preferable. She couldn't face Anderson. She drove back to Jerusalem and sat in the walled garden.

Dexter turned up at Anderson's apartment at ten in the morning. He carried a black document case which he handed over along with a small card which read: 'J. D. Dexter, Shipping Agent'. 'When you have an answer, ring me at that number,' he said. 'Hiram's coming off duty now but you won't be alone.'

'Thank you,' said Anderson, not quite sure if he meant it but supposing that he did. He made coffee and took it out on to the roof to begin work on the papers. When he opened the case he was alarmed at the thickness of the file, but when he flicked through it he saw that much of it was repetitive. The papers were the monthly accounts of a research lab for the last six months.

Anderson got his answer within fifteen minutes. It came from the list of chemicals ordered. Most of them were standard laboratory reagents but each month an order was placed with a small specialist company for 'restriction enzymes'. These could only be used for cutting open DNA molecules. Anderson searched the lists for the other telltale order. There it was! An order to the same company placed some three months ago for 1,000 units of T4 ligase, the enzyme used for rejoining open DNA molecules after the insertion of foreign material. There was no doubt that the lab was engaged in DNA manipulation, gene cloning, genetic engineering, call it what you would. No doubt at all.

Mirit arrived as he was sifting through the rest of the material. She stood quietly at the roof door, watching him, until, conscious that he was no longer alone, he looked up. His face broke into a huge smile. 'Mirit! What a lovely surprise.' Putting down the papers he gave her a big hug. 'A false alarm? You're back on leave?' he asked, willing her to say 'yes'.

'I'm back on leave,' said Mirit.

'There's nothing wrong, is there?' Anderson asked, thinking that he detected a note of reservation in her voice.

'No, nothing.'

Anderson told her of his visit from the CIA and of the chase that had taken them all over Tel Aviv.

'At least they didn't open your head wound again,' said Mirit.

'I think one of them is acting as guardian angel,' said Anderson.

'I know. I saw him.'

'You saw him?'

'Sure. Grey suit, button-down collar. They merge into the background like blood on snow.'

'How come your intelligence people allow the CIA to operate here?' asked Anderson.

Why did he ask that? Was there something behind the question, Mirit wondered, or was it her imagination born of guilt? 'We have a special relationship with the United States,' she said.

'You too?' said Anderson, but didn't elaborate. He was wondering why Mirit's eyes had avoided his when she answered the question.

'You have a long shopping list,' said Mirit, looking at the papers. Anderson told her what the CIA had asked him to do.

'And is it the lab?' she asked.

'It could be. They are definitely in the gene business.'

'Which lab is it?'

'They wouldn't tell me.'

'Any clues in the accounts?'

'That's exactly what I'm looking for,' smiled Anderson. 'I'll get us some orange juice and we can both look.'

After twenty minutes or so, Anderson said, 'Have you ever heard of the Jan Kouros Hospice?'

'No, why?'

'Every month this lab pays money to the Jan Kouros Hospice. There's no indication why.'

'Do you think it's important?'

'I don't know. How can we find out about it?'

'I'll make some calls.'

Mirit went to use the phone while Anderson continued his audit. She returned ten minutes later. 'It's a charitable organization in the desert. It's a refuge for poor people suffering from incurable diseases.'

'I wonder what the connection is.'

'Ask the CIA.'

Anderson considered the suggestion. 'I might just do that. I'll have to call them anyway. If they tell me, well and good. If they don't? I'll know it's worth following up.'

'Are you collaborating or competing with the CIA?' asked Mirit.

'If the Klein gene still exists I'd like to get there first, destroy it before the button-down collars get to it. Does that make sense?'

'Yes,' said Mirit, kissing him on the cheek. 'I'll help you all I can.' Anderson smiled but didn't say anything. He was wondering why Mirit had just avoided his eyes again.

'Dexter, shipping agents,' said the female voice. It could have been worse. Anderson couldn't have kept a straight face if he'd had to use code words or enquire about the brand of cigarettes used by his second cousin twice removed.

'Mr Dexter, please.'

'Who's calling?'

'Dr Anderson.' A pause.

'Yes, Doctor, any luck?' said Dexter's voice.

'This could be the lab. They're definitely involved in DNA manipulation.'

'Excellent. I'm obliged.'

'But not obliged enough to tell me which lab?'

'No.'

'Can you tell me why the lab makes a regular payment to the Jan Kouros Hospice?' asked Anderson.

'The hospice is a refuge for incurables. The money is apparently a charitable donation.'

'Thanks.'

'You're welcome. We'll be in touch.'

Anderson returned to the roof, deep in thought.

'Something wrong?' asked Mirit.

'I'm not sure. They said the payments were a donation.'

'So, it's a donation. What's the problem?'

'Look at the sum. It's an uneven amount. People make donations to charity in nice round figures, not—' Anderson referred back to the papers— 'not numbers like three thousand, two hundred and forty-nine. I just don't buy the donation story. I think they're paying for something specific.'

'You think that the CIA were lying?'

'I don't know. Maybe they believe it. Either way it's worth investigating. Can you find out more about the hospice?'

'I'll try.'

Mirit didn't return until early evening. When she came in, Anderson suggested that they drive down to Jaffa for dinner and discuss their progress afterwards, a suggestion readily agreed to by Mirit who said that she knew just the place. She did. The restaurant was high above the old harbour and cut into the rock, affording them views along the shore to the lights of Tel Aviv as they sat in the heavily scented air of a roof garden.

'Find out anything?' asked Anderson.

'Something. The hospice is in the desert about forty kilometres from Hadera. It's totally isolated, for obvious reasons, and is run by some obscure sect of the Coptic Church,' Mirit said. 'Have you had any more thoughts?'

Anderson ran his finger slowly round the edge of the glass. He said, 'The more I think about this "donation" business, the less I like it. Research labs don't make donations. They receive them.'

'But what could they possibly buy from such a place?'

'No idea, but I'm convinced it has something to do with the Klein affair.'

'So, what now?'

'I want to see this place. I'm not sure why, but I do.'

'We can go tomorrow, but what about your "guardian angel"?'

'What about him?'

'He'll follow us.'

'I hadn't considered that. Do you think he will?'

'Of course. He is here tonight.'

'What?' exclaimed Anderson in surprise. 'God, I'm such a novice in this game.'

'Behind you and to your left, dark-blue suit and sunglasses.'

Anderson didn't bother to sneak a look at the man he knew must be Hiram. 'We'll have to shake him then,' he said, feeling suddenly self-conscious at having used an 'in' term. He saw Mirit smile. 'Is that what you say?' he asked.

'Yes,' she said, 'we'll have to shake him.'

'Shaking' Anderson's watchdog proved not to be a problem when, next day, they left the apartment. They simply walked along the flat roof of the French Building and descended, using the stairs of the Italian Building at the end of the block. They left the compound by a side entrance and picked up the car which Mirit had parked in a suitably discreet place. After all, Anderson's minder had no reason to suspect that they would be trying to avoid him.

It took them a long time to find the hospice for there was no good reason for it to advertise its presence with road signs. Eventually, knowing the distance that they had travelled from Hadera, Mirit decided on a desert track which was barely differentiated from the sand itself. Doubts about her choice were just beginning to arise after five kilometres of barren scrub when they came to a sign and an arrow. It said 'Jan Kouros Hospice 1 Km.', although the writing was barely legible on a wooden board that had been bleached by the sun and scratched by wind-driven sand.

They stopped the car and took swigs in turn from an army-issue water canteen that Mirit had insisted they would need. She had been right. Anderson's throat was as parched as the land around them. 'Do we drive straight up?' Mirit asked.

'No,' said Anderson. 'They can't get too many passers-by out here. We'd stick out like sore thumbs.'

'Then what?'

Anderson thought for a moment before saying, 'It's too hot to walk far. What do you say we climb that ridge and have a look from there?'

'Sound military strategy,' said Mirit.

The climb was agony in the heat. Their feet kept slipping on the sand and made the ridge twice the height it actually was. Just before the summit they lay down to regain their breath and take another drink from the canteen. Mirit took binoculars from the leather case that hung round her neck and handed them to Anderson. 'You'll need these.' They wriggled up to the top of the ridge on their elbows and looked down on the Jan Kouros Hospice.

Anderson found the sight to be movingly pathetic. The hospice consisted of a number of wooden huts huddled together in a compound that even here in the wilderness was fenced off. Skull-and-crossbone motifs were dotted around the perimeter on notices that warned travellers to stay away. Inside the compound, Anderson could see through the glasses a number of shuffling figures moving about. Each was dressed in a long brown robe fitted with a voluminous hood. There was a depressing aura of suffering and hopelessness about the hospice which Anderson found disturbing. For a moment he wished that he had never seen the place, for now that he had, the image would always be with him. Even on lazy summer days when eating strawberries on English lawns he would know that such a place existed. When pushing his car from winter snow in Dumfries he would know that it existed.

One of the inmates stumbled and fell in the compound. As he got up, the hood fell back from his head causing Anderson to gasp. 'Good God Almighty!' he said in

182

horror, 'he hasn't got a face!' He handed the glasses to Mirit who gave a little swallow.

'Yes,' she said quietly, 'he's a leper.'

Anderson turned his back on the awful tableau of human suffering and lay in the sand while Mirit looked at the compound. 'What a place,' she said, with the same mix of distaste and guilt that Anderson felt within him.

'But what a place to carry out secret experiments,' murmured Anderson.

Mirit dropped down below the top of the ridge and joined him in the sand. 'Do you really think so?' she asked.

'I think that the money given to this place is some kind of rent,' said Anderson, 'rent for secure facilities in the middle of nowhere. A place that no one ever comes to through choice.'

'But how can you prove it?'

'We'll have to get in there.'

'You can't be serious,' said a shocked Mirit.

Anderson's silence said that he was.

'But how?'

'I was rather hoping that you might tell me that,' said Anderson.

Mirit raised the glasses again and scanned the perimeter of the compound. 'Well, it's not exactly a military install-ation. But then, it has no need to be. No one in their right mind would want to get in there. You can't go in over the gate, they've cleared all the scrub away from that area; you'll be seen. There's a clear view down the drive from the buildings.'

'At night?'

'The drive is lit at night. See. Two floodlights each side.'

Mirit handed Anderson the glasses. He saw the tall, wooden posts with the lamp housings on top. He returned the glasses. Mirit said, 'We can go in through the fence at the bottom left-hand corner. There's a dense patch of scrub between the wire and the buildings; it would give us cover.'

'Doesn't look like the kind of fence you "go through" easily,' said Anderson.

'We'd have to cut it,' agreed Mirit.

'But they would know,' said Anderson.

'Depends how often they inspect the fence. By the look of it, not that often.' Mirit adjusted the focus on the glasses. 'I think we can get away with just cutting the bottom strand. We can scoop away the sand below it and go in underneath.'

'Couldn't we scoop away even more sand and go under without cutting the wire at all?' asked Anderson.

Mirit shook her head. 'Too difficult. It's all right going down on one side but it's extremely difficult to come up the other. You have to move much more earth than you think.'

Anderson took her word for it. 'What about guards?'

'There's no sign that they have any,' said Mirit. 'No guardhouse, no towers, no men patrolling. I suppose they don't need any.'

'Not normally,' agreed Anderson. 'But if something else *is* going on there, outside interests might have put a few around the place.'

'No sign,' repeated Mirit.

Anderson accepted it. 'Maybe they just rely on the isolation and very nature of the place,' he said.

'Good enough for me,' said Mirit. 'Are you sure you want to do this?'

'I have to know.'

'All right. We'll do it.'

'What do you need?'

'Wire cutters, bridging cable, crocodile clips, that's about it.'

'How long will it take to get them?'

Mirit checked her watch and said, 'It's too late to try tonight. I suggest we get what we need tomorrow morning, drive up late afternoon and try to get in tomorrow night.'

'Agreed.'

'And we'll need some dark clothing,' said Mirit, looking at Anderson's white shirt.

'It might be an idea to get one of those robes that the inmates wear, then even if someone spots me they might not suspect an intruder.'

'We can buy them at the Arab market tomorrow.'

'Just one,' said Anderson, 'there's no sense in both of us going inside. I know what I'm looking for. You don't. If you can get me into the place I'll do the rest.'

'Makes sense,' agreed Mirit quietly.

'You mentioned bridging cable and clips. What are they for?'

'In case the fence is electrified,' said Mirit.

'Is that likely?'

'You were the one who brought up outside interests.'

'Let's go.'

They returned to Jerusalem.

On the following morning they travelled from Mirit's home in Jerusalem to the Arab market in Jaffa where they bought a robe of the type they had seen the inmates of the hospice wear, and stuffed it in the back of the car along with the hardware that Mirit had already decided they would need. They left their departure for Hadera as late as possible. In the late afternoon they drove slowly along the shore road to Tel Aviv and sat by the marina drinking cold Maccabee beer and listening to the tinkling sounds of the yachts at anchor. The noise was hypnotic. It acted as white sound to quell unspoken anxieties about the night to come. They left Tel Aviv at seven and spoke little on the journey north.

As they passed through Hadera and drove out on the desert road, Mirit, who was driving, slowed down so that they would not miss the turn-off. 'How are you feeling?' she asked.

'Awful,' said Anderson. They lapsed into silence again till they both saw the turn-off at the same time.

'Got it,' said Mirit. They were now slowed to walking pace, seeing boulders and potholes only as they came into range of their dipped headlights. 'We can't risk main beams,' said Mirit, 'they light up the sky a long way off.'

'Maybe we should leave the car a good bit from the hospice. Walk the rest?'

'I think so,' said Mirit. 'We can drive till we get to the one-kilometre signpost then hide the car somewhere around there.'

Anderson peered out of the windows at the sky. 'Moon's coming over the ridge,' he said.

They hid the car in a gully between two sand dunes where it could not be seen from the track and collected their gear from the back. The moon had now cleared the ridge and lit up the desert with a pale, shadowy light that allowed them to see their way. Anderson thought that their surroundings looked like the surface of the moon itself, but did not say so. His stomach was in no mood for small talk.

They came to the foot of the hill near the hospice that they had climbed on the previous day. 'Do we go up again?' asked Anderson.

'Yes, we'll have to observe the place for a while before we make a move.'

At night the climb did not prove as unpleasant as it had the first time in the blistering sun. Anderson found that he actually enjoyed it. If nothing else it took his mind off things for a while. They got to the top and looked down on the hospice, its tiny cluster of lights in the black sea of the desert at night made it seem the loneliest place on earth. The drive was lit as were three of the buildings. Anderson looked at his watch and rolled over to lie on his back. Mirit continued to keep watch. 'Shouldn't be too long,' she said quietly.

At midnight there were still three lights burning in one of the buildings. 'Come on . . . go to bed,' urged Mirit.

'Sssh,' said Anderson. 'Listen.'

They both listened and heard the sound. 'A car is coming,' said Mirit.

'Sounds too heavy,' said Anderson.

The noise grew louder and headlights came into view along the winding track. 'It's a truck,' said Anderson as the vehicle passed below them and stopped at the gates of the hospice. A man ran down the drive from the lit building and opened them.

'Strange time for deliveries,' said Anderson.

Mirit, who had the glasses to her eyes, said, 'They are not delivering. They are collecting . . . people.'

Anderson took the glasses and saw a single file of robed inmates emerge like penitent monks from the lit building and get into the back of the truck. The man who had opened up the hospice gates closed them again as the vehicle lumbered out into the night. Shortly afterwards all the lights in the hospice were extinguished.

'What was all that about?' whispered Anderson. Mirit shook her head.

'How long do we wait?'

'An hour.'

At a quarter to one the wind got up. At first it was a gentle breeze that flitted across the dunes but, within minutes, it had risen to whip up the sand in its fury and throw great clouds of it across the moon. Mirit signalled that they should make for the fence for speech was impossible. They stopped for a few moments at the foot of the hill to rest in the shelter of a boulder before crossing the final scrub to reach the wire, wriggling up the last few metres on their stomachs.

Mirit clipped the bridging cable on the bottom strand and the sound of the cutters on the wire was lost in the maelstrom. Another few minutes and they had cleared away enough sand for Anderson to get in. Mirit kissed her fingertips and placed them on Anderson's lips before he gathered the folds of his robe and crawled under the wire.

He stayed on his stomach and crawled round the edge of the dense scrub between him and the huts to reach the shadow of the first building. The wind dropped as suddenly as it had risen, its scream becoming a low moan that was still sufficient to cover any sound that Anderson's feet and robe made as he crept along the sides of the dormitory huts, hugging the contours of the walls. He knelt at the corner of the bottom hut and looked over to what he felt must be the main building. There was no safe way of approaching it; he would have to take the risk and run across the open compound.

He gritted his teeth, sprinted over the sand to the verandah and pressed himself into a corner, looking back for any sign that he'd been spotted. Nothing stirred. He sidled along the front of the building and tried the door; it was unlocked and creaked back on its dry, sand-filled hinges. He stepped inside and closed it quickly behind him, searching in the folds of his robes as he did so for the torch that Mirit had given him.

The first room he searched was an office. He sifted through papers and files but, finding that most of them were in Hebrew, he cut the search short and moved on to the next room which turned out to be a well-organized dispensary. He ran the torch beam down the labels but found nothing out of the ordinary and moved on again. Anderson recognized the smell of dusty books in the darkness. He was in a small library of mainly medical and religious books although his torch beam did fall on a red leather-bound edition of *David Copperfield* by Charles

Dickens. He recognized Manson's book on tropical diseases and the *Manual of Clinical Mycology*, both books he had himself.

At the end of his search Anderson had found only one room in use as a laboratory. It was about two metres square and was equipped for elementary urine and blood analysis, the sort of work that would be done in a side ward back home. He had been wrong. Utterly wrong. There was no way on earth that sophisticated genetic engineering experiments were being carried out in this place. The hospice was exactly what it purported to be, a refuge for some of the most unfortunate people in the world.

Anderson let himself out and flitted quickly back across the compound and into the shadows of the dormitory huts, feeling depressed. He had only a few moments to contemplate his failure, however, before the compound lights were switched on. He flattened himself against the hut wall like a rabbit caught in headlights and felt sure that he had been discovered. But there was no sound to be heard. No anxious cries, no running feet. He recovered from the paralysis of fright and dived into the patch of scrub nearest the hut. He heard the sound of an engine approaching and realized that the lights had been switched on for the benefit of the truck they had seen earlier. It was returning.

Anderson lay still in the scrub, pressing his body to the ground while he watched the sorry spectacle of the returning lepers disembarking and filing into one of the buildings. A brief word passed between the driver and one of the staff before the truck left and the gates were secured. It was another ten minutes before the compound was in darkness again.

Anderson got to his feet, realizing that he had lain in one position for a very long time without moving a muscle. His limbs were stiff. He stretched his arms but scarcely had time to feel good before an arm encircled his neck and drew him backwards into a miasma of foetid breath. Anderson gasped for air as he desperately tried to break the grip of the powerful man that held him, but the arm was huge, unnaturally huge, and covered in scaly skin. The thick, swollen arm of a leper held him fast.

Anderson let go of the arm and hammered back both elbows into his attacker's midriff. This was his last chance and he knew it. All his energy was channelled into the successive blows that he kept slamming into the man's stomach until at last he felt the grip weaken and he was free. He swung round, filled with fear and revulsion, the heavy torch held high in his right hand ready to strike. He didn't deliver the blow. In the thin silver moonlight he saw that his attacker was blind. There were no pupils to his eyes, just thick white cataracts which caught the light as he groped the air in his effort to find Anderson. The man made no sound and Anderson guessed that the disease had destroyed his larynx. He melted back into the shadows, leaving the awful spectre circling with outstretched arms.

To his shame, Anderson was sick in the scrub behind the huts. Inside he knew that it wasn't because of the fight or the violence but because of the man's disease. Here he was, a doctor, on his knees in the sand and vomiting because of the revulsion he felt at having been in close contact with a leper. Anderson was disgusted with himself. Once more, Israel had stripped him bare of veneer and shown him an inner self that he would rather not have known. He made for the perimeter fence and left the compound, knowing full well that his attacker would have no way of telling what had happened.

He lay in the sand for a moment outside the wire, trying to calm himself and rein his imagination. He was grateful that Mirit was not waiting there and deduced that she had probably moved further along when the compound lights had come on. He scooped out a hole in the ground and buried his robe in it. He was desperate for water – not to drink but to wash in. He wanted to scrub his skin till there was no trace left of the leper's horny touch, except for the guilt; that would remain for a long time. Mirit crawled towards him. 'Are you all right?'

'I'm fine,' said Anderson, 'let's go.' They returned to the car in silence. When they reached it Anderson said, 'Have you any water?' Mirit handed him a canteen. 'No, more than that.'

'There's a can in the back,' said Mirit, looking puzzled.

Anderson stripped to the waist and scrubbed himself with meticulous care while Mirit watched in silence. She knew that something was wrong but didn't dare ask. Anderson finished his ablutions and put the can back in the boot of the car. He got in and looked straight ahead. 'OK,' he said. 'Let's go.'

Mirit didn't speak until they had reached the highway. Then she said, 'Was that the place?'

'No,' said Anderson, 'I was wrong.'

Mirit sensed that he was still deeply upset about something but didn't feel that she could reach him. She said softly, 'Where shall I drive to?'

'Jerusalem,' said Anderson, 'I want to sit in your garden.'

'Of course,' said Mirit.

When they got to the house, Anderson showered and changed. He was sitting in the quiet of the walled garden when Mirit came out and handed him a cold drink. 'Want to talk yet?' she asked softly.

'Yes,' said Anderson. He told her what had happened with the leper and of the revulsion he had felt.

'But that's natural,' Mirit said, to no effect.

'But I'm a doctor. I shouldn't feel like that about any disease. Don't you understand? I thought I was a good doctor, but I'm not. I'm a sham.'

Mirit encircled him from behind with her arms. 'Don't be silly, Neil. Being a doctor doesn't make you superhuman. You just behaved like any normal human being in the circumstances.'

'No, I'm a coward.'

'Don't be ridiculous,' said Mirit firmly. 'What's really bothering you is that your own image of yourself has been dented. You've been forced to admit that you are vulnerable like everyone else. Macho man and little tin god have taken a bit of a knock.' She took his face between her palms and said, 'Look. It's the real Neil Anderson that I love, the vulnerable one, the one with doubts and fears. Don't play a part for me, Neil.'

Anderson held her tightly. 'God, I feel awful.'

'I know, I know,' Mirit soothed. 'But let me tell you this. If you had really been a coward you would have struck that man with the torch. You would have struck him over and over again and destroyed him for showing up your cowardice. But you didn't, you were in control, you backed off, and what's more, you showed compassion . . . real compassion when you were filled with fear and revulsion and your animal instincts screamed at you to kill him. You did the right thing, Neil. You were in control and you did the right thing.'

Anderson managed to raise a wan smile.

As they held each other tightly in the peace of the Jerusalem garden, it was Mirit's eyes that showed a flicker of pain and doubt.

CHAPTER NINE

Mirit and Anderson spoke no more of the Klein affair for the rest of the day, but spent the time relaxing in the garden and recovering from the horrors of the night. At one point in the afternoon both of them fell asleep and didn't wake until the sun had sunk low in the sky and the garden was in shadow. Mirit woke first and decided to leave Anderson sleeping while she went inside to start dinner. She kissed him lightly on the forehead before she left him. She couldn't say so but she was delighted at Anderson's failure to find the secret laboratory. If he didn't find the source of the Klein gene she couldn't deceive him and that was all she now wanted. The mere thought that she might have to betray him had become an almost unbearable burden to her over the past few days, and she now knew that if it ever did come to the point where she had to hand over the gene to her superiors, she would never be able to see Anderson again. There was no question of doing it secretly behind his back and carrying on as before. She just couldn't do that.

Anderson came in from the garden yawning.

'I think that garden is enchanted,' he said. 'That was the best sleep I've had since I came to Israel.'

'I *know* the garden is enchanted,' said Mirit. 'The cares of the world just can't live in it!' Anderson watched her as she prepared the food. He leaned against the kitchen door and felt a lump come to his throat. He had never been in love with anyone the way he was with Mirit, but in the odd moments when he could think clearly he had to be honest and admit to himself that he couldn't see the proud, independent Israeli girl organizing summer fetes at St Thomas's. Mirit had more than a career – she had, or thought that she had, some kind of mission in life, almost a vocation to be pursued with missionary zeal. Anderson had always been reluctant to talk to her about it because he had sensed that it might be a dangerous subject to tackle, but he had recently begun to wonder what might happen should a conflict of interests arise. It hadn't been an idle thought. It had been triggered by Mirit's behaviour after her brief recall from leave. Something had happened back at the base, something that she hadn't told him about, something that disturbed her, something that made her look away when before she would have looked directly at him with the challenging honesty of her dark eyes, something . . . to do with the Klein gene?

And yet, just now, she seemed relaxed, like she had been at the Red Sea. Oh God! What he'd give to recapture those hours. If he had but one wish before he died it would be to return to the shooting stars and coral reefs with Mirit. Maybe when this business was all over? Maybe it *was* all over. But no, the CIA had something on a lab that they wouldn't tell him about. If there was the slightest chance of beating them to it, he must go on. It was something Anderson had accepted without really considering why. Now he thought about it. Was he really doing it for altruistic reasons? Or could it be that it was an excuse to delay leaving Israel because he knew in his heart of hearts that Mirit could never marry him and that when he left Israel it would all be over? The Klein gene had brought them together. Perhaps when it was gone . . .

'What are you thinking about?' asked Mirit.

'I was thinking how nice you looked.'

'Would you like to have dinner in the garden?'

'Yes.'

'Put some music on, would you.'

Anderson browsed through the shelf of albums by the stereo system and chose Mozart. The sound filtered out

194

through the open french windows as they ate below. Mirit looked at Anderson and decided that he had recovered sufficiently from the ordeal at the hospice for her to return to the subject of the Klein affair. 'What are you going to do now?' she asked.

'I don't know,' he said. 'If only I could find out from the CIA where these accounts came from, but they're not going to tell me. You wouldn't have a way of finding out, would you?' he asked.

Mirit looked doubtful but she was playing for time. She was considering whether or not to ask Mossad if they knew who the CIA target was or where the accounts originated. But would they tell her, and if she did come up with an answer wouldn't Anderson know immediately of her involvement with the Intelligence Service? Maybe that was why he had asked. Maybe he was testing her. Maybe he suspected her. This can't go on, thought Mirit. Feeling guilty was a new experience to her and it was eating her alive. 'I don't think so,' she said.

There it was again, thought Anderson, the reluctance to look him in the eye. 'What's wrong, Mirit?' he said gently.

For a split second Anderson saw her look like a frightened rabbit before she recovered and got up from the table. 'Nothing,' she laughed, but it sounded hollow. 'I'll get us some more coffee.'

Back in the kitchen Mirit put down the coffee pot and held her hand to her head while she recovered her composure. The prospect of continual deceit and evasion was making her ill, but now as she stood there she saw the way out. She wouldn't betray Neil Anderson; she would give him up! She would tell him that it was all over between them and that she didn't want to see him again. But could she do it? She did love him. Yes, she decided, for after that he would go home and he would be safe. He would be back in his leafy Surrey lanes where he really belonged and he would get over it in time and so would she, however badly she felt. What's more, she would be able to live with herself. With Neil gone, Mossad would have no further interest in her. The Klein gene would be someone else's problem. She returned to the garden with the coffee and took a long time stirring hers. She was aware that Anderson was watching her and steeled herself to look him in the eye.

'Tell me,' said Anderson.

'We have to talk,' said Mirit quietly. Anderson waited for her to go on. 'I think it's time,' said Mirit. Her voice had dropped to a whisper.

'Time for what?'

'It's time that we said goodbye. We both knew that our time together was limited despite the talk of marriage. It just wouldn't work. You must leave Israel. Forget the Klein affair. Let the professionals get on with it. Go back to what you know.'

Anderson felt as if his insides were being removed without anaesthetic. 'Are you saying that you don't love me enough?' he asked quietly.

There was an agonizingly long pause before Mirit said, 'Hurting you is the last thing in the world I would ever want to do, but . . . yes, I suppose that is what I am saying.'

Anderson stared down at the table for a moment before looking up and smiling broadly. Mirit's eyes opened wide with surprise.

'Now I know you're lying,' said Anderson.

'What . . . ?'

'You love me as much as I love you. There's something else going on.'

'Of all the arrogant . . .'

'Not arrogant, just observant. You have been under some kind of strain since you were recalled from leave.

Something happened up in Hadera, something to do with me . . . Is that it? They asked you to spy on me? Report back on what I did and said?'

Mirit diverted her eyes and stayed silent.

'Something more serious than that?'

'I can't tell you,' said Mirit, still avoiding his eyes.

'Then I am right,' said Anderson in triumph. 'So what can it be? They want you to kill me . . . '

'Don't be ridiculous.'

'But it's something important enough to make you feel so bad that . . . I know. They want you to get the Klein plasmid for them!' Anderson saw by the look on Mirit's face that he was right. He leaned back in his chair. 'So that's it. The military have ordered you to get the plasmid for them when we find it and you couldn't bear the thought of betraying me. So rather than face that prospect you staged this touching little goodbye scene.'

Mirit offered no argument.

'It didn't work, Mirit.'

'No, it didn't, did it,' she said.

Anderson took both her hands across the table and said, 'I understand the problem and I can see how it's eating away at you. I will make a bargain with you. I think that the Klein thing is evil and should be destroyed, but if and when we find it you disagree and feel that you should hand it over to the authorities, I won't stop you.'

'Do you mean that?' asked Mirit.

'I do.'

'Neil, I love you.'

'I just told you that.'

They sat and talked in the garden. There suddenly seemed so much to say now that the strain of Mirit's guilty secret had disappeared. 'Do you realize that the CIA have probably been scouring Israel for you?' she said.

'I'll go back to Tel Aviv tonight and confess all, say I

197

sneaked off to have a night of love with a beautiful Israeli lady.'

'Good thinking,' said Mirit. 'They're Americans. They'll accept that without question. A man's got to do what a man's got to do and all that. What then?'

'I want to talk to Professor Strauss again. Now that he's had time to think after I told him that Cohen was innocent, he may have some ideas.'

'But he may be the guilty one, Neil.'

'I thought we'd agreed that he wasn't.'

'*You* decided that he was innocent,' insisted Mirit. 'I've seen no proof.'

'All right, my decision,' conceded Anderson. 'What are you going to do?'

'I'll try to find out if the CIA told my people what they wouldn't tell you.'

They arranged to meet in Tel Aviv for lunch on the following day.

Anderson was walking up Einstein at seven-thirty when a car pulled up beside him and Dexter got out. 'Where the hell have you been?' he asked angrily. 'We thought they'd got you.' Anderson apologized for his 'thoughtlessness', saying that he'd 'been with a lady'.

'We can't protect you if you keep sneaking off like that,' Dexter lectured.

Anderson adopted what he felt was a suitably contrite expression, pleased that, just as Mirit had predicted, the American had accepted his explanation without question. 'I'll try to keep you informed of my movements. Any progress with your investigation?' he asked.

'No. Our man on the inside reports nothing unusual. You've told us that they're buying the stuff they need, but they don't appear to be using it.'

'Wouldn't it be a damn sight more sensible if you were to

198

tell me where this place is and who it is that you suspect?'

'Can't do that.'

Anderson decided on the spur of the moment that he wouldn't wait till morning to contact Jacob Strauss. He would telephone him and suggest that they meet that same evening. The embarrassment at having been caught in Strauss's office was rekindled in Anderson as he dialled the number and he wondered if he would ever be able to think of the incident without getting that feeling. Perhaps that was his real reason for contacting Strauss again. He wanted to exorcize the ghost of that bad experience, seek absolution.

'Jacob Strauss,' said the voice in the earpiece.

'Professor? It's Neil Anderson.'

Strauss interrupted him before he could say anything else. 'Dr Anderson! I've been trying to reach you. I must speak with you.' Strauss sounded agitated.

'That's just what I was calling about,' said Anderson. 'Perhaps we could meet this evening?'

'Yes, yes. I think I know what's been going on. Come round to my house, Doctor.'

'I'll be there about nine.'

Anderson put down the receiver and faced his next problem. What did he tell the CIA man? If Strauss really had come up with something he didn't want any button-down collars around to steal the advantage. He'd go out over the roof again.

A cat was scratching away at a corner of the roof when Anderson left his apartment. It was trying to get at a large cockroach that was sheltering in a crack in the parapet wall. He watched it for a moment, fascinated by its appearance. It was an alley cat, very lean, almost scrawny, its hair ruffled and matted by its dustbin life. Anderson wondered how it would view the smooth, plump, tinkling tabbies of home. The cockroach stupidly left the safety of the crack and paid with its life.

'*Bon appétit*,' murmured Anderson, wondering if he himself were leaving the safety of a crack in the wall. He moved quickly and quietly across the flat roof in the starlight and descended via the stairs in the Italian Building to leave the compound by the side entrance. He found it easy to get a cab in the lull between people going out for the evening and coming home again, and gave the driver Strauss's address. He'd abandoned the T-shirted casualness of the day in favour of a proper shirt and a light jacket in deference to Jacob Strauss's unavowed, but none the less obvious, adherence to standards.

Anderson asked the driver to let him off at the beginning of the avenue where Strauss lived. He wanted time to get his thoughts in order, stretch his legs, feel the night air before he sank back into the Klein affair. As he got to the gate of the Strauss villa he thought that he could hear music and paused to listen. It was coming from the house across the street. A teenage girl was sitting at an electric organ in a ground-floor room. She was playing from music and kept leaning forward to study the score in her halting progress through some vaguely familiar pop tune. Anderson walked up the path and knocked on Strauss's door. There was no answer. He tried again and this time he heard someone coming. It was Jacob Strauss.

Anderson smiled and stepped inside, but immediately began to feel uneasy as Strauss seemed surprised that he had done so. A bad start, he thought, feeling as if he'd eaten with the wrong fork. He turned in the hallway and waited for Strauss to direct him to a room. 'Eeer . . . you'd . . . eer . . . better come in here,' said Strauss, opening a door and fumbling on the wall for the light switch. Anderson was confused. Why was Strauss behaving as if he'd just turned up out of the blue. Dammit! He'd been invited.

Strauss indicated a chair. 'Please sit down,' he said, while crossing to a writing bureau and closing the lid. Anderson took the gesture personally. Just in case I start prying, he thought. Strauss was now standing in front of the bureau, rubbing his hands together nervously. He said, 'I am afraid I have asked you here on a false errand, Doctor.'

'False errand?'

'Yes.' Strauss attempted a smile but failed. 'The imagination of an old man, I'm afraid. I thought that I had deduced something but I had not . . . '

'What did you think you had discovered, Professor?'

'That is now irrelevant.' Strauss said it finally and stared at Anderson, making him feel uncomfortable. It was as if the old man was attempting to move him by telekinesis.

'Well, in that case . . . '

'Yes, indeed, I'm sorry to have troubled you, Doctor.' Strauss was already herding him towards the door. Anderson found himself back out on the avenue breathing the warm, humid air and listening to a halting rendition of 'If I Were a Rich Man' from across the street.

So what the hell was that all about? thought Anderson as he started out down the avenue. Talk about the bums' rush! He didn't believe for one moment that Strauss had changed his mind about what he had deduced. The only logical explanation that Anderson could see was that Strauss had changed his mind about trusting him with the information. He had had second thoughts about trusting a man who would rifle through his desk drawers. Anderson added depression to the embarrassment that he already felt over the deterioration of his relations with Jacob Strauss. He had nourished a hope that his meeting with Strauss would have done much to repair the damage done by the break-in, maybe even have restored the possibility of a friendship which Anderson would have liked. But now the hope was so remote as to make it seem ridiculous, ridiculous enough to make Anderson wince when he thought of it in the green Mercedes taxi that took him back to Einstein. He was still thinking about it when he got out at the foot of Einstein and started walking up to the side entrance of the university residency. Was there any need for Strauss to have been so rude? Even if he didn't trust him any more he could at least have been civil; in fact, it didn't seem like Strauss at all. He had never seen the old man like that . . .

'Well, it's nice to be home again,' said a sarcastic American voice behind him, interrupting his line in self-pity. Anderson turned to find Hiram there; he was still wearing sunglasses.

'You followed me?' asked Anderson.

'Sure did. You don't catch us that way twice. We now cover all the exits.'

'I just went to visit your target,' said Anderson, hoping for a lucky break.

'No shit,' said Hiram, not giving him one.

Anderson smiled. Maybe Hiram wasn't that dumb after all. 'Goodnight,' he said.

''Night.'

Anderson returned to thinking about Jacob Strauss as he climbed the stairs. The last time he had visited the house, the old man and Miriam had been the very essence of good manners. Anderson stopped on the steps as if he'd walked into a wall. He hit the heel of his hand into his forehead in frustration at his own stupidity. 'You fool!' he said out loud. Miriam Strauss! He hadn't seen Miriam Strauss! Strauss's odd behaviour and his anxiety to be rid of him had nothing to do with whether he could be trusted or not. If he hadn't been such a self-centred clown he would have seen that earlier. There was something wrong in the Strauss household. The time he had taken to answer the door, his strange manner, his reluctance to say anything. God! It all seemed so obvious now. Strauss hadn't been alone in the house. There had been an intruder somewhere in the background and it was now Anderson's belief that he had been holding Miriam Strauss hostage.

The stairs flew up at him as Anderson hurtled back down them four at a time. He burst out through the glass door at the bottom and found Hiram still there. 'Hello again,' said the American. 'Change our mind, did we?'

'I'm going back to Professor Strauss's house. If you are going to follow, why don't we both go in your car?' suggested Anderson.

'Suits me,' said Hiram. 'What's the problem?' he asked, seeing how agitated Anderson was.

Anderson told him on the way over and elicited an immediate change in Hiram's manner. He now asked question after question about the layout of the Strauss villa, impressing Anderson with his professional single-mindedness. As they neared the avenue where Strauss lived, he said, 'Look, if I have a headache I'll ask your advice, but this kind of thing is my game, OK?'

'Agreed,' said Anderson, seeing the sense.

Hiram parked the car at the foot of the avenue and said, 'On foot now.' They walked towards the Strauss residence as Anderson had done earlier in the evening, but this time for a different reason. 'Cross here,' said Hiram, and Anderson saw the logic in crossing to the side of the street that would keep them out of view from the villa for as long as possible.

The young organist was still labouring through her repertoire; she was maiming Lara's theme from *Dr Zhivago* when Hiram signalled Anderson to get behind him. 'Take the left side of the house,' he whispered. 'I'll circle to the right. Look and listen but don't make a sound! We'll meet at the back.' Anderson nodded his understanding.

Hiram, still wearing his dark glasses, moved quickly out of the shelter of the bush and ran across the front of the

203

house in a crablike sideways run. For a big man he was surprisingly quiet and agile. Anderson knew that he was watching a professional. He'd have to be more polite to Hiram in future – if he was to have a future. He himself did well until he reached the wall of the house but, in ducking down into its shadow, he caught the toe of his shoe on the path and scraped along it for a metre or two. It made a sound like tearing cardboard. Anderson's lips formed the first 'F' of the expletive but he recovered enough not to compound the damage with a curse.

He listened for any sound coming from within. Nothing, only the chirruping and whirring of insects in the garden and the umpteenth halting chorus of Lara's theme from over the road. He moved further along the wall and stopped again beneath a window. There was no light coming from it but Anderson reckoned that it had to be on the stairway and that he should be able to hear any sounds coming from the hall. Again, nothing. He paused once more at a small wire-meshed window near the rear of the building before turning the corner and seeing the shadow of a tall figure standing there in the darkness. Anderson's heart missed a beat before he realized that it was Hiram. He wasn't crouching; he was standing upright and looking in through patio doors at the back of the house. Anderson stood up and walked towards him, feeling a bit silly at having maintained what he felt had been a professional crouch throughout.

'Nobody here?' said Anderson, trying to sound cool.

'Oh yes, they're here,' said Hiram, without moving his eyes from the glass. 'Take a look.' Anderson's blood went cold at the tone of Hiram's voice. He looked in through the doors and saw Jacob and Miriam Strauss. They were hanging by their necks from a wooden beam in the dining-room, their faces blackened, tongues swollen and protruding. Their corpses rotated slowly backwards and forwards as if keeping time in some hellish dance to the music outside. Anderson turned away and screwed his eyes tight shut. 'Fuck! Fuck! Fuck!' he said in successive explosions of breath. 'What a waste! What a useless, fucking waste!'

'Friends of yours?' said Hiram.

Friend? thought Anderson. The word seemed far too small and personal for a man like Strauss. He said, 'This world only gets one or two people like that man in an entire generation.' Grief welled up within him again and he slammed his fist into the bark of a tree.

'The woman. His wife?' asked Hiram.

'Yes, that's Miriam.'

'OK. Let's go.'

'Go? But we can't just go!' exclaimed Anderson.

'Yes, we can,' said Hiram. 'We can't bring them back, Doc, and the aftermath is none of our business.' Anderson reluctantly saw that the American was right. They walked round the side of the house as Lara's theme ended and the theme tune from *The Godfather* took over. They could see the girl through the lighted window, oblivious to everything around her and totally unaware that her music had probably been the last sound that Jacob and Miriam Strauss had ever heard.

'Christ, I need a drink,' said Anderson as he got into the car.

'Beer?' asked Hiram.

'No, a real drink, but you can never get one in this . . . ' Anderson dismissed all the adjectives that sprang to mind and just said, 'country'.

'You can if you know where to look.'

They drove back to town and the American led the way up a side-street to what looked from the outside to be a small nightclub. 'The American Bar,' said Hiram as they descended some stairs into a smoky room. 'What's your pleasure?'

205

Anderson took a great gulp of the whisky he'd asked for and felt the fire burn his throat. 'That's better.'

'So who killed Strauss?' asked Hiram.

'I wish I knew who was behind it. I suppose that person or someone working for him killed him to shut him up.'

'Or you did,' said Hiram.

Anderson almost choked. 'What do you mean?'

'You were in the house about forty minutes before the Kleins were found murdered.'

'But I didn't kill them! I loved the man,' said Anderson.

'I know you didn't kill him, Doc,' said Hiram. 'I saw Strauss see you to the door when you left.'

'Then why . . . ?'

'If I hadn't been following you, you would be the number-one suspect. Get the point?'

'I get the point,' sighed Anderson. He finished the whisky that remained in his glass. 'Same again?' he asked. Hiram hesitated. Anderson pushed. 'I'd like to buy you a drink.'

'OK, same again.'

The memorial service for Jacob and Miriam Strauss was Anderson's first experience of a synagogue. He attended with Sam and Myra Freedman as Mirit had never met Strauss and didn't feel that she should go. Anderson arranged to meet her afterwards.

'What can you say about a man like Jacob Strauss?' said Sam Freedman, and Anderson knew exactly what he meant. There was no way that they could communicate their real sense of loss to each other. Myra stood quietly, holding her handkerchief to her face, and Anderson noticed Sam give her hand a comforting squeeze before men and women were separated as they entered the synagogue.

Anderson asked Sam Freedman who the tall, distinguished man in the front was.

'Dov Strauss,' said Freedman, 'Jacob's son.'

Anderson remembered how Strauss had looked away when Miriam had mentioned their son Dov at the house. 'He's a biologist, too, isn't he?' he said.

'Yes.'

'In the States, I understand.'

Freedman looked at Anderson. 'Miriam told you that?'

'Why, yes.'

'Dov has been back in Israel for some time,' said Freedman. 'He's director of Comgen, one of the myriad genetic engineering companies thrown up by American venture capital.'

'But why would Miriam say . . . ?'

'She probably didn't know that Dov was back in Israel. Jacob obviously didn't tell her.'

'I don't understand,' confessed Anderson.

'Jacob and Dov never saw eye to eye. The first big break came when Dov gave up his academic post and went to work for a pharmaceutical company in the States. Selling out to mammon and all that. Then, when Dov wrote and told his father that he was coming back to Israel to set up Comgen and asked for his help with DNA expertise, Jacob really blew his top. Told him he was a scientific prostitute and that he never wanted to see him again. The breach was never healed.'

Anderson could hardly believe what he had been hearing. Jacob Strauss's own son was head of a genetic engineering concern here in Israel. He had come all this way in the Klein affair without knowing that. As the 'kepa'-covered heads of the congregation began to bow and bob, Anderson's imagination was taking him along a road he had no wish to travel.

'His own son?' exclaimed Mirit, seeing the implications

of what Anderson had told her. 'You think his own son killed him?'

'God, I don't know. But it's something we must consider. The circumstantial evidence is almost breathtaking – even the CIA angle, if you think about it.'

'Explain.'

'Strauss's son spent some time in the States. Maybe he got up to something there that interested the CIA and they are still interested in him.'

'I see, but why would Langman and the CIA be interested in you and Strauss's laboratory in Tel Aviv when there was no contact between Dov Strauss and his father? That doesn't make too much sense.'

Anderson agreed with a thoughtful nod of the head and said, 'We'd better check it out anyway. Can you find out about Comgen?'

'On my way.'

Anderson walked slowly back to his apartment, not at all sure what he was going to do till Mirit returned. He still had not come to terms with the news about Dov Strauss. If only he had known about this sooner. Had Strauss himself suspected his own son? Had he known all along? Is that what he was going to tell him the night he got killed?

There was another question that bothered Anderson. If Sam Freedman knew that Dov Strauss was back in Israel, then Myra must have known too. Why had she not said anything? He was trying to think of an answer when he heard his name being called on the paging system. He went to the phone. 'Neil Anderson.'

'My name is Dov Strauss,' said the voice. 'We haven't met but I think that we should talk.'

Hellfire, thought Anderson. What next? He paused for a moment to conjure up a neutral tone for his voice. 'Very well,' he said with a constricting throat. 'What do you suggest?'

208

'Do you have transport?'

'No.'

'Then I'll come to you.'

'Do you mean now?'

'Yes, I thought as I was still in Tel Aviv . . . but, of course, if it's not convenient . . . '

'No, no problem. I stay in the university apartments in Einstein.'

'Ten minutes then?'

'Ten minutes.'

Anderson went downstairs to find the duty CIA man. It was still Hiram. He told him that he was expecting a visitor and requested him not to shoot. 'Very funny,' said Hiram. 'Who is she?'

'He . . . Dov Strauss.' Anderson looked for a reaction but couldn't see Hiram's eyes for the dark glasses. So that's why he wears the bloody things, he thought, as he returned upstairs.

'I'm afraid my apartment isn't up to entertaining in,' said Anderson, as Dov Strauss reached the head of the stairs. 'Perhaps we could talk outside on the roof.'

'Of course, whatever you like.'

Anderson brought out a chair for Strauss while he himself opted to stand, leaning against the parapet wall. Strauss opened conventionally, saying, 'I expect you are wondering why I have come here.'

Anderson countered obligingly, 'Yes, I am.'

'Quite simply, I came here to save you the trouble of coming to see me.'

'I don't understand.'

'I think that you do, Doctor. You found out today that my father had a son who ran a genetic engineering company. I know why you came to Israel so it was quite obvious what your next step would be. You would start investigating me to find out if I was responsible for the death of your medical student, Martin Klein.'

'And were you?'

'No, Dr Anderson. I was not.'

'How did you know that I had found out about you today?'

Strauss smiled. 'The Freedmans told me. You see, although my father and I did not see eye to eye, I've always been friendly with Sam and Myra. When Myra told me about the English doctor who had come to my father's lab and why, I saw right away that you would suspect me so I asked Myra to say nothing about my existence. But today, when you asked Sam in the synagogue about who I was, he felt that he could not lie. He called me afterwards and told me what he'd done. So here I am, Doctor. What would you like to know?'

Anderson decided to be equally direct. 'I would like to know if you collaborated with Martin Klein in the construction of a plasmid carrying a foreign gene . . . the Klein gene.'

'No, I did not. I never even met Martin Klein.'

'But your company carries out experiments in gene manipulation?'

'Yes, but there is nothing illegal in that. We are trying to clone the nitrogen-fixing genes from bacteria into cereal crop plants so that they could grow well without the use of fertilizers.'

Anderson whistled in admiration. 'That would go a long way in solving the food problems of the Third World,' he said.

Strauss smiled. He said, 'I am not a hypcrite, Doctor. I am a businessman. If we succeed we will make a great deal of money. We won't be giving the plants away.'

Anderson nodded but didn't comment.

'Doctor, may I extend an invitation to you to visit my laboratories? You may search at will, investigate any culture that you find, ask my staff anything that you like. I will rely on your discretion when it comes to anything that might be commercially advantageous to a competitor to know.'

'Thank you,' said Anderson. 'But I think I believe you. You may have disagreed with your father but you are very much Jacob Strauss's son.'

'I am glad to hear you say that,' said Strauss.

'You must have been proud of your father in spite of your differences,' said Anderson.

'I was. I loved him very much. But believe me, Doctor, having a saint for a father is not easy. You are always so much nearer the devil than he is, whatever you do.'

'I think I understand,' said Anderson.

'I'm not sure that you do,' said Strauss, 'for as well as having a tremendously high moral sense he was, of course, academically brilliant. There was no area in which I could compete. I got a first-class degree from the same university where my father had obtained a double first. I won the Siemens Medal. My father had won it twice in his day.'

'I get the picture. But you have a business brain.'

'Yes, it was the only way that I could escape from his shadow. My father had no interest in commerce at all so there was actually a chance that I could start running in a race where I had a chance of winning instead of coming second from the word "go".'

Anderson nodded. 'And you are obviously very successful.'

'I see nothing wrong in honest business, Doctor.'

'Thank you for coming,' said Anderson.

When Mirit returned she looked so tired that Anderson felt embarrassed about what he had to tell her. She plumped herself down on the bed and lay back with her head on the pillow. 'Well, I found out about Comgen,' she said. Anderson opened his mouth but no sound came out.

Mirit was concentrating on the ceiling. She said, 'Their research labs are in Jerusalem. It's quite a small company employing about twenty people and, as of yesterday, they are solvent and thought to be doing quite well. Dov Strauss is the managing director and . . .'

'I know. He was here,' said Anderson.

' . . . there are two other dir . . . What did you say?'

Anderson told her of Strauss's surprise phone call and subsequent visit.

'Do you mean that I have been . . .'

'I'm afraid so, but never mind, I'll take you out to dinner. I might even pay.'

'Where does that leave us?' asked Mirit as they sipped their coffee.

'Back at square one,' said Anderson, 'unless your people come up with something on the CIA target.'

'There's no chance,' said Mirit. 'I tried. They wouldn't tell me.'

'Did they know?'

'I don't even know that.'

CHAPTER TEN

The unease that Anderson felt at no longer having any clear objective or obvious course of action began to gnaw at him as they left the restaurant and walked down the steps to the marina promenade. The shore was the only place in Tel Aviv where he could find any respite from the humidity. They walked out along the breakwater and sat down on the rocky wall near the harbour light, hoping to catch the slight breeze that flitted over the dark water to set the yachts tinkling as they bobbed at anchor. There was never enough wind to break the surface of the water; it remained smooth and calm, reflecting the lights of the water-front hotels and bars like a huge oily mirror.

'What did you think of the synagogue today?' asked Mirit.

'It was an experience,' said Anderson.

'Too vague. What kind of experience?'

'Historically interesting, aesthetically unpleasing.'

'Go on.'

'You want the view of an outsider?'

'It's the best one to have.'

'To see ourselves as others see us . . . '

'Pardon?'

'Nothing. I was impressed more with the idea of the rituals I was watching than the sight itself. There's nothing inspiring in men of any religion dressing up in funny clothes and genuflecting to unseen deities, but I had to acknowledge that what I was seeing was a continuation of an idea, a belief that has spanned more than three thousand years. Only an arrogant fool could dismiss that without being moved.'

213

'What did you find "unpleasing"?'

'The music. There wasn't any. I like church music. It has an intrinsic value which I find soothing, reassuring, even inspiring on occasion, but discordant chanting I find hard to take . . . especially in Hebrew! You could do with some music lessons from Rome!'

'And your Scottish psalms?'

'Same thing,' conceded Anderson, 'a monkey with a mouth organ could have written them.'

'Oh dear,' smiled Mirit.

Anderson threw a small pebble into the water and watched the ripples upset the reflections like a spreading earthquake.

'So where do we go from here?' asked Mirit.

'I'm trying not to face that.'

Mirit sensed that something was wrong. She looked on as Anderson picked up another pebble and threw it in. 'I don't understand,' she said softly.

'I've been pretending to myself that I didn't know what to do next. I've been pretending to myself that I am relieved that Dov Strauss had nothing to do with his father's death when all the time I am disappointed, because if he had been guilty it would all be over now, and I would not have to consider going back to the Jan Kouros Hospice to find out why they bus around a bunch of lepers in the middle of the night . . . ' Another pebble splashed into the water.

'We have tended to ignore that question,' said Mirit quietly. 'Not just you.'

'We have to find out,' said Anderson.

'I know. When do we start?'

'Tomorrow.'

They deliberately planned a lazy day, knowing that they would be up for most of the night. After a late rise they drove up to Herzliyya and swam in the sea before eating a picnic lunch on the beach and having a snooze in the shade of a beach umbrella. It seemed important to soak up as much warmth and light as possible before night fell and they had to face what the darkness held for them.

Mirit stretched out her hand and intermingled her fingers with Anderson's. 'It might have been a one-off event with the truck,' she said, without opening her eyes.

'True,' said Anderson without conviction.

Mirit tried again. 'Or it may have been that the truck had been due much earlier and had broken down on the way. That was why it only got there at midnight.'

'But they still went,' said Anderson.

'What?'

'The lepers. They still got into the truck and went wherever it was they were going.'

Mirit rolled over on to her stomach and supported herself on her elbows. 'And the question is, where?'

'And why,' added Anderson quietly.

'Come swim with me,' said Mirit.

They ran down the sand and plunged headlong into the first breaker to emerge, shaking the water from their ears and eyes.

'Puts a different perspective on things, doesn't it?' gasped Mirit as another wave lifted her up on its crest.

'Sure does,' agreed Anderson, swimming towards her in a lazy crawl.

At three-thirty they showered in fresh water to rinse away the stickiness of the Mediterranean salt, before dressing to drive down to the Arab market to buy two more robes. 'Just in case we ever have to mingle,' said Mirit.

At nine-thirty they left for the hospice, still undecided as to their best course of action. 'If we drive right up to the hospice someone will see the headlights and raise the alarm. But if we leave the car where we left it last time we

215

couldn't get back to it in time to follow the truck. What do you think?'

'I think we should gamble on the truck coming straight back down the track from the hospice to join the road,' said Anderson. 'We're going to have to follow without lights and that might not be possible on the rough track; we might hit a boulder or something. But if we hide ourselves somewhere near the main-road turn-off we can follow the truck when it reaches the tarmac.'

'Good thinking,' said Mirit.

They were in place at the intersection at eleven o'clock. Anderson got out to stretch his legs on the barren lunar landscape while they waited. He leaned against the back of the car and looked up at the stars in a cloudless sky. Mirit joined him. 'What are you thinking?' she asked.

'I was just thinking how bright the stars were.'

The sound of an engine sent them scurrying round the front of the dune they had hidden the car behind, to take up a position where they could see the road. It was the truck they had seen last time. It slowed as it came to the turn-off, and the driver made three crunching attempts at selecting a lower gear before the truck snorted and started its long climb up to the hospice. Anderson looked at his watch. 'Should get there about midnight, same as last time.'

As the time drew near for the truck's return, Anderson and Mirit left their car and came round the front of the dune.

'Any minute now,' said Mirit.

'Look,' said Anderson, pointing to the horizon and a dancing white haze. 'Headlights.'

When they could hear the sound of the truck's engine, Mirit left to get back in the car. Anderson stayed to see the vehicle rumble up to the intersection and turn right. He noted with dismay that it only had one rear light. He ran to join Mirit in the car. 'They turned right. You'll only see one red light; it's the left one.'

Mirit, having memorized their route round the dune and up on to the road, accepted the information in silence and concentrated till their wheels were on the tarmac. She caught up to within a hundred metres of the one red tail light then held station.

'They're heading towards Hadera,' she said.

They continued in convoy for fifteen minutes before Anderson said suddenly, 'They're slowing.'

Mirit took her foot off the accelerator and dabbed the brake hesitantly. 'Are you sure?' she said. 'It's difficult to tell.'

Anderson began to have doubts himself when suddenly he was reassured by a swing in the truck's headlight beams. 'Yes. Look, they're turning off the road.'

Mirit said something in Hebrew. Anderson could see her point. If the truck had turned off on to another rough desert track it was going to be very dangerous trying to follow without lights.

'Our only chance is to get close to them,' said Mirit, 'close enough to benefit from their headlights. There won't be enough light from their one tail light to show us up in their mirrors.'

'If you say so,' said Anderson.

'It's getting close that's the problem,' said Mirit through gritted teeth. 'Starlight may be romantic, but for desert driving . . . ' She swung the car off the road and headed for the single red light that was now some two hundred metres ahead, although an accurate estimate was impossible. The car picked up speed as Mirit took the blind chance. It almost came off. They had closed to around fifty metres and Anderson was considering relaxing his white-knuckled grip of his seat, when the left-hand side of the car suddenly dropped a metre and their progress came to a bone-jarring halt. Their seatbelts held them but their heads were flung violently forward on to their chests. The engine revs began to scream. Mirit turned the key and there was silence. 'Are you all right?' she asked.

'I'm OK,' said Anderson, rubbing his neck. 'You?'

'Me too.'

They got out to inspect the damage by torchlight. The left front wheel had gone straight down a pothole deep enough for the far side of it to have impacted the body of the car against the tyre.

'We'll have to bend that away from the wheel before we can move,' said Anderson. Mirit opened up the back of the car and brought out a spade. She handed it to Anderson and held the torch while he tried to insert the blade between the wheel and the bodywork. 'Try turning the steering wheel to the left,' he said, after a first failure. Mirit pulled hard on the wheel but with little effect. 'Again,' said Anderson. The wheels moved very slightly but it was enough to allow him to insert the spade. 'Now we have some leverage,' he said, putting all his weight against the handle to force the twisted body panel away from the wheel. Steady pressure was not working. He changed to violent, intermittent stabs at the handle. The metal began to yield.

'It's moving!' said Mirit, shining the torch on the working area.

Anderson took five more stabs at the handle then stood back, wiping his brow. He took a closer look at the wheel arch and said, 'That should do it. Now to get out of this damned hole.'

'We'll have to cut away the ground from the back of the hole,' said Mirit. 'Make it a gentler slope so we can reverse out.' She took the spade from Anderson and started clearing away dirt behind the wheel. Anderson took over after a few minutes and found it progressively harder going.

The desert floor was only soft for the first few inches through erosion. Beneath was rock hard. He was breathing heavily when Mirit said, 'I think that might do.' She got into the car and started it up. Anderson put his weight against the front of the car as she engaged reverse gear and slowly let out the clutch. The car began to inch out backwards as the revs rose to an insistent snarl. Anderson spreadeagled himself against the hood and heaved with a final effort as success came within reach. The air all around was filled with the smell of burning material from the clutch's friction plate, but the car was back on level ground.

Anderson let himself fall to the ground and sat there listening to his own breathing, looking up at the heavens. Mirit got out to join him and ran her fingers through his hair. 'As I see it,' she said, 'we have two choices. One, we go back and try again tomorrow or two, we turn on our lights and find out where the track leads us.'

'Let's find out,' said Anderson, getting up from the ground.

After ten minutes he asked, 'Have you any idea where we are headed?'

Mirit said, 'We were making for Hadera when the truck pulled off to the left, but now the track is winding back to the right again. I would guess at somewhere north-east of Hadera, assuming the truck hasn't already turned off and we missed it.'

They found themselves heading down a steep gully through lines of giant boulders and between towering dunes. Mirit almost had to slow to a crawl to negotiate the final hairpin bend that brought them to the floor of the canyon. Anderson suddenly said, 'Stop!' Mirit brought the car to a halt. 'Up there, look!' Mirit couldn't see anything. Anderson said, 'Look at the top of the ridge. There's a sort of glow.'

Mirit saw what he meant. 'Lights maybe? Lights on the other side?'

Anderson nodded. 'I think so. Can we dump the car somewhere and take a look?'

Mirit came off the ascent road and drove fifty metres or so along the base of the canyon. 'Look, there's a gap in the dunes,' she said, 'we won't have to climb up.' They got out and approached the narrow gap. They could now see the source of the lights. They were looking at a long, low building surrounded by a perimeter fence.

'There's the truck,' said Mirit. Anderson saw it parked by the fence, halfway along and outside a small gate. The driver was leaning on the front fender talking to a man dressed as some sort of security guard. They were smoking.

Mirit looked at Anderson; he seemed to be staring into space. 'What's the matter?' she asked.

'I know this place,' said Anderson slowly, 'I've been here before. It's the Kalman Institute. We're at the back of the Kalman Institute . . . '

Mirit looked again at the shape of the building and regarded it with reference to the lights of Hadera beyond. She said, 'Yes, I think you're right. But doesn't that mean that your friends the Freedmans are involved?'

The euphemism seemed to make the implications all the worse for Anderson. 'It would mean,' he said, 'that Sam Freedman, the brilliant Sam Freedman, the respected Sam Freedman, was the brain behind the whole nightmare.' Anderson's voice was dull with shock.

'And Myra?'

'She too,' said Anderson flatly. 'God, what a fool I've been. It was she not Cohen who set the acid trap for me. She came in that morning "to set up something for Strauss", she said. Cohen must have suspected as much and challenged her when they were working together, so she killed him with a hypodermic full of toxin.'

'But Langman, the CIA man?'

Anderson shook his head in despair. He said haltingly, 'I thought she was my friend. I told her just about everything. I told her that there was an American in my apartment block who kept asking questions about the Klein affair . . . I even told her that I was going to see Shula Ron. I sentenced that kid to death . . . '

'And Professor Strauss?' asked Mirit softly.

'When I told him that Cohen had been murdered he must have deduced that the cloning had been done by the Freedmans. That's what he was going to tell me when he phoned, but they got to him first. All these people, killed through my meddling interference.' Anderson put his fingertips over his eyes for a moment. Mirit put her hand on his arm. 'Not your fault, Neil. You were only doing what was logical. How does the the CIA involvement fit?'

'It fits,' said Anderson. 'The Freedmans were American citizens until three years ago when they came here. Sam Freedman would be the "prime target" they wouldn't tell me about. Myra, his wife, would be the secondary. Langman was using me to keep tabs on Myra Freedman.'

'And the accounts you saw?'

'Must have come from here, the Kalman Institute. The restriction enzymes for DNA work, the payments to the Jan Kouros Hospice . . . it all fits.'

'But what are they doing in there?' asked Mirit.

'That's what we still have to find out,' said Anderson with bitterness in his voice.

They settled down in a crevice behind a boulder to watch the rear of the Institute. Anderson noted that in the building itself only the basement lights were on. He remembered that Sam Freedman had told him on his tour of the place that that was where their maximum-containment suite was situated and how they had no occasion to use it. 'Bastard,' he said under his breath. Mirit heard but did not enquire.

'Something's happening,' said Mirit.

Anderson saw the back door of the building open and a group of robbed figures emerge to shuffle back across the grounds to the gate. The truck driver put out his cigarette and prepared to see them on board while his erstwhile companion opened the gate. The driver secured the back of the truck and shouted something to the guard.

'What did he say?' whispered Anderson.

'He said, see you tomorrow,' replied Mirit.

The heavily laden truck groaned and stuttered away up the desert track, and Anderson and Mirit watched as the guard checked the gate and disappeared into the building.

'What are our chances of breaking in there?' asked Anderson.

'Not good,' said Mirit. 'The man on the gate and the large open space between the fence and the building are the problems.'

Anderson thought for a moment before asking, 'How many patients would you say were in the group tonight?'

'Fifteen? Twenty? Hard to say. Why?'

'I was thinking that, in a group that size, two more or less might not be noticed . . . '

'Go on.'

'We know that the truck parks outside the fence and the patients go in through the gate and walk across to the building. If somehow, wearing our robes, we could tack ourselves on to the group, we could get into the Institute that way.'

Mirit considered the idea for a few moments before conceding that it was a possibility. 'We would need a diversion to distract the driver and the guard while we joined the group, and what if one of the lepers raised the alarm?'

'We'll just have to risk that,' said Anderson. 'Do we try?'

'We try.'

They discussed possible diversion tactics for the following night.

'Can't we talk about this on the way back?' said Anderson, as the wind started to moan and the sand around their feet showed signs of movement like ripples on a pond.

'It's best we do it now while we can see everything,' insisted Mirit. Anderson pulled up his collar and agreed reluctantly.

'What we need is some kind of natural diversion,' she said, looking about her for inspiration.

'I don't understand,' said Anderson.

'If we start a fire somewhere or cause a small explosion it will certainly create a diversion, but the wrong kind. People will come running from all over the place, alarms will start ringing and suddenly everyone will be on their toes. That's the last thing we want.'

'I could sneak out and stick a knife in one of the truck's tyres,' suggested Anderson.

'You'd break the knife,' said Mirit.

'Only a suggestion,' said Anderson, pretending to take offence. Mirit broke her concentration and smiled. She didn't say anything. Anderson crouched down behind one of the boulders as he felt sand whip up into his face. He sat down and leaned his back against the rock, moving slightly as he felt a sharp piece dig into him. It gave him an idea. 'The boulders!' he said. 'What if one of these boulders should roll down the dune and hit the fence? It could happen quite easily and the guard and the driver would be sure to have a look at it.'

'But it wouldn't cause any alarm . . . Perfect!' said Mirit. 'A natural diversion. No need to inform anyone inside the building immediately. Just one of those things. Something for Maintenance to deal with in the morning.'

They set out to look for a suitable boulder for their purpose and decided on one. It would have a clear roll down the dune and would hit the fence some thirty metres along from the gate. The problem now was to ensure that it could be persuaded to move at the right moment.

'We'll have to excavate most of the sand from the front of it tonight,' said Mirit.

Anderson nodded. 'I thought you'd say that.' The night suddenly seemed much blacker as the last light in the basement of the Institute went out. It was followed shortly by the sound of two cars leaving the front of the building, then all was quiet. 'I'll get the spade,' said Anderson.

They undermined the ground in front of one half of the boulder at a time, using a smaller stone as a wedge under the first half in case they should misjudge it and the boulder should topple early. When Anderson had finished cutting the vee for the remaining section he packed it lightly with brushwood and added pebbles to the top. Mirit spread the material he had removed so as to make the area appear natural. 'The sand will do the rest,' she said as another cloud enveloped them. 'Till tomorrow then.'

Neither of them slept much that night. It was a relief when dawn broke and sounds came from the streets to distract them from thoughts of all the things that could go wrong.

'What would you like to do today?' Mirit asked.

Anderson looked up at the ceiling and said, 'I would like to lose myself in old Jerusalem with you. See the colours, hear the sounds, eat where we ate before, those sort of things.'

Mirit leaned over and kissed him lightly on the forehead.

From their position up on the dunes, Anderson and Mirit saw the lights go on in the basement of the Kalman Institute shortly before midnight. Anderson took this as his cue to leave Mirit and move along to the boulder they had primed to fall. He had just wriggled up behind it when a door at the back of the Institute opened and yellow light spilled out on the sand. A man stood framed there for a moment before he closed the door again and walked slowly across the compound to the gate. As he came nearer, Anderson could see it was the guard from the night before. The man looked at his watch and lit up a cigarette, flicking the match away in a lazy arc over the gate before turning his back and leaning against it.

Anderson began clearing away the peeble-and-brush camouflage from the leading edge of the boulder, his face muscles tightening as he concentrated on the need for silence. The vee was now clear apart from the smaller rock that he had inserted as a wedge. He circled his arm round the stone and pulled it slowly away from the boulder's path, hugging it into his chest. He had just begun to relax when he heard the first sounds of the truck approaching.

It seemed to take an age before the truck finally appeared from behind the dunes and drew to a halt where it had stopped the night before, beside the gate. The driver got down and slammed the door behind him before walking over to the guard, his hands deep in his pockets. They exchanged a few words and laughed together while the gate was opened.

As the driver opened up the back of the truck and the patients started to climb out, Anderson put all his weight against the back of the boulder. It didn't move. The patients were now all out and congregating beside the gate. Anderson felt panic threaten. Timing was everything. Once more he put his back to what was beginning to feel like a cathedral and strained until the veins stood out on his forehead. He was at maximum exertion, on the knife-edged interface between defeat and victory, when he felt the boulder loosen its grip on the dune. He only had to maintain his effort for a few seconds more before gravity freed him from all responsibility.

As the boulder began its run down the slope, Anderson rolled over the crest of the dune and scrambled back to join Mirit. From the blind side he heard the boulder hit the fence and the startled cries from below. He rolled back over the crest and slid down to where Mirit was crouching.

'Are you all right?' she whispered, only managing to pick out the word hernia from the string of expletives that came in reply. Together they saw the guard and the driver walk along the fence to inspect the damage, while the leper patients remained in a group between the truck and the fence.

'It worked,' hissed Anderson. 'Come on.'

Adrenalin coursed into their veins as they pulled up the cowls on their robes and half crawled, half slid, down the slope to the shadow of the truck. From along the fence they could now hear laughter as the two men thought what they were supposed to think. Mirit was about to circle round the back of the truck when Anderson tugged at her sleeve and drew her round the front. He edged out and saw that he was right. From this side the patients had their backs to them. Silently they moved out and casually stood at the back of the group, hoods well forward, faces looking down.

The guard came back and led them across the compound, keeping at what he obviously felt was a safe distance. Although he felt reasonably sure that the group would not be counted, for they were patients not prisoners, Anderson was still glad to see that the group did not string out in single file. Amorphous huddles of people were less likely to attract numerical curiosity.

The guard knocked on the door of the Institute and it was opened by another man who took over, indicating that they should enter and follow him along the tiled corridor they were now in. Anderson and Mirit made sure that they were the last in line to enter, and Anderson risked a look back to ensure that they were not being followed from behind. The hallway was empty.

As the group passed a corridor leading off the main one, Anderson shot out his hand and gripped Mirit's shoulder, steering her off to the right. They stood absolutely stock still, listening to the shuffling footsteps receding, faces pressed against the white tiles. Anderson let out his breath slowly. Mirit gave a tight, nervous smile.

Their relief at being free of the group was quickly replaced by feelings of vulnerability at standing still in a well-lit corridor. They sought refuge in the nearest darkened room and closed the glass-fronted door behind them. The light from the corridor was reflected in rows of gleaming trays lying on a long wooden table. 'Surgical instruments,' whispered Anderson. Mirit wrinkled up her nose at the smell in the air.

'Ether. They're running some kind of clinic.'

They took off their robes and stuffed them out of sight in a cupboard under a sink. 'What now?' said Mirit.

'We find the stairs leading up to the main building. I want to get into Freedman's office, find written evidence about what's been going on.'

They took a few moments longer to compose themselves before gingerly opening the door and stepping back out into the corridor. They approached the main hallway on tiptoe and peered out, Anderson to the right, Mirit to the left. Anderson signified that he had seen the bottom of the stairs and pointed to the left-hand side, halfway along. Mirit nodded. Anderson asked her with his eyes if she was ready and she nodded again. They ran along the thirty metres of open corridor and ducked into the relative darkness of the stairwell, once again flattening themselves against the wall and taking time to calm down. Mirit led the way up the stairs, cautiously pausing each time they came to a blind turn to peer round before committing herself. Anderson constantly glanced back, but more out of nerves than caution. They found their way barred by a locked door. Mirit tried the handle both ways, then the original way again. She shook her head. Anderson felt his stomach become weightless. He placed both palms against the door and appreciated just how solid it was. Double mortise locks denied them the other option.

'Back down?' whispered Mirit.

Anderson nodded. He was cursing himself for not having foreseen that movement between the upper and the lower halves of the building would be denied to most people if what went on in the containment suite was to be kept secret. As they approached the bottom of the stairs, he was feverishly trying to think of an alternative course of action when the initiative was taken from them. A man was waiting there, pointing a gun at them. Anderson's shock was amplified by the fact that it was the man who had pushed Shula Ron off the walls of Jerusalem. The man acknowledged the fact that he had recognized Anderson with the merest trace of a smile before he indicated the direction they should move in with the muzzle of the gun.

'Sorry,' said Anderson to Mirit.

The man said something that Anderson did not understand.

'He says, put your hands on your head,' said Mirit.

'Oh, shit,' said Anderson quietly as they were herded along the corridor. He had just noticed the closed-circuit television camera on the end wall. It had been covering the entire length of the hall.

'Halt,' said Mirit, translating the Arab's command. The man circled round from behind, keeping the gun on them all the time and feeling for the handle of a door without diverting his eyes. The door opened to reveal a flight of stairs. Again the man motioned with the pistol, and

228

Anderson and Mirit descended into a sub-basement which, unlike the rest of the building, did not seem to be air conditioned. The man followed them down and opened up a further door, that of a small, stuffy storeroom. They were directed inside.

As they went through the doorway Mirit signalled with her eyes and a slight movement of her head that Anderson should move to the left. He complied and was aware of the Arab saying something sharply to him. Still not understanding what was going on, Anderson turned to see that Mirit had moved to the right, thus dividing the man's attention momentarily. The Arab was indicating that Anderson move back beside Mirit, assuming that the man would be the greater threat, but, while his attention was with Anderson, Mirit swung the edge of her hand at the man's throat. The blow missed his windpipe but connected with the side of his neck, sending him reeling against the edge of the door. The gun flew from his grasp and clattered over the floor to slide past Anderson and lodge between two crates of plastic containers.

Anderson was aware of Mirit swinging her foot at the man's groin but failing to connect as he himself made a dive for the gun. He heard Mirit cry out in pain behind him. He discovered that he could not get his hand between the crates to grasp the gun and tugged frantically at one of the crates with his right hand to increase the space. He managed to insert his left and pull out the weapon.

As he did so, the Arab reached him and brought the heel of his shoe hammering down on Anderson's left hand, making him scream out in pain. He was aware of the metacarpal bones being splayed out and the flesh parting in a splash of red as nausea hit him like a white wall. The man bent down to retrieve the gun and Anderson made a last desperate attempt to hit him with his good hand. The punch connected, but only weakly, and the Arab stood back to

229

aim another kick at Anderson who tried to avoid the blow but took it high up on the head. Suddenly, pain and nausea became black nothingness.

It was so dark that Anderson considered for a moment that he had gone blind. But even a consideration of that magnitude took second place to the agonizing pain he felt in his left hand. He tried to move it and immediately the pain soared through the agony barrier. It was so intense that he didn't cry out. His reflexes had bypassed that response and gone directly to throat paralysis and cold sweat. He now realized that his hands were tied together, the slightest movement of his right hand inducing the fires of hell in his left. His throat muscles relaxed enough to permit a single, shivering curse.

'Neil, are you awake?' said Mirit's voice in the darkness.

Anderson had to concentrate hard before he could manage a reply.

'Are you injured?' asked Mirit.

'My hand is damaged,' said Anderson, turning understatement into an art form.

'Badly?'

'Could be. How about you?'

'I was knocked out but I'm all right. My hands are tied behind me but I'm working at it.'

'Any luck?'

'I think the rope is loosening a little.'

'Good,' said Anderson quietly, realizing that he should have said something more encouraging or enthusiastic but pain was weakening his spirit.

'What do you think they will do to us?' asked Mirit.

'They will kill us,' said Anderson weakly as nausea threatened him again. 'They have to. We know too much, and that man was the one I saw kill Shula Ron.'

Mirit was quiet for a moment then she said with

conviction, 'Then we have to get out of here.'

Anderson felt himself teeter on the brink of acquiescence. It scared him. It reminded him how he had almost given in high up on the walls of Jerusalem and let himself fall . . . calm acceptance of the seemingly inevitable. He began to fight back. 'How are you getting on with those ropes?' he asked Mirit.

'I could do with some hand cream,' she replied. 'This would be a lot easier.'

'How about oil?' asked Anderson, with a flash of inspiration.

'What do you mean?'

'The containers in the crates. They were full of centrifuge oil!'

'Lubricating oil?' said Mirit in disbelief.

'Yes,' said Anderson.

'Do you think we can . . . ' started Mirit, but she stopped herself. 'Ssh, there's someone coming. Pretend you are still unconscious.'

Anderson closed his eyes and feigned unconsciousness as the key turned in the lock, but felt sure that whoever was coming in must hear his heartbeat. Through his closed eyelids he was aware that the room light had been switched on. Footsteps came nearer to him and stopped. Oh God, he prayed, don't let them touch my hand! A foot was kicked into his side. He didn't move. The footsteps moved across the room to where Anderson knew Mirit must be. He took the opportunity to open one eye slightly and orientate himself. He saw the crates of centrifuge oil and memorized their location. Behind him, Anderson heard their visitor say something in Arabic and thought for a moment that he had found Mirit out; but no, the man grunted, switched out the light and locked up the room again behind him.

'What did he say?' whispered Anderson.

'Sleep of the dead,' said Mirit.

Anderson asked her if she had managed to open her eyes at all. She said that she had and confirmed that she knew where she was lying in relation to the door.

'The crates are in the corner to the right of the door,' said Anderson. 'I'm sorry I can't be much help.'

Mirit rolled across the floor and followed the line of the wall past the door until she contacted the crates. She manoeuvred herself up into a sitting position with her back to one of them and reached through the bars with her bound hands to make an attempt at forcing one of the bottles up and over the edge. She succeeded at the third attempt. Anderson heard the bottle drop and Mirit's sigh of satisfaction. 'Well done,' he said. 'Can you get the cap off?'

Mirit did not reply; she was concentrating on using what little flexibility she had in her fingers to best advantage. The seconds seemed to race by, heightening Anderson's appreciation of the passage of time to a hitherto unbelievable pitch before Mirit said, 'It's done. I've got the oil on my wrists.'

Anderson could only continue to wait impotently in the blackness, listening to the sound of Mirit trying to free herself. He knew she had won when he heard her throw her ropes across the room and get to her feet. 'I'm free,' she whispered. 'Can we risk the light?'

'Yes,' said Anderson, 'we'll have to.'

Mirit sucked in her breath when she saw Anderson's hand, still tied behind him. She smoothed the hair on his brow and said, 'I'll be careful.' She picked at his bonds with great care until the first knot was undone, then she gently undid the others. Anderson brought his hand round slowly and examined the damage.

'Well?' she said softly.

Anderson dabbed the blood away gingerly till he could see the exposed bones and connecting tissue. 'I'll have to set them,' he said, 'or it might be ruined for good.'

'But the pain?' said Mirit in horror.

'No other way,' said Anderson. 'If I pass out, bring me round.'

He stuffed a handkerchief into his mouth until he was satisfied that he couldn't cry out, then bit down hard on the remainder. He started to move the displaced bones with a quick, deliberate movement that made stars explode inside his head and sent showers of shrapnel into his nerve ends. He rested for a moment, mutely looking at Mirit and unashamedly aware of the tears that were running down his cheeks. Mirit looked on helplessly, feeling the pain herself, as Anderson made three more setting manoeuvres before letting his head roll forward on to his chest. She thought that he had passed out but it was just the sudden wave of exhaustion that follows severe exposure to pain. Anderson recovered and took the handkerchief from his mouth. 'It's over,' he said. 'Tear me some strips, will you?'

Anderson finished binding up his hand and let Mirit tie the final knot. It felt much more comfortable with everything in the right place. 'Now to get out of here,' he said, although his eyes searched for sleep.

'We'll surprise that man when he comes back,' said Mirit. She looked around the room for something to use as a weapon and selected a piece of steel conduit piping, part of a bundle of steel and copper tubing standing in one of the corners.

'This should do,' she said, slapping it into the palm of her hand. She knelt down in front of the door and moved back till she was satisfied with the range and the freedom of movement she had. She stood up and nodded in satisfaction.

'Can I help?' said Anderson, not sure what she was planning.

'Rest,' said Mirit, 'I can manage.' Using a piece of rag, she reached up and removed the light bulb. 'Now, we wait.'

Anderson heard footsteps approach. They stopped out-side the door and the key went into the lock. The door swung back to reveal the figure of Shula Ron's killer, silhouetted against the hall light. His hand came in and felt for the light switch which did not respond to the click. He said something in Arabic, but at that moment the pipe hit him. Mirit had ensured that the heavy pipe had been swung at maximum arc and its one-metre length meant that the tip was travelling at ninety miles per hour when it met teeth.

The man dropped to the floor like a felled bullock and lay still. Anderson helped one-handedly to pull him into the room. Mirit replaced the light bulb and searched through the man's pockets for keys and weapons. She found keys but no weapon; he had been confident that, tied up, they had posed no threat to him. She took the keys and switched out the light before opening the door and looking out into the passage to find it empty.

There were three more doors in the sub-basement. They discovered that two of them led to further store-rooms, one to a laundry and one to a large cellar where the ventilation machinery for the building was housed.

'We're still trapped,' said Anderson. 'As soon as we go upstairs the TV camera will pick us up.'

They huddled together at the foot of the stairs. 'If it comes to it we might have to take on the next man who comes, try to get his weapon and fight our way out,' said Mirit.

Anderson could tell from the look in her eyes that she had as little optimism for that course of action as he had. 'I can hear something!' he said.

They waited with held breath as the sound got louder, then Anderson recognized the sound of trolley wheels. He relaxed a little. Whoever was coming would not try to bring a trolley downstairs. He stretched out prone on the steps and crawled up enough to see round the corner up to main corridor level.

Two attendants, dressed in surgical green, wheeled a trolley past the head of the stairs. The patient lying on it looked directly at Anderson, giving him a bad moment, but there was no reaction. Anderson recognized the thickened features of one of the lepers from the hospice and guessed that he was under some kind of premedication. He sank back down and told Mirit what he had seen.

'What's "premedication"?' she asked.

'It's a kind of sedation they give to patients before they go to surgery.'

'You mean they are operating on these people?'

'Seems like it. But it can't be anything major. We know that they're only here for a couple of hours.'

The sound of the trolley had faded into the distance when Mirit said, 'We must be running out of time. They'll be coming to look for that man.'

'If they send two men we'll have no chance. I vote we make a run for it.'

Mirit stood up and took a deep breath. 'I'm ready,' she said.

'Wait!' said Anderson suddenly. 'The laundry! We could get a couple of the uniforms I saw the attendants wearing. We'd have a much better chance walking along the corridor in those.'

They turned the door that led to the laundry and went inside.

'Green or white?' asked Mirit.

'The ones I saw were wearing green.'

Mirit had just finished tucking her hair into her surgical cap when they heard raised voices a long way off. Anderson took his hand off the doorhandle. 'It's too late,' he said. 'They're coming.'

They looked around desperately for anything they could

235

use as a weapon in a last-ditch stand, but found the search hopeless. Anderson was considering hiding in laundry baskets when he saw the chute protruding from the wall above one of them. He examined the angle of its slope and said, 'We can do it.'

Mirit looked up inside the chute and agreed that there was room enough. 'But where does it go?'

They could now hear voices in the corridor outside, accompanied by the intermittent slam of doors. A distant yell told them that the man they had knocked out had been found. It dispelled any further consideration of where the chute led to.

'In you get,' whispered Anderson.

Mirit clambered inside the mouth of the chute and started moving up the forty-five-degree incline. Anderson waited until she was ten feet inside before crossing the room to the light switch. He paused to memorize his return route then switched it off.

For Anderson, climbing into the chute in darkness with only one hand was no joke. At his first attempt he slid back down into the laundry basket. He was unhurt, but the voices outside said that he might have run out of time. He had just managed to get up into the chute when he heard the laundry door being opened. Mirit heard it too. They froze like statues in a party game.

The room light was switched on. Anderson could see the lit square of floor at the end of the chute below. He could hear three separate voices raised in argument, urgent, angry voices.

Anderson felt his green surgical cap slide down the back of his head. It had been knocked askew in his struggle to get into the chute and he hadn't been able to adjust it. It was going to fall off and there was nothing that he could do about it! He couldn't take his hand away from the wall of the chute or he'd fall. Desperately he hunched his shoulders and tilted his head in a succession of angles to provide a platform for it, but his final effort just made things worse. The cloth cap tumbled off the back of his head and rolled off his shoulder. It fluttered gently and silently to the floor below.

Anderson couldn't take his eyes off it. It was his death warrant. The argument still raged below but Anderson saw a foot move into the square of light, then a shoulder and an arm as a man bent down to retrieve the cap. Oh, Christ, here it comes! thought Anderson. But the man below was still intent on pursuing his argument. He had picked up the cap and accepted it as nothing out of the ordinary. Almost absentmindedly he pushed a wicker basket under the mouth of the chute and, still shouting the odds, he and his companions switched off the light and left the room. Anderson offered up a silent prayer and, looking up into the darkness, said, 'OK, on we go.'

The darkness offered no distraction from the almost unbearable heat in the chute as Mirit and Anderson inched upwards, their thigh muscles feeling the strain of constantly having to maintain friction between their feet and the smooth metal walls. Their breathing was now heavy and laboured as their lungs demanded more and more oxygen from the static, unyielding air.

Anderson could now see Mirit up ahead; it was getting lighter; they were getting near the top. Mirit stopped moving and looked at Anderson coming up behind her. Neither spoke but they knew that they had to rest before the final climb to the top. Anderson let his head rest on his chest, gazing idly back down into the darkness while he waited for his pulse rate to drop and his breathing to quieten. Sweat dripped from his forehead and fell audibly on to the metal wall of the chute like the ticking of an erratic clock. When all was quiet again he looked up and nodded to Mirit.

Anderson had thought that it would get much lighter as they neared the exit of the chute, but it didn't. For some reason that he didn't yet understand, the lighting remained subdued, even when they got to the mouth itself. It was as if the room they were about to emerge into was lit by candlelight. He saw Mirit pull herself slowly and carefully out of the opening and stand up on the floor. She turned to help him with his one-handed effort.

Anderson had almost succeeded in getting out of the chute when the sound of voices startled him and he lost his balance. He had to throw out his injured hand to save himself from tumbling back down and felt the pain burst like an exploding shell as the metal corner of the chute exit gouged into the raw, bleeding flesh of his hand. Sweat poured down his face in a river as he locked his jaw in a desperate attempt to remain silent. Mirit slid her hand beneath his left armpit and allowed him to take some of the strain off his hand. She whispered encouragement to him. 'Concentrate on your feet!' she urged as she took control of the top half of his body.

Anderson regained ground with pained slowness but gradually moved upwards till his centre of gravity tilted in his favour. He rolled out of the chute and lay on the floor clutching his injured hand.

Mirit removed her cap and gently mopped his forehead with it while cradling his head in her arms. The pain ebbed slowly like the tide going out, leaving Anderson exhausted but well enough to take stock of his surroundings. The strange light in the room was actually coming from next door. There was a glass fanlight some three metres up the wall which was allowing light to come in along with the intermittent sound of voices.

Anderson could see another room which adjoined theirs and which was being dimly lit from the same source. He recognized it as a surgical recovery-room where patients

238

would be taken after their operation while they came out of anaesthesia. The room that they had emerged in was part of a surgical theatre complex and the light, Anderson guessed, was coming from the theatre itself.

Anderson patted Mirit's arm to signify that he'd recovered and got to his feet. Mirit rose with him and looked into his eyes to be sure that he was all right. She touched his cheek and Anderson wrapped his good arm around her. He indicated with sign language that they should try to get a look at the theatre through the fanlight and looked about him for something to stand on. There was nothing available but Mirit disappeared into the recovery-room and returned with an instrument trolley. She moved very slowly to avoid noise and parked it directly below the fanlight, gesturing to Anderson that he should get on to it.

Mirit held the trolley steady while Anderson sat on it and swung his feet up. He took the strain with his good right hand on a wall joist and pulled himself slowly and painfully upwards till he could see through the glass. He had been right; it was an operating theatre. The source of the light was a large, shadowless Mannheim theatre lamp which he was now almost directly above as he looked down on the table and the patient who lay on it.

Three people in anonymous surgical garb were concentrating on the exposed left leg of the patient which was badly swollen and infected. Anderson saw the surgeon scrape material from an open sore with a steel curette and deposit the exudate in a small glass container that one of his assistants held out to him. They were collecting leprous body tissue. Anderson sank slowly down from the fanlight and whispered to Mirit what he had seen.

'Why?' she asked.

Anderson shuddered inwardly. He said, 'They're collecting the bacteria that cause leprosy. That's where the foreign DNA must have come from for the cloning

239

experiments. The Klein gene must come from the leprosy bacillus.'

'That's horrible!'

Anderson stood up again on the trolley and continued watching. They had finished collecting the infected material and the assistants were now bandaging the patient. So that's what the payments to the hospice were for, thought Anderson. They were buying leprosy! The surgeon removed his cap and mask and Anderson saw that it was Sam Freedman. The last vestige of hope that, somehow, he could be horribly mistaken about the Freedmans' involvement had now disappeared.

Anderson suddenly realized that they might want to use the recovery-room, but then thought not. The surgery involved was very minor and although he couldn't see the patient's face for the wide disc of the lamp, he reckoned that the procedure was being carried out under sedation and local anaesthetic. But they couldn't take that chance! They'd have to get back into the laundry chute for the moment.

Getting into the downward-sloping chute was a good deal easier than the upward journey. Mirit got in first and moved down to let Anderson in. She looked up questioningly to see if she'd moved far enough. Anderson signalled with his head that she had. He himself was now about three metres down from the mouth. They held their position and listened until it became clear that the recovery-room was not going to be used. Anderson could hear movement from another direction and deduced that the patient was leaving theatre by another route. A few moments later he was about to start moving up the chute when the room above filled with light as someone came in.

Anderson froze as a shadow came over the end of the chute, then realized, almost too late, what was happening when a cascade of soiled linen fell on him, smothering his face in wet, sticky cloth. He had to fight the urge to tear it from him lest he lose his grip and fall on to Mirit, but revulsion filled his throat as he shook his head violently to escape the clinging embrace of the diseased dressings.

Anderson held on desperately till the light above went out. As it did so, Mirit lost her grip in struggling with the soiled laundry and slid down the chute in a tumbling flurry of arms and legs. Anderson followed her in slightly more controlled fashion but was still relieved to reach the floor without further damage to his hand. 'Are you all right?' he asked Mirit.

'Yes. You?'

'Yes. Let's get cleaned up.'

They were safe for the moment. The laundry had already been searched and it had no windows so they could put the light on in confidence. What was more, it had plenty of sinks and running water. Mirit listened at the door for a moment before saying, 'Nothing.'

They washed and changed into clean surgical overalls that Mirit fetched from the rack. They stood there looking at each other.

'Neil, are you scared?' asked Mirit.

'Shitless,' said Anderson.

'Pardon?'

'Very,' said Anderson.

'Me too,' said Mirit. For a moment she seemed very small and vulnerable, just like a little girl.

CHAPTER ELEVEN

Anderson said, 'There was a ventilation shaft running along the outside wall of the theatre. It looked big enough to get inside. If we can get into the system perhaps we can make it to the upper levels of the Institute.'

'Where do we get in?'

'Down here on this floor.'

Anderson listened outside each door in the cellar corridor till he heard what he was looking for, the sound of large fans. The noise coming from the electric motors was almost deafening when they got inside. Anderson pointed to a ladder leading up to an inspection hatch in the trunking and climbed up to draw back a canvas screen. The wind velocity this close to the fans was close to gale force and he had to lean heavily against it as he crawled inside the trunking. Mirit followed and replaced the canvas screen behind her before starting out on a long horizontal crawl following the line of the main shaft as it hugged the cellar contour before branching out to all corners of the building. There wasn't enough room to turn round so Anderson decided on his own which path they should follow. He chose the central supply route, reasoning that it would probably be larger and offer them their best chance of reaching the upper levels and the possibility of a telephone call or even freedom.

They weren't in complete darkness, for every ten metres or so a grid would admit corridor light where fresh air was released from the shaft. As they came to the first vertical section of the trunking the wind had dropped to a gentle, pleasant breeze. Anderson found no difficulty in finding footholds in the frequent sectional joins of the trunking and climbed easily, even with his injured hand, to the next level. He looked back over his shoulder and could see that Mirit was keeping up. She tapped his trailing foot with her hand to indicate that all was well.

Anderson stopped moving when he heard voices and trained his eyes on a grating some two metres in front of him. He saw a trolley, escorted by two attendants, pass along the corridor below as they took another patient to theatre. One more level, thought Anderson, and they would be in the Kalman Institute proper! He continued to crawl as soon as the voices had faded, now anxious to reach the next vertical section. Two more gratings and he saw the base of the shaft that would take them upwards. He looked back at Mirit and smiled but didn't risk saying anything. They were so near; they mustn't take chances.

Anderson pulled himself into the vertical section of the trunking and looked up. His heart stopped! A face was looking down at him! There was a man in the shaft and he was coming towards them. He saw Anderson below and stopped moving. Through his fear Anderson suddenly got the impression that the man seemed as surprised and afraid as he was himself. 'Who the hell . . . ' he said.

'You're English?' said the man in astonishment. Anderson didn't argue the point. 'You must be Anderson?'

Utterly confused but delighted at being alive, Anderson repeated his question.

'I'm Shamir, CIA.'

'You're the inside man that Dexter mentioned?' said Anderson.

'Yes. I finally worked out that there was something going on in the basement at night but I could never get down here.'

'Can we get out?' said Anderson.

'Up or down?' asked Shamir.

'Most decidedly, up.'

They climbed out of the shaft where Shamir had entered in one of the animal-preparation rooms and found the smell of mice and wet sawdust strong in their nostrils as they descended the ladder that Shamir had left propped against the wall. They stretched their limbs and dusted themselves down, not quite sure where to begin.

'What's down there?' asked Shamir.

Anderson told him, watching his face mirror his disgust. 'Leprosy! What the hell are they doing with that?'

'I think they're cloning genes from the leprosy bug into other vectors.'

'Germ warfare?'

'Looks like it.'

'What do you do here?' Mirit asked Shamir.

'I'm a maintenance technician. I've been on the staff for six months but haven't been able to find out a thing. I was beginning to think that Freedman was innocent when Dexter told me about your conclusions from the accounts.'

'Why are the CIA interested in Freedman?' asked Anderson.

'He didn't leave the States of his own volition.'

'But he was an American citizen,' said Mirit. 'You couldn't deport him from his own country!'

'Let's say it was a high-level compromise,' said Shamir. 'Freedman had been carrying out genetic experiments in contravention of the law, to such an extent that he was liable to a long jail sentence. He didn't want to go to prison and the US government didn't want the scandal of an Ivy League and influential professor in court. Freedman suggested that as a Jew he could apply to Israel for naturalization under the Israeli government's policy to accept all Jewish immigrants. He and his wife would go there, settle and never come back. The US government agreed.'

'What about the Israeli government?' asked an outraged Mirit.

244

Shamir looked embarrassed. 'They weren't told,' he said quietly.

Mirit's eyes saucered. 'You exported a criminal to Israel?' she asked incredulously.

'I suppose you could say that. But we've been keeping an eye on the Freedmans ever since they arrived.'

'And not telling anyone why!' added Mirit.

'We couldn't risk the scandal,' said Shamir.

'And having the Freedmans sent right back!'

'No. Nothing would change,' said Shamir quietly.

'What do you mean?' demanded Mirit.

'Captain Zimmerman,' said Shamir, acknowledging for the first time that he knew who she was, 'the difference between us is that you are an idealist and I am a realist. In many ways I wish it were different. The simple fact is that even if your government found out about the real reason for the Freedmans coming here, it would change nothing. America couldn't tolerate the affair becoming public.'

'So what?'

'Israel needs America more than America needs Israel. Pressure would be applied, irresistible pressure, and nothing would change.'

'But Israel wouldn't . . .'

'Morality only exists at our level of society, Captain. Up top it's a luxury they do without.'

Mirit looked to Anderson for support. 'I suspect he's right, Mirit,' he said gently.

Shamir changed the subject. He asked Anderson, 'Did you find out everything that you wanted to know down there?' Anderson replied that he'd still like to get his hands on Martin Klein's notes and would like to search Freedman's office. 'OK, why don't you two do that now while I call up the infantry.'

'Loud-mouthed Yank!' hissed Mirit as she and Anderson crept along the darkened ground floor of the Kalman

Institute. Anderson smiled in the darkness. He was glad to see that Mirit's spirit was back. They reached the reception area which Anderson recognized with its ornamental pool and tasteless abstract sculpture. 'Freedman's office is up there,' he said, pointing to the circular stairs which looked ethereal in the pale moonlight that filtered in through the glass cupola. 'Let's go!'

They ran quickly and quietly upstairs, anxious to be exposed for only the minimum of time. They flitted across the landing like two spectres of the night and tried Freedman's door. It was unlocked. They went inside and closed it.

'Use the torch,' said Anderson, not wanting to risk anyone seeing a light from outside. Mirit turned on the beam and they began a systematic search of drawers and filing cabinets. Ten minutes later they stopped. There was no trace of the book.

Anderson slumped into the chair that he'd sat in on the last occasion he'd been in Freedman's office and faced Mirit's unspoken accusation that the book did not really exist. For some reason he thought about the accident Freedman had had with the whisky. Had that been a misunderstanding or something else? If so, what? Could Freedman have kicked over the tray deliberately to create what Mirit termed a 'natural diversion'? But why? What had Anderson been about to do at the time?

Anderson thought hard. He remembered that he had been on his feet when he had heard the crash behind him. He had been making for the bookcase to look at the titles.

'Give me the torch,' he said to Mirit. He went over to the books and played the beam along the rows. The light tracked back and stopped. Anderson cursed softly under his breath. There, next to *Gene Expression*, was a dark-blue notebook. It had St Thomas's Medical School crest on it.

'What is it?' asked Mirit.

'Klein's book,' said Anderson quietly. He flipped open the cover and saw again the immaculate handwriting of Martin Klein. 'That look on Freedman's face,' said Anderson, 'he must have thought for a moment that I'd seen the book when I was here last.'

'Maybe you did,' said Mirit, 'but it didn't register at the time. The crest is so familiar to you. But it might have registered one day, and that was a chance that Freedman couldn't take. That's why he still tried to kill you at the Red Sea.'

Anderson sat down in the chair again and read by the light of the torch. Mirit kept silent in the semi-darkness until, after ten minutes, he slapped the covers shut.

'Was it what you thought?' she asked.

'He was extracting DNA from the leprosy bascillus and cloning it into PZ9.'

'That's it then?'

'I suppose so,' said Anderson thoughtfully and feeling vaguely deflated. 'We'd best get back to Shamir.'

Anderson had not told Mirit everything he had learned from the book. Klein had carried out his experiments with leprous material obtained from a number of patients and someone, presumably Freedman, had ringed one of the names in red. Anderson reckoned that there must be a good chance that this was the patient that the Klein gene had come from. He had memorized the reference number: 6713. When Shamir's infantry arrived he would try to locate reference 6713 and destroy it before the CIA could get their hands on it. There was, of course, the agreement with Mirit . . .

They returned along the route they had come, hurrying through darkened corridors till they reached the prep-room in the animal labs.

'I got it!' said Anderson as they entered.

'Did you indeed?' said Myra Freedman quietly.

Anderson's blood turned to ice at the sight of the gun that was trained on his stomach.

'And little Miss Israel too . . . do come in.'

The man who had captured them, and whom Mirit had felled with the pipe, moved forward to ensure that they didn't back out. The malevolence that shone from his eyes above a bloody and toothless mouth made Anderson wish that Mirit had incapacitated him more permanently while she had the chance. 'God! What a fool I was,' he exclaimed, looking at Myra.

'I won't argue,' said Myra.

'But why? For God's sake, why?'

'Perhaps I can best answer that,' said Sam Freedman, coming into the room. 'For the advancement of science and medicine.'

Anderson was outraged. 'Do you call biological warfare advancement?'

'Don't be stupid, Neil,' said Freedman as if he were chiding a small child. 'Don't be a complete cretin. The Klein gene was an accident.'

'An accident! How could it be an accident when I've just seen you collect leprous material for cloning!'

Freedman adopted a patronizing grin as if Anderson were a mental defective. 'I'm working on leprosy, Neil. I'm working on a vaccine, a vaccine against leprosy!'

'But how . . .' stammered Anderson.

'No one has been able to grow the leprosy bacillus in the lab so there's never been enough material available to work on a vaccine against it. We've been cloning genes from leprosy into plasmids so that we can bypass the growth problem and produce all the antigenic material we need in other vectors. We are very close.'

'And Klein?'

'One of the patients from the hospice was a serum hepatitis carrier. Klein cloned a gene from the hepatitis virus by mistake. As luck would have it, it was the gene for the viral toxin. An accident, just an unfortunate accident, that's all.'

'That's all!' exclaimed Anderson. 'Do you realize just how many people have died because of your unfortunate accident?'

Freedman pursed his lips and sighed. He said, 'How I'm sick of people whining about other people. People are the most plentiful commodity on earth! Do you honestly expect me to give up my work over a few interfering people?'

'And what do you expect to get at the end of it all?'

'I expect to get the Nobel Prize. I expect to be celebrated as the man who wiped out the scourge of leprosy. I expect to take my rightful place among the great names of science.'

'And the Klein gene? What will happen to that?'

'When I'm ready I'll destroy it.'

'And you are a part of all this?' Anderson asked Myra.

'Of course. Do you think that I want to spend the remainder of my life in this fly-ridden patch of desert? When Sam takes the Nobel Prize, the US authorities won't dare touch him. We'll be able to go back.'

'But you are Jewish,' said Mirit softly and with astonishment on her face.

'So, I'm Jewish. Personally I've had enough of building other people's pyramids.'

'What's to happen to us?' asked Anderson.

'Abbas is going to kill you.' Freedman said it as if he were cancelling a dinner appointment.

'Because we got in the way of your ambition?'

'If you like,' said Freedman, not rising to the bait. 'People with no brains always seem hell bent on obstructing those of us who have.'

The toothless man made to grasp Mirit. Anderson said,

'Do you know that that bastard threw a kid off the walls of Jerusalem?'

Freedman shrugged and said, 'I don't concern myself with the details as long as the end result is achieved. Good help is so hard to find . . .'

Mirit cried out as the man dragged her towards the door in response to Freedman's nod. Anderson automatically lunged forward to help her but had only covered a couple of steps before something came crashing down on his head and everything went black.

Yet again, Anderson woke in darkness to wonder where he was, his head a cage of pain which showed no inclination to escape. He wondered if Mirit was anywhere near and called out. No reply. His hands were tied behind his back and he appeared to be lying on something soft, soft but lumpy. He considered that it might be a bed but that didn't seem quite right. It was just too lumpy and uneven. There was a burning smell in his nostrils which irritated him because he felt that he should recognize it but didn't. The other strong smell was that of animals. He must still be in the animal labs of the Institute. A bed in the animal lab? Didn't make sense. He tried feeling underneath him with his good hand and touched something soft and furry. Yet here and there it was wet . . . and sticky.

He gave an involuntary cry as a stab of pain shot through his left hand from trying to move his right too much, and stopped the exploration. Outside the room a light was turned on and a faint glow entered through the door crack. Anderson turned his head and could see that he was not alone. A dull, glassy eye stared back at him. He recoiled and sucked in breath against a spasm of fear. He now knew what he was lying on. They had dumped him on top of a pile of animal corpses in the experimental lab. The burning smell was coming from the incinerator.

Anderson was filled with fear and revulsion. And Mirit, what had happened to her? The awful possibilities tortured him as he lay there, struggling ineffectually with his bindings, thrashing his feet into the yielding flesh of his mattress in a subsconscious effort to avoid the final thought that Mirit was already dead.

The door opened and the light came on. The toothless man was there, a spectre of malevolence, looking at Anderson but not saying anything. He crossed the room to the back wall and took down a long fire rake from its mounting.

Anderson could see now that there were two loading hoppers for the incinerator. He was lying on top of a full one, the other was empty. He stared at the empty one. It contained only a few smears of blood on the sides and the dissected body of a mouse that had avoided cremation by sticking to the bottom. Anderson felt anguish push him to the bounds of reason as he considered that Mirit might have been lying on top of the other bin. He tore his eyes away from it.

The Arab opened the fire door and shielded his eyes for a moment before inserting the rake and retrieving it slowly with great care. Anderson found himself mesmerized. What was coming out was a skeleton, a human skeleton. The man wanted him to see it in its entirety so that he would know . . . know what? The answer paralysed him.

The Arab moved the skeleton along the hearth plate so that he could wheel in the other hopper. Anderson felt the jolt as it began to move and looked blankly up at the ceiling. With Mirit dead nothing really mattered any more. He made one last decision. As the fire door opened he would deliberately wrench his wrists against their bindings. He felt sure that the surge of pain from his fractured bones would push him into anaesthetized oblivion before he met the fire.

The hopper engaged noisily in front of the furnace and Anderson opened his eyes for the final act. He saw a vision. There was a man's face in the ceiling, a man with a gun, a man wearing sunglasses. The gun jerked mutely, like an air pistol, thought Anderson, and the Arab fell dead. The vision was Hiram.

The American dropped from the ventilator shaft and freed Anderson gently from his bonds. 'Jesus,' he whispered when he saw his damaged hand.

Anderson sat up on his animal mound and looked at the skeleton on the hearth. He got off the hopper and said to the American, 'Can I have that?' nodding to the gun.

Hiram handed him the weapon without speaking and watched as Anderson stood over the Arab's body and aimed. He went over and said quietly, 'You have to take this off.' He released the safety catch. Anderson squeezed the trigger three times and handed the gun back.

He knelt down by the skeleton and reached out his fingers. He didn't touch the bones; he just held his hand near. He couldn't say or do anything, but he wanted to. He wanted to scream, to shout, to accuse, to fight, to run . . . anything but float weightlessly on this agonizing ocean of grief. Then he saw. He couldn't believe it at first but there was no mistake.

'It's not a woman,' he said. 'It's not a woman.'

'Of course not,' said a puzzled Hiram quietly. 'It's Shamir.'

Anderson was reborn in the ashes of the hearth. 'But I thought . . .'

'Oh, my God,' whispered Hiram as he realized. 'You thought it was Captain Zimmerman?'

'I thought it was Mirit,' repeated Anderson quietly.

'Cap . . . Mirit's OK. The bastard was keeping her for something else.'

Anderson had never known such joy. His hand was

shattered, his skull felt fractured, he was covered in animal blood and tissue and he was deliriously happy. Hiram could hardly believe the change that had come over him. 'Guess you like her a lot,' he said with awe-inspiring inadequacy.

Mirit didn't seem to notice the mess that Anderson was in. She kissed him full on the lips as if she would never breathe again. 'Oh, Neil . . . never leave me.'

'We'd best get you to a hospital, Doc,' said Hiram. Anderson said that he'd like to wash and change first.

'I'll help,' said Mirit. They walked along to the laundry-room and stepped inside.

The weariness that Anderson had displayed suddenly disappeared. 'Mirit — the cultures. We've got to get them!'

'You'll kill yourself!' protested Mirit.

Anderson ignored her. 'Do you have Klein's book?'

'Yes. I picked it up when the CIA freed me.'

'Good. Destroy it!'

'What?'

'Destroy it. It has the reference number of the Klein gene cultures in it.'

'But . . .'

'I haven't forgotten my promise but I don't want the CIA to get the Klein gene.'

Mirit began tearing out the pages and sluicing them down a laundry drain while Anderson put on fresh clothes. 'We'll have to be quick before Hiram suspects!' he said.

For practically the first time in the Klein affair, things went smoothly. They located the cloning lab and found the culture store. There were eight vials labelled 6713. Anderson put them all in his pocket and closed up the fridge. 'Back to the laundry-room. Quick!' They returned without being seen and Anderson brought out the vials from his pocket. He held them out and said, 'Now tell me that you want to hand these over to the authorities.'

Mirit looked him in the eye. She said, 'It is my duty as an Israeli officer to . . .'

Anderson interrupted her. 'That wasn't the bargain. I don't want to know what the Israeli army or the Israeli government think. I want *you* to tell me that *you* want to hand the Klein gene over.'

'You don't understand!' Mirit protested.

'Yes I do. You are hiding behind your uniform, your rank, your "duty" and if the worst comes to the worst you can always say that you were only obeying orders!'

'How dare you!'

'Tell me!' insisted Anderson. 'Tell me that Mirit Zimmerman thinks that the Klein gene should be kept in existence!' He pressed one of the vials into her palm. 'Go on! Tell me!'

Mirit clutched at the vial as her mind reeled. She watched as Anderson packed the other seven cultures into pockets of the soiled clothing that he then picked up in a bundle saying, 'We'd best get back to Hiram.'

'Feel better?' asked Hiram, as Anderson entered the incinerator-room.

'Much,' said Anderson, approaching the fire door. Hiram crossed and opened it for him, a gesture which brought a faint smile to Anderson's lips. He flung the bundle into the flames.

'Wait!' said Mirit, as Hiram made to close the heavy iron door. She came over and flung the last of the Klein cultures into the furnace.

'What was that?' said Hiram.

Mirit ignored the question and stared into the flames.

'I've just come of age,' she said. Anderson smiled at her and nodded his approval.

'Neil?'

'Yes?'

'Surrey isn't all that bad . . . is it?'